Copyright © 2022 by Rod P. Couser

First paperback edition June 2022

Book design by Rod P. Couser
Photo 31956828 / Space © Abidal | Dreamstime.com

ISBN 978-1-7376917-8-5 (Hardcover)
ISBN 978-1-7376917-9-2 (Paperback)
ISBN 979-8-9858281-0-8 (eBook)

Prologue

Sergei Omelchenko glanced through one of the tall windows that overlooked the grounds of his estate. It was dusk, and the skies were heavily clouded, with rain forecasted. Despite the thick bullet-proof glass, he did not dwell long at the window. The house of Basque design was built on a small hill in Rublyovka, a ritzy suburb fifteen kilometers west of Moscow's third ring, and this prized lot included a sizable forest that went down to the Moskva river.

Omelchenko, a former KGB agent and Minister of Energy before the 1991 breakup, toiled these days as CEO of Geoentergetics, the third largest energy company in Russia. A large man in all aspects, he was in his early seventies, although most would agree he looked younger. Standing over six feet tall, he was nearly three hundred pounds and balding without embarrassment. Like many larger men, he had presence and commanded authority the moment he stepped into any room.

Unlike his contemporaries, he had not fled Russia, having no desire to be one of the 'Londongrad' crowd, the slang term for areas of London taken over by wealthy Russians who had self-exiled. Instead, he savored being Russian and surviving the former USSR. A realist, he also knew few with his past survived as long as he had, inferring that someday, his luck would give out.

A knock at the door interrupted his thought, and seeing the familiar face on the video monitor, he pressed the access button. His head of security, Dima Ivanov entered quickly and without warning said, "Sir, please enter the safe room immediately, we've had a security breach on the grounds. I will contact you shortly." And abruptly left.

Omelchenko didn't hesitate and pulled back his desk pad, entering a code on a hidden keyboard underneath. Within seconds, a single section of a bookcase across the room rose into the ceiling to reveal a door which he entered after a thermal scan allowed his palm print. Hearing gunfire outside, he quickly entered the room and closed the door. The bookcase lowered back into place, leaving what appeared to be an empty study. Behind the facade was a fifty square meter impenetrable apartment where he could stay for weeks on end if needed. He sat and opened communication with Ivanov, waiting for this new threat to play out.

It was over two hours later when Ivanov contacted him and said the property was secure. They had located three armed men. One was dead and two were subdued, awaiting instructions. Omelchenko reversed the process and exited the safe room, heading to the basement where such threats were usually held. At least the ones still alive.

When he exited the elevator, he entered a room and observed the two men sitting at a small table in a solid concrete room next door through a two-way mirror. Ivanov entered.

"Who do we have here?" Omelchenko asked him.

"Unclear. The assault leader was killed as he tried to fight his way out. These are just hired hands."

"Let's address them." They both rose and entered the room. Ivanov did not approve of Omelchenko's hands-on approach, but this was something he clearly enjoyed.

The captured men looked up at him in surprise. Omelchenko calmly asked, "So, you have come to kill me, yes?"

The smaller man prisoner smirked, "Yes, and there are others. You will die tonight."

Omelchenko paused, then smiled. "Maybe. Who sent you?"

"I don't recall."

"You are honestly of no interest to me. Tell me who sent you, and you are both free to leave." Both men looked at each other clearly unsure if they believed him. The shorter man was visually reluctant, but his partner nodded as if to say yes.

The short man stopped him and said, "We are professionals, we would never betray our client."

Ivanov knew the drill and silently walked behind the smaller man. Omelchenko looked at him, amused. "Would you care to rethink your answer?"

"No, you dead pig."

"So be it," as Omelchenko simply nodded. Ivanov grabbed the prisoner's head and violently snapped it to the left, breaking his neck instantly. His body hovered and then slumped onto his partner, who screamed. Omelchenko switched focus to him. "Your partner was willing to die to protect someone who cares nothing about you. I assume you are more reasonable."

"And... if I tell you, you'll let me go?"

"Of course. I am a man of my word."

"I'm not positive but I overheard it was a Frenchman, Bouvier... Aldéric Bouvier." Ivanov looked at Omelchenko who nodded. They both knew who he was. With that, Omelchenko rose and left the room to return to his study.

After ten minutes, Ivanov escorted the prisoner up to the ground floor. He walked him to the door, opened it, and gestured for the man to exit. He was hesitant, but then rushed out into the dark and began running down the long drive toward the exit. The door closed.

As Ivanov headed to the second floor, the sound of vicious dogs running from behind the house to the front became loud. Their barks and frenzied howls almost masked the screams of a man caught in their assault.

Back in his study, Omelchenko poured a small glass of vodka from the beautiful crystal decanter and took a sip. Despite his wealth, Beluga Epicure vodka from the Mariinsk Distillery in Siberia was a treat even for him. Retailing for as much as ten thousand dollars a bottle, he reserved it for special occasions, such as surviving another attempt on his life.

He picked up his tablet computer and went back to the email he had been reading earlier from a private banker in Hong Kong, Nigel Corbyn. Years earlier, he had been working with Corbyn on investment opportunities in China primarily so he could convert a massive number of Russian rubles into alternative currency. Corbyn suggested the Chinese telecom industry.

Back then, China Telecom still ruled fixed telephone services while mobile communication was split between China Mobile and China Unicom. That changed when Datang Telecom, a subsidiary of state-owned China Academy of Telecommunications Technology, completed the development of China's 3G TD-SCDMA technology. Its existence allowed the rise of the modern smart phone in China with a potential market valued at over three trillion Chinese Yuan Renminbi (CN¥) or a five-hundred billion dollars at that time.

Although foreign companies were certainly going to try, a local subsidiary of Ningjin Heavy Electronic Company, Realtime, was poised to become the domestic leader in smartphone production, and they were quietly seeking private capital. After a few months of negotiation with the owner of Realtime, Dr. Shen Zhou, Corbyn made a five-hundred million dollar investment in Realtime on Omelchenko's behalf.

As predicted, China recorded over a billion new cellular subscribers over the next five years. Everyone had a mobile phone even though most had never owned a landline phone.

Not long after, however, the Chinese Ministry of Industry and Information suddenly proclaimed they were intent on doing away with foreign investment in the telecom industry as a matter of national security. They set the valuation of Realtime at six billion dollars and forced Realtime to buy out all foreign capital holders and soon after, Corbyn received payment of just under two billion dollars, which went directly back to Omelchenko. Corbyn made one percent on the net profits and happily refilled his dwindling bank account. To him, the sale was welcome news.

Omelchenko thought differently. Making three times his investment over five years was excellent, but why would the Ministry of Industry and Information suddenly care about foreign capital in this sector? And why now, when the industry was reaching its zenith? If they wanted to do something like this, it should have been years earlier, so he told Corbyn to hire someone to investigate how such a decision might have been made. That was thirteen months ago.

Omelchenko took another sip of vodka. Corbyn's recent email revealed two things. First, the Shanghai firm hired by Corbyn had concluded that it was Shen Zhou himself who lobbied the government for the change in foreign investment. Second, Realtime had just been sold pending approval by the Ministry of Finance to a Chinese consortium for eighty billion CN¥, or thirteen billion dollars. While Omelchenko had made a handsome return, he would have made twice that amount on this revised valuation.

Was Zhou a nationalist under pressure from his government? Or was he a shrewd business owner who had just screwed him out of several billion dollars? He assumed the latter, which was unfortunate for newly minted billionaire, Dr. Shen Zhou.

They had history between them, so when the opportunity arose, Omelchenko would teach Zhou a lesson he would never forget, and maybe just kill him.

Northwestern Region, Iceland

Dressed in thermal pants, mud boots, a wool sweater and a large, bright red parka, recently adorned Dr. Sara Ricci sat inside her unheated hut at a small makeshift desk, contemplating whether to attempt data entry with her mittens on or off. The answer was obvious, given she couldn't very well type with them on, but her brilliant mind was rejecting this. The ambient temperature outside was in the low teens, but the wind was fierce today, bringing temperatures to harmful single and even negative digits.

Sara, the scientist, intuitively knew the ridged framed hut, a series of aluminum arched trusses with a heavy rubberized nylon outer barrier, was engineered for weather considerably worse than this, but honestly, the sound of the wind made her think the entire structure would lift into the heavens at any moment... with her still inside it. Unsettled, she continued to focus on her task, recalling her first day in Iceland when someone mentioned there was no such thing as bad weather in Iceland, only bad clothing. She zipped her jacket up further and reluctantly yanked off her mittens.

Born in England and raised in Italy, it was understandable Sara would dislike the extreme cold. She easily adapted to rain and Scotch mist, but weather like this was unbearable. Inside the hut, which was purposely kept cold to protect their frozen core samples, Sara shared with Fridrika Gunnarsson, a master's student from the University of Iceland. A second team member, Lars Copeland, from the Massachusetts Institute of Technology (MIT) was pulling samples inside a second hut, one kilometer away and Sara would have to trek over and retrieve his data in an hour, which she did twice a day.

Several years earlier, a student at the University of Iceland noticed core samples from the permafrost, that earthen layer under the topsoil which, regardless of topical conditions remains frozen year-round, contained higher levels of magnetism. This expedition, sponsored by the MIT, was an attempt to understand why, and Sara was a co-leader of the field project. This was her first assignment since obtaining her PhD from Sapienza University in Rome months before.

It was also her first time working since she had almost been killed and her boyfriend, Jason Sykes, had been seriously wounded. Truth was, she only accepted this assignment to stay sane, waiting for word of his condition.

The project itself was nearing the end of its stated two-month duration. MIT had established sixteen locations around Iceland, all in the lowlands, a mixture of flat to rolling tundra and wetlands. Although northern Iceland lies just below the artic circle, the weather there was surprisingly moderate. The sea surrounding the island lies directly in the upward path of the North American current, where the warm waters from the Gulf Stream intersect the Norway Current and flow counterclockwise around the entire island. Because of this relatively warmer water, in its shallower depth, rain is far more common than snow and wind is almost always present. All of which fuels the juxtaposition of its name, Iceland, which is almost entirely green, and its neighbor, Greenland, which is almost entirely ice.

Fridrika Gunnarsson handed the last of her data sheets to Sara, who was typing them into a database and asked, "Fridrika, is that all the samples for NW1?" Sara practically yelled to be heard over *Riders on The Storm* by the Doors, Fridrika's favorite band, named after Aldous Huxley's book, *The Doors of Perception* in the 1960s.

"It is all I have right now. I might have one more before dinner. Are you heading over to NW2 soon?"

"Yes. It's going to be a cold walk. I hope I don't get blown over."

Fridrika smiled and patted her ample behind. "Here you need meat on your bones, skinny one. A year with me and I'll make you healthy," she laughed. She was constantly teasing Sara that she was too skinny, although in Sara's mind, she had never weighed so much.

Sara smiled and shook her head at Fridrika as she closed her rugged Panasonic Toughbook and placed it into an insulated bag. She put that into her backpack and replaced her heavy mittens, waving to Fridrika as she headed out the door. Setting her sights on the hut to the west, Sara began walking towards NW2, and it took all she had to not blow over, frequently stopping with her legs spread and her arms out like wings to stay balanced.

As Sara neared the hut in the relentless wind, she stopped,
thinking she had heard a helicopter. That was not uncommon as
they were at least fifty miles from any navigable roads, although
given the high winds, it seemed risky to travel in this manner
now. She was almost to the hut when she heard the sound again
coming and going with the wind. She looked up and sure
enough, the expedition's red AS350 ASTAR helicopter slowly
came into view.

She watched it gingerly touched down, and a heavyset man
in a red parka exited and stooped low as he walked away from
the rotor wash. When he was out of harm's way, the helicopter
rose, and he advanced towards Sara. She waved, realizing it was

the expedition leader, and motioned to the hut just a hundred feet from her. She was not being rude; it was just too cold out in the open to wait. Sara turned, entered the research hut and unzipped her coat when minutes later, the door opened and Dr. Uggi Sigfusson came in, quickly doing the same. Sigfusson was also a professor at the University of Iceland.

Sara greeted him, "Dr. Sigfusson. Hi. How can we help you? It must be important to come out here in this weather?"

"Good afternoon, Dr. Ricci, and pay no mind to the wind. A helicopter does not much care as long as it is airborne. Well, at least if the pilot is skilled. Anyway, I just flew in from the university and need you to accompany me there. We have an important donor who wishes to speak to you. I will call the pilot to return. Yes?"

Although it had not always been the case, Sara had a strong mistrust for important donors, which was code for wealthy donors. The events of the last few years had done this to her, and she yielded. "Dr. Sigfusson, we are quite busy. I really cannot make the time."

"Sara, I understand your concerns, but this visitor is beyond reproach. I must ask that you reconsider," he said with a frown, his bushy eyebrows twitching, visibly annoyed.

"Dr. Sigfusson, you know we are behind even working twelve hours a day. There is just no time for frivolity, or we'll have to extend the expedition, which I'm sure MIT will not be willing to do," she replied confidently.

"Sara, MIT is funding this expedition with a grant from the man wanting to talk to you. I suspect he would fund another six months if needed and not think twice about it. Please, it is just a twenty-minute flight and I'll bring you right back, weather permitting."

She had no idea who this person was, but understood the inference. In research, funding was a major obstacle and required researchers to spend a fair amount of time not researching but fund raising. She sighed, grabbed her coat, and reluctantly put it back on as she told Lars Copeland she would return in a few hours. Together, they left and walked across the hard volcanic field where the helicopter was now approaching. She watched it gyrate, just hoped she wouldn't throw up.

The University of Iceland is a public research university in the capital city of Reykjavik, founded over a hundred years ago. Sixty percent of the Icelandic population live here in the capital, although its density is nothing compared to most modern cities. The helicopter slowed and circled as it came to the university grounds. Some of the newer buildings on campus were architecturally stunning, with strong roots in modern Danish and Norwegian design. As she glanced down, she noted the main university building, which was more like an eastern bloc government building.

The helicopter lowered onto a small heliport to the side of the Radisson Blu Saga hotel, which was just off the campus grounds. They debarked and Sara, feet wobbling, headed towards the lobby with Dr. Sigfusson.

Entering the hotel, they removed their coats, and Sara immediately went to the restroom to compose herself with a splash of cold water on her face. When she returned, some color had returned to her cheeks, and they walked to a small conference room. A short man in his early 60s stood on her arrival. With the build of a laborer, he wore a well cut dark gray suit, his dark skin framed by the blackest of hair, which he wore longer than most his age. With his firm walk and pronounced black with gray eyebrows, he came toward her and extended his hand. "Dr. Ricci, it is an honor to meet you and I very much appreciate you granting me a few minutes of your time. I know you are very busy."

Sara, unsure of what to say, reached to shake his hand, which felt like fire compared to her icy digits, and replied, "Merhaba" or *hello*, the only Istanbul Turkish she knew.

"Nicely done, and thank you for the interest in my country," he replied. "I am Dr. Demir Caliskan, founder and co-chair of the Solak Group. Have you heard of us?"

"I have not. What is this regarding, if I might ask?"

"I obviously have you at a disadvantage, as I know much about you."

"And your inability to answer my question makes any concerns I have even more relevant." Sara took a step back as Dr. Sigfusson glanced at her.

"Dr. Ricci, my apology. I come with only the best of intentions. You know, not all people of wealth are evil." He laughed. Not getting a reaction he continued, "Might we have some tea and discuss the reason I am here?"

Sara reluctantly nodded yes. Although she would have preferred coffee, tea would have to do. After all, it was hot, and she didn't want to be rude. Moments later, three tulip shaped glasses of Turkish tea were served without milk as Dr. Caliskan motioned for them to enjoy. He explained this was his own personal blend brought with him from the Rize Province on the eastern side of the Black Sea. Sara took a sip of the rich black tea, which was strong but quite good, and wrapped her hands around the hot cup, warming her instantly.

"Dr. Caliskan, I am told that you are funding this project. I was led to believe MIT was doing so?"

"Both statements are accurate. MIT is funding this on a grant from the Solak Group. As with all of our projects, we prefer to stay in the background to allow a focus on the science and not our group."

"As a scientist, that is refreshing. How might I help you?"

"Well, perhaps you can first give me an update on this project. I am told you and the students may have developed a hypothesis."

"Ah, yes, possibly. We are almost complete with data verification and validation from the original field data, and some of the team have returned to analyze what they found. As you are likely aware, some sample data from the original source was used, while other data was re-verified or re-taken before submission. Armed with that perfected dataset, early research suggests microbes within the samples hold encoded proteins involved in iron metabolism, a fancy way of saying the microbes appear to be using iron based minerals as an energy source. We theorize this process is altering the magnetism and the returning teams are creating the design-of-experiments to test this."

"Fascinating," as he took a sip of tea, savored it, and placed the cup back on its saucer. In Turkey, tea was not just a pastime, it was an experience. "My family's business, Caliskan Holdings is in heavy construction and at one time, I must confess, we paid little attention to environmental concerns. It was considered a burden to our profession. Times change and nine years ago, I was urged to join a consortium for the environment. There I met a Chinese business executive, Mr. Shen Zhou, who now runs the Sunset Foundation, a rare non-profit company in Shanghai and is also my co-chair of the Solak Group. An amazing and provocative thinker, I found him intellectually superior to those around him. A few days with him allowed me to view this group differently." Caliskan took a sip of tea, again savoring it.

"Dr. Ricci, in that audience were some of the richest people in the world whose combined wealth rivaled nations. If they choose, they could do many things governments could not, or would not, regardless of the reasons. With that in mind, I founded the Solak Group. It is not a company, per se. We are a group of like-minded persons who hope to save earth from destruction."

"Destruction? From what?" Sara asked.

"Ourselves, Dr. Ricci."

"Ambitious." Sara chuckled.

"Yes, perhaps. Consider this, CO_2 levels on planet earth have been calculated between one-hundred-fifty to three-hundred parts per million (PPM) over the last 800,000 years. Since the start of the Industrial Revolution, that average level has increased to over four-hundred PPM. Unfortunately, less than sixty percent is absorbed by our oceans, flora, and soil. The remaining twelve billion metric tons, stays in our atmosphere annually. Without radical actions, some models suggest humankind may not survive beyond the year 2150; a truly deadly discovery."

"So, your group is a crusader of renewable energies?"

"More or less. We focus on water and renewable energy approaches to better our world and are soon to undertake carbon reduction projects."

"Dr. Caliskan, that is admirable, and I certainly hope you succeed, but what does any of that have to do with me?"

"As we see it, most climate change and geopolitics of the last century were shaped largely by the importance of fossil fuels. Looking forward, geopolitics will soon be shaped by the struggle to move away from them."

"That makes sense, but again, how does this involve me?"

"Dr. Ricci, consider this an informal interview." He paused and took a sip of his tea. "You have been recommended to lead a group within one of our most ambitious projects, Project Solaris, a space-based solar power system that will collect solar energy and beam it back to earth. I am here to see if you are worthy of such a recommendation."

Sara looked at Dr. Sigfusson who sat like a proud father. Flabbergasted, she turned back to Caliskan and replied, "Wow, I'm flattered and not sure what to say. If I may ask, who recommended me?"

"I'm sorry, Dr. Ricci, but I cannot discuss this. Our membership is private. I can only say it is a member of the Solak Group. Someone that knows you and admires your work."

"Dr. Caliskan, thank you again, but if you have researched my past, then you know that my experience with billionaires wanting to change the world has been anything but kind. I'm afraid I cannot help you. If that is all, I have much work to consider."

"Sara, are you at all interested in why we consider you a prime candidate?"

"I can only assume it is related to my PhD thesis and my earlier work on beamed energy."

"Well, yes, these are mere qualifications, but the more fundamental reason is simply you Dr. Ricci."

"I don't understand. What about me?"

"Dr. Ricci, all members of the Solak Group share some common experiences. Most were born poor. Almost all have witnessed death. Some were, at one time, persecuted. Others lost their entire families to conflict. But rather than complain, become angered or feel sorry for themselves, they all took the extreme negatives life had dealt them and by themselves, turned life positive on a grand scale. I see that same quality in you. Your ability to rise and keep fighting no matter what comes at you."

"Dr. Caliskan, there was a time I might have agreed with you, but that is no longer the case. Thank you just the same." As Sara said these words, she looked down with some embarrassment, wishing she were anywhere but there.

Dr. Caliskan was silent as he looked at her deeply, his face reflecting sorrow. Dr. Sigfusson stood next to him, clearly trying to consider something to say to ease the tension, when Caliskan smiled. "Well, perhaps I was mistaken Dr. Ricci. It would appear you could not move beyond your recent past. Thank you for your time."

Within ten minutes of being dismissed, Sara was eagerly back in the helicopter, preparing to return to the research area. Her insides churning, she looked out the window and saw Dr. Caliskan and Dr. Sigfusson looking at her through a window. Caliskan's words hurt, but he was not wrong. She had not risen above the terror several months before and she wasn't entirely sure why, or if she even could?

From the large balcony, the views of the Rodrigo de Freitas Lagoon and the Atlantic ocean were spectacular. The residence, with its modern Spanish decor was high up Rua Victoria Regia street in the Lagoa neighborhood, just over the hill from Copacabana. No structure here looked alike, as the land you had available dictated the shape and size of any dwelling.

This home was long and narrow, and the architect had made up for this with four stories, each larger than the one below it, like an inverted pyramid. Laundry, storage, and rooms for the staff were on the first floor. The second floor contained secondary guest rooms and a six car-garage while the third floor was living space, a chef's kitchen, two VIP guest rooms and held

24

access to the two lap pools and a spa. The top floor, accessed only by a special card, or invitation, was a three-hundred square meter space that contained the master bedroom, master bath, and an expansive office with an extended balcony overlooking the view below.

It was here that Cristiano Marcon was seated in his office, admiring the scenery as he took a sip of Bowmore Mizunara Cask Finish Scotch, an exotic Japanese style whisky made in Scotland on the island of Islay. Marcon was no stranger to nice things, and this was one of them.

Marcon had handsome Brazilian features and a strong physique he honed daily. A former member of the Brazilian Special Operations Command, COPESP, he could be summoned to use his previous occupation as a commando when appropriate and the COPESP motto; "any mission, in any place, at any time, by every way," was very much his attitude toward business and life.

Although wealthy, very few knew the boundaries of his legitimate versus illegitimate businesses. Outwardly, Marcon was known as a serious businessperson, the head of Povos Engeria (Peoples Energy), but as to the entirety of how he made his money? That was for him to know and to keep others from finding out.

Sitting across from him was his confidant and love interest, Izabel Vargas. Attractive by any measure, she was also quite intelligent, and like Marcon, dangerous when she chose to be. It was her mind that Marcon was most attracted to. She was one of the very few he talked things over with, and she did not abuse this. Izabel was well aware of who he really was and helped him in many ways, but also played it safe to avoid her own death.

Izabel smiled at him when the phone rang. Marcon had not expected a call, but noted the call was coming from Russia. He picked up and casually said, "Marcon."

"Mr. Marcon, a friend in Russia wishes for your presence tomorrow. Can you arrange this?"

Knowing he was referring to Sergei Omelchenko, Marcon simply replied, "Yes."

"Once you land, I will text with the meeting location."

"Thank you." The call disconnected.

Marcon put down the phone and looked over at Izabel who asked, "You're leaving me again?"

"Yes, our friend in Russia has asked to meet."

"Please be careful."

"Always." Marcon said as he rose and went to pack a few things before heading to Santos Dumont airport where he would use his NetJets license. He could probably afford his own plane, although he liked the anonymity and flexibility of any plane, any time.

The Gulfstream GV touched down at the Domodedovo Airport in south Moscow after a refueling stop in Germany. Marcon took a hired car to Neskuchny Garden, the oldest park in Moscow, dating back to 1729. There he headed for the grotto at Count Orlov's Summer House, which was currently closed to visitors. Omelchenko's security was at every entrance and exit, so he simply presented himself to them. They knew exactly who he was, and once past the mindful security precautions, he was allowed to proceed. Omelchenko sat calmly on a bench feeding pigeons near the grotto and former bath house, its edges still frozen over. Marcon came forward and sat down, acknowledging him. "Sergei, you look well."

"Thank you, Cristiano. You as well. I trust business is doing well during these troubled days."

"Yes, I am fortunate to be in the trouble business."

Omelchenko nodded and explained the situation involving his investment, buyout, and subsequent sale of Realtime by Shen Zhou.

Marcon asked, "And you think the timing was deliberate?"

"Yes."

"So, is this about money or payback?"

"An interesting question, but I think this is a matter of honor, Zhou knew exactly what he was doing even if he did not know the investment was mine."

"What is your wish?"

"I'm not sure. He has two passions. First is the Sunset Foundation. Once he sold Realtime, Zhou took on the Giving Pledge, that ridiculous notion to give away your wealth that makes Gates and Buffet so proud. To accomplish this, he has two hundred employees whose sole job is to research ideas and give away his money. The second is the Solak Group, a partnership he has with a Turk, Demir Caliskan. Quite secretive, I'm told the group is perhaps a hundred wealthy individuals who fund various projects to save the world." He shook his head and laughed before adding, "I tried at one time to join them, but Zhou said I was not what they were looking for. He actually said this. I should have just killed him then. The problem there is I know the Caliskan family. Good people, so I can't imagine hurting Zhou via the Solak Group without hurting Caliskan, which I prefer not to do."

"But the crux of the assignment is to affect Zhou's standing in the world. Not necessarily to get back the money you lost." Marcon said, for clarity.

"Yes. My priority is to punish him, so he understands his place. If this action recovers any of my losses, that is fine, but that should not be the goal."

"Very well. After research, we can discuss scenarios. Give me a few months."

"Excellent." As Omelchenko rose and walked away. Marcon stayed seated, typical for these meetings. Once Omelchenko and his teams were gone, he could leave.

4

Levent, Istanbul, Turkey

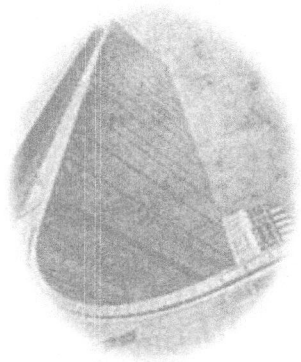

The Istanbul Voltaire was an elegant structure in Levent, the central business district of Istanbul. The 54-story modern and uniquely shaped building was quite an achievement, especially considering where it was. A city of enormous culture and history, Istanbul started its life as Byzantion or the latinized version, Byzantium. It then became Nova Roma, or New Rome, capital of the new Roman Empire, before being renamed Constantinople. In 1930, it became Istanbul, the new capital of the Republic of Turkey, where its mass splits Europe and Asia at the Bosphorus Strait.

Dr. Demir Caliskan stood overlooking the sea and surrounding city from his office at the Solak Group on the penthouse floor. The office here was modest but well-appointed and given this was not a traditional company, most rooms, other than his and that of Dr. Shen Zhou, were not individual offices but a series of conference rooms, cubicles for members and places for entertainment. The genesis of thought happened here, but actual work was done elsewhere.

With annual revenues in the billions, Caliskan Holdings built significant things. Buildings like the Istanbul Voltaire, major roadways and massive pipeline systems around the world. The business had recently turned a hundred years old and Caliskan's three brothers worked there, allowing him considerable time away from it. Although as the eldest son, he held the presidential appointment, but was paid just one Turkish Lira per year. The Solak Group received most of his attention, although he remained on Caliskan Holdings board of directors and was an active member of their finance committee.

After meeting the young scientist in Iceland, Caliskan had been both pleased and disappointed. He was progressive and tried to look beyond his upbringing, which said that women were less capable than men, and certainly not leaders. Caliskan knew this was thinking from a different time, as he had met several very impressive women. Many of them were leaders of organizations larger than his own. To that point, he thought of Dr. Ricci as intelligent and extremely capable. But her abduction and near death by Maximillian Drummond, and then the sister,

Bridget, six months later, had changed her. The promising young researcher was finding it difficult to navigate in the real world, and that was unfortunate for him and her.

Caliskan had known the Drummonds personally. They were energetic and interesting to talk to, clearly intelligent, but their focus was only on money. When you met them, their goals were obvious, never what you could do, only what could you do for them.

Ironically, it was actually the story of Sara's abduction by Maximilian the year before that led Caliskan to know of her. He knew she had been an MIT PhD student and had called a member of the Solak Group in Boston to learn more about her. That member referred him to her PhD chair, Dr. Adrian Zimbrean.

When Caliskan finally contacted him, he learned Zimbrean was still acting as her mentor. He noted how protective he was of her and her story, but also sensed a certain admiration he held for this gifted student. When Caliskan spoke of her current state, Zimbrean, with some prodding, postulated that her PhD goal may have acted as a motivator and perhaps without that now, she could not get past all that had happened. Caliskan was not privy to the details of her most recent troubles, those involving the sister, Bridget, but knew Sara's life had been threatened, and several were wounded, her boyfriend, seriously. He had not yet recovered.

He was about to close the blinds for the evening when the door opened, and an aide said that Dr. Zhou had arrived and wished for a few moments. He smiled and said he would be right there.

Dr. Shen Zhou's height overshadowed his unremarkable Chinese appearance. Tall with a mesomorph body, he uncharacteristically walked with feline grace, and some would even say he had outwardly feminine characteristics, although it was assumed he was metrosexual. Educated in Beijing, Zhou had also attended Oxford and it was there he honed his mastery of English. He could speak almost without an accent, a laborious task for someone born and raised in China, which caught most people off guard. And he used this and his height to his advantage.

Born in the agricultural town of Ningjin, in the Hebei province, Zhou's family was poor and lived a sustenance lifestyle, as most did before the economic revolution of the mid-1990s. As foreigners came to Ningjin to build factories on former crop fields, intent to capitalize on inexpensive labor, the Germans, Dutch and Americans had impressed young Zhou. He studied their mannerisms and worldly ways, and was most impressed that mere foreign managers wielded the power to make enormous decisions.

In time, he would leave the family farm to work at the Ningjin Heavy Electronic Company. Although he paid much of his earnings back to his father to compensate for his loss in the fields, his intellect and education eventually allowed him to take the company over. He had since succeeded spectacularly, but never forgot who he was or where he came from.

Caliskan entered the room and walked to Shen Zhou, giving him a warm embrace. "Shen, you look peaceful."

"And you do not, Demir. You worry too much of things you cannot change."

"Perhaps. Your raw intellect allows you to absorb information differently. Unfortunately, I must worry in order to understand." Caliskan replied.

"That is untrue Demir. You simply refuse to train your mind. I presume Project Solaris is still at the forefront of your thoughts?"

"Yes. Although we now have a leader for the Energy Collections committee, I still want the young girl, although she remains lost."

"Demir, she is no child. She is twenty-eight years old and any attempt to change her mind before she is ready will only foster her weaknesses, never her strengths."

"I am aware of your feelings, but I believe she can get beyond this. I just don't know how or when? In any case, the team has a leader."

"If I read her dossier correctly, Dr. Ricci only trusts her father and her mentor at MIT, Dr. Zimbrean. They are perhaps the key, but until she is ready, this project is too important to risk on an emotional and unfocused mind."

Caliskan simply nodded. He knew this as well.

5

Sapienza University, Rome, Italy

The campus of Sapienza University lies within the heart of Rome, a short distance from the main railway terminal and the Vatican City. Founded in 1303 by Pope Boniface VIII, it was one of the dozen medieval universities in Europe and one of the largest when online and campus enrollment was considered. They offered many curriculums, many in Italian, but most were in English to lure higher paying foreign students. The energy of a new school year, which had started just days ago, could be felt on any square of the campus.

Sara had recently returned from Iceland had accepted an opportunity to teach as an adjunct professor, meaning she was not on a tenure track and only worked part time. That assignment had been scheduled to start the semester before, but the attempts on her life and the Iceland assignment made that all but impossible. On campus, almost no one knew her actual story, but Sara realized she was not acting like the person she had once been, and largely took the teaching assignment only to create a routine and bring some formality to her life. If not, she might never move forward.

Standing at the lectern, she watched the students entering the amphitheater style room on this third day of PHYS1022 *Introduction to Electromagnetism*. Voices slowly died down as students found seats and Sara flew a quick hand through her long brown hair and exclaimed, "Ciao, everyone. When we last met, we talked about the relationship between magnets and electricity, and we covered the reason a wire containing an electric current, when placed above a magnetic needle, would deflect that needle by 90 degrees. Can anyone remind me why the deflection is precisely 90 degrees?" She looked at the students and several raised their hands.

She pointed to a freshman from France who stood and said in broken English, "Magnetism is the circulation of electrical currents at right angles to the poles of the magnets."

Sara looked at him and said, "Excellent, please stay standing." He had sat, but stood back up and she asked him,

"Why would that experiment bring such a uniform reaction when magnetic forces all around us do not?" As she waved her hands wildly through the air.

The class laughed at her hand gesture, and he replied, "Magnets, because of their geological properties, arrange molecules so that their electrons spin in only one direction. The magnetic reactions all around us don't, because most often, the magnetic field is coming from electrons that are spinning wildly around the nucleus of atoms in random directions."

"Very good, and so electricity and magnetism, once thought of as separate phenomena, are now known to be components of the unified field of electromagnetism. Particles electrically charged interact by an electric force but charged particles in motion, produce, and respond to magnetic forces as well. We also discussed the basic math behind electromagnetism. And those would be?"

A young girl, Sara thought was Finish, stood awkwardly and with a very strong accent, replied, "The four Maxwell Equations and the Lorentz Equation."

"That is correct, and it is worth knowing that these five non-quantum equations describe our knowledge of electricity, magnetism, light, sound, and radiation. The very components of electromagnetics and classical physics."

For the next hour, Sara led a participative class, and as the students were leaving, she realized that not so long ago; she had been one of them.

The only child of Italian parents, Giovanni and Annini Ricci, the family moved to Milan from the United Kingdom back to Milan when Sara was thirteen. A dedicated student, she excelled in her studies and completed her undergraduate degree in geoinformatics, and then her master's in physics, two years later. She had started her PhD not quite six years ago at MIT.

Grabbing her papers to exit, Sara noticed her current boss and former thesis chair, Dr. Emilio Ferrera, walking down to the lectern as students were heading up. An older man in his late fifties, he looked much younger than his age, his deep Italian features characteristic of his Sicilian roots. Sara had been pleased to learn he was not only a friend of her previous thesis chair at MIT, Dr. Zimbrean, but his father had actually studied under her great-great-grandfather, Gilberti Ricci prior to his death in 1943. Dressed in a nice suit with a pale blue shirt and conservative tie, he walked with confidence toward her as she waited for him.

"Dr. Ricci, that appeared to be an excellent start."

"Yes. They are becoming more engaged, which I like."

Ferrera chuckled and replied, "Yes, it helps. The reason I came by was to say that Dr. Zimbrean called and wanted to know if you could call him. I think he has an opportunity for you."

"Thanks, Dr. Ferrera. I knew he wanted to talk, but have been busy since returning from Iceland and starting here."

"I understand and only mentioned it because he asked. On a more personal note, have you been able to reconnect with Dr. Facciolo?"

"Um, no. Not yet." He was referring to Dr. Bianca Facciolo, a psychologist the university had recommended when she initially returned to Rome after her troubles.

"She can help you, Sara." She smiled and told him she would call her. They parted, and as Sara neared her office, her cell vibrated. It was her dad, Giovanni.

"Hi Dad, how are you?" as she switched her notebook into her other hand.

"I am well, my special girl, and you?"

"Good, my class went well. Any plans to come down to Rome?"

"Yes, perhaps in a few weeks. The reason for my call is we released our first book today."

"Oh, that is fantastic news," she said with hope. Sara's mom, Annini Boscolo Ricci had passed suddenly two years before of cancer and was an author of twenty-five children's books and even a weekend cartoon she wrote and produced. After her death, Giovanni had created a charitable foundation and a group of her friends that previously helped her with story ideas forming a new entity, "Amici di Annini", *Friends of Annini.* They intended to create new books under this revised name on her mom's behalf. It was a very sweet gesture.

"Yes, I am thrilled about this. Well, I didn't want to bother you, but that's our little excitement here in Milano."

"You never bother me, Dad. Thanks, and I hope you have a great weekend. Love you, ciao," Sara disconnected and thought of him. He had recently retired and started to see someone, Chiara Bulgari, a member of the famed Carabinieri Art Squad. Sara had met her once and, although awkward, since it was hard to picture him with anyone other than her mom, she was also happy for him. He was so full of life, he deserved to be happy.

Weeks later, Sara reluctantly entered the calming foyer to Dr. Facciolo's office and introduced herself to the receptionist. She had come here for two previous sessions before the Iceland assignment, but had not been back in the three weeks since she returned. The receptionist took assurance that her information had not changed and promptly took her into a room before exiting and closing the door. Facciolo entered moments later, stylishly dressed, as always, and motioned for her to sit. "It pleased me to receive your call, Sara."

Sara looked down like a child in trouble and replied, "Thank you. My apology, but I needed to prepare for classes."

"Sara, there is no need to apologize. You're the one working through some issues, not me. Where is your mind these days?" Sara actually preferred direct communicators and took no offence at the brash, opening remarks. She explained her routine and how staying busy helped, but she was still ignoring those closest to her. Facciolo replied, "So, I take it you have not tried to contact Jason?"

"No, I really can't. He has to contact me." Facciolo looked at her notes and saw that Sara could text him, but said nothing.

"And Dr. Zimbrean?"

"No, not yet."

"Your circumstance is unique, but know that it is natural after such an event to shield yourself from those that really know you. This is your way of protecting yourself and not allowing yourself to become vulnerable."

"Perhaps?"

"I imagine you let yourself be vulnerable with Jason and feel you have got the short end of the stick." Facciolo was referring to Sara finally accepting Jason, but he was now in a military hospital.

"It sounds selfish when you say it like that."

"How would you say it, Sara?"

"I wouldn't say anything. He is the one suffering?"

"But am I wrong? Do you not feel the outcome is less than satisfying given you finally let your guard down?"

"I don't know how I feel, just that something is missing."

"Sara, whatever you currently feel, it is simply a feeling. It is not reality, and it will not hold up with the passing of time. You need to surround yourself with those who care for you."

"It's easier to be robot girl. The only time I didn't, look what happened." Sara was referring to a nickname given to her by a former roommate at MIT because she could shun emotion and focus completely on her studies... like a robot. The term had stuck.

"Sara, although you are actually making my point, you are also too smart to believe that. You ceased being robot girl because you finished your PhD, and had real feelings for someone else. I recall this was a first for you."

"Yes... And now I'm just empty."

"So perhaps that is a better descriptor. You don't feel that you got less by exposing the real you, you feel empty because it cannot continue in the current state."

"Maybe, but it's more than that Dr. Facciolo. You're right in that my PhD was a driver. Without that, I definitely feel less motivated and less grounded."

"Without that, you also, for the first time, must face real life. Real emotion. Real decisions. Scary stuff for someone with your isolated background."

"Perhaps."

"Let's change topics. What do you think Dr. Zimbrean wants?"

"Oh, I know what he wants. He is trying to get me back to work."

"And you don't think a new project might help? Iceland seemed to help you. It sounds exactly like something robot girl would do—throw yourself into your work."

Sara smiled and replied, "True. But I keep thinking I need to be here if Jason has a breakthrough and besides, the university feels safe."

"Sara, the world is full of good and evil. Please recall that you and those that care for you defeated evil multiple times. You didn't back down or hide. That is your true self. Not the one you are hiding behind now. You have created this set of responses to cope."

"You sound just like Dr. Caliskan."

"I don't know who that is, but it is true."

Sara looked at her. "One thing I can't get past is that people were actually hurt because of me."

"Forget the others for a moment. How did you feel when evil was after you?"

"I was scared, but to be honest, I was mostly annoyed because it was disrupting my PhD effort. The fear went away quickly, and I just moved forward."

"Based on what you have said previously, I would agree."

"But seriously. Jason is forever changed because of me. His sister was wounded and may not be able to do a job she loved. Because of me. People risked their careers and lives… because of me."

"Sara, what happened is unfortunate, but you did not ask them to solve this problem for you. They offered because, frankly, they are soldiers. It is what they do."

"I understand that, but here's the thing. I put myself in that position. When I knew I shouldn't, I went to New York and trouble found me there. I went to Canada, knowing I shouldn't. Surprise, trouble was there. I keep thinking I could have stopped all this by just not moving forward. That bitch, Drummond, was bad news, and I knew it, but I practically put myself at her feet, regardless. That forced others to fight for me." Sara cried.

Facciolo, while pleased to get this out, also knew this was an important stage in her development. A mistake here could cause a setback, and she said softly, "Sara, you can say that now only because you have the hindsight of knowing what happened. You cannot live and act thinking you'll know every outcome of today's actions. As smart as you are, even you are not clairvoyant."

The scientist in Sara nodded. Dr. Facciolo rose and said, "Sara, please try to get hold of Jason any way you can, and if you can't, just keep trying. Second, contact your mentor, Dr. Zimbrean. These will become very important conversations for you, more than you might realize right now. Once you have done so, we'll talk after that."

Sara acknowledged her but said nothing.

Dr. Adrian Zimbrean had retired at the end of the school year when Sara had left MIT. He was now a distinguished professor emeritus and kept an office on campus going in two to three times a week. The last time Sara spoke to him was a few weeks before Iceland. A widower, he was sitting in his modest home of thirty years on Soden Street in Cambridge, when Sara called. "Sara, my goodness. It is wonderful to hear your voice. Thank you for calling me back."

"Dr. Zimbrean, I'm so sorry for the delay. I've been busy, and it's been kind of hard for me to reach out."

"Well, I'm old enough to understand some mechanisms the human mind uses to defend itself, so I do not take it personally. I wanted to talk to you however about another assignment."

"I kind of assumed that, but it's more difficult now that I'm teaching."

"Yes, I realize that, but what I propose can be done largely from Rome and before you ask, I have already discussed this with Dr. Ferrera, and he has no objection."

She smiled. "Can you provide me with any details?"

"Yes, of course. It involves the Solak Group."

Recalling the name, she replied, "I've met Dr. Caliskan. Did he put you up to this?"

Zimbrean laughed. "Well, yes, and no. I must confess, we have known each other professionally for several years and it was that knowledge that led me to ask you about Iceland, not as a favor to him, but what I viewed as a much-needed opportunity for you. I was not aware until after the assignment he had approached you for a grander role within his organization."

"A role you feel I should have taken."

"A role for which you are capable."

"And you want me to consider it now?"

"No, that position has since been filled. What he and I are suggesting is an opportunity to help them rather than lead an element of the project itself."

"How well do you know Dr. Caliskan?"

"Compared to you, not well at all. I am somewhat familiar with the group itself, as a former student is a member. The Solak Group has an impressive resume even though almost no one knows who they are."

"You know what I'm asking."

"I do, but I cannot answer that, Sara. Are they evil? Do they do good things so they can secretly do bad things? I cannot know this but doubt it very much. You'll just have to trust my instincts."

"I do. So, how would this work? I mean, what are the next steps?"

"I would reach out to them to state your interest, and someone from the group would approach you at your university and explain the details. This is an exciting opportunity that will allow you to expand your mind and at the same time, be comfortable for you. You know this material quite well."

"All right. Let them know I will consider it and thank you for always thinking of me and trying to help. I appreciate it."

"Sara, please call me after you have spoken to them and remember, there are no obligations. Only do what you feel is right."

"I will. Talk to you soon, and thanks again." Sara hung up and poured a glass of Kokomo, Red Zinfandel, from Sonoma County in California. It was difficult to find in Italy, but a superb wine at a moderate price, and these days, Sara was committed to excellent wine. Life was too short to do anything else. As she held her glass, she could feel her mind slowly returning to science.

Richard "Rottweiler" Chase was reading in front of a dwindling fire in the living room of his modest log cabin in Kalispell, Montana. God's country as some say. A private man in a security business that catered to high-wealth clients, Chase's private cell phone suddenly rang, which aroused his curiosity. Few had this number. He glanced at it and smiled. "Sara?"

"Mr. Chase, how are you?"

"I'm fine, and after all we have been through, please, it is Richard. How are you doing?" Richard had been with Jason the night he was shot and knew what she was going through.

"I'm surviving. Listen, the reason for the call is I want to hire you."

Assuming she was in danger once again, Chase tensed and said tersely, "Sara, what happened?"

"Oh, nothing. I'm sorry. I didn't mean to alarm you. I am considering an opportunity and wanted to hire Fortitude Security to investigate a man, Dr. Demir Caliskan, and a foundation he runs called the Solak Group." Sara spelled out both and continued, "Both are out of Istanbul, Turkey. It is a great opportunity, but I am weary of such men and power. Can you help me?"

"Sara, I'll put a team on this right now and get back to you as soon as I have something."

"I can't thank you enough. I am trying to get on with my life but... sometimes I don't think I know how. Anyway, please let me know how much this will be."

"Sara, I know the situation is tough, but Jason will hopefully be out of the hospital soon, and things will improve. As far as payment, I insist on doing this for you. If it gets too involved, we'll work something out. Okay?"

"That is more than fair. Thank you as always. How is Nathan?" She was referring to Richard's son, who was soon to graduate from MIT and had been Sara's lab assistant the year before.

"He is good, very busy, and can't thank you enough for helping him with his capstone project. With less than a semester to go to his master's, he has a serious case of senioritis."

"Boy, do I understand that." She said with a chuckle.

"I can imagine. Okay, I'll get the team on this and get back to you. Goodnight, Sara." Chase hung up, and his mind went back to that horrible night.

Chase, a former navy seal, now ran a specialized security company for high wealth clients, Fortitude Security. Together with Jason's dad, Harley Sykes, a former Sergeant Major in the army, they had formed a raid party with a plan to apprehend Bridget Drummond in Sweden before she went underground forever. Governments wanted her but were unwilling to push the issue past diplomatic efforts, none of which were working. Although not sanctioned by any government, the group was provided intel by the CIA and SIS suggesting tacit approval to move forward. During the raid, Drummond refused to be apprehended and tried to kill them. Thankfully, they got her first, but not before she shot Jason's sister, Rachael, and then Jason, when he dove to save her from a second shot. Rachael had more or less recovered, but Jason, shot in the head, was having a tougher time of it. He had lost several months of his memory and was having small but frequent brain seizures at a military hospital in Germany. Sara wasn't allowed to visit, and neither was anyone else.

Richard Chase was in his office at Fortitude as six faces looked back at him on the large monitor. The faces belonged to various analysts who, for the past forty-eight hours, had been researching Dr. Demir Caliskan and the Solak Group. They had done a lot of work in a short time, revealing a man of wealth and power, and without a serious blemish on him or the group he managed. The family business, Caliskan Holding, was as expected, not as clean, but his brothers more or less ran this.

The research on the Solak Group had led them to a second individual, Dr. Shen Zhou, who also proved to be a man of his word, dedicated to his new non-profit business, the Sunset Foundation. He had made his money by turning a small electrical equipment company into one of the largest cell phone providers in China.

Using this information, Fortitude created a dossier for Sara, but Chase was asking the team on this video call to verify everything they had written. Sara had been through a lot, and he didn't want to arm her with the information to join them if they were not as they appeared. They had backed up their findings and not revealed any concerns.

The last analyst offered some additional information. "It's in the report, but I hacked a few sources and located a hand full of Solak Group members. This is not something you apply for; an existing member must nominate you. They are all extremely wealthy, and the best I can tell, they are all self-made and fought for what they have. I suspect that is at least criteria of how members are selected. That said, these individuals are not as clean as Caliskan or Zhou, but similarly, any negatives appear in their distant past. Nothing present. Should I try to locate more members?"

Chase replied, "Yes, but be careful. I suspect they'll know if someone is looking."

Sara had just finished class the following day when her cell rang, and it was Chase calling and she answered. "Sara, it's Richard. I have sent you a dossier on what we found regarding Caliskan and his co-chair, Zhou, as well as the Solak Group and Zhou's Sunset Foundation. They and both entities appear legitimate."

"Thank you. I will be in my office shortly and will look through it. I may have a few questions if that is okay?"

"It is, and call me anytime. I also have a researcher staying on this as we are trying to understand the makeup of the estimated one-hundred members of the Solak Group. Unlike Zhou's foundation, which is basically a philanthropy outlet intent on spending his own money, the Solak Group meets twice a year to discuss environmental and humanity enhancing opportunities. They vote and seek a seventy-five percent majority. If a project gets consensus, it is officially budgeted, and each member must pay presumably one/one-hundredth of the total where the denominator is the size of the group. We believe that if you don't pay, you're out."

"So, the group is all about its members, hence your concern."

"Possibly, although we have found nothing and certainly nothing out of the ordinary for people in this wealth category. We won't know until we have a more complete list, but also interesting is that each of the members comes from a different country. If this trend continues, it will show this is not a random group at all, but one that a set of criterion has created. As we get more, I'll keep you informed."

"Thanks." Sara hung up and went to her office to read and review the report. Just as Chase described, it was uneventful and without a major concern. She set it down and thought about the reality if she accepted the assignment. At a minimum, it took two items off her list with Dr. Facciolo. She had called Dr.

Zimbrean and had likely worked out a job opportunity, but one item remained. Talking with Jason.

An hour later, Sara remained unmoved, still under a blanket atop her chaise lounge. There was no wine, no music, and even her tablet computer was powered down. She was contemplating contacting Jason. It was true she could not call him, only he could call her, but she could text him using a special, untraceable application that Chase had put on her phone, Jason's phone, and his dad and sister, Rachael.

From the time before Iceland until now, they had spoken twice. Jason had struggled during both calls, and had no recollection of what they went through during their two months together in Seattle let alone the raid in Sweden.

She summoned her nerve and simply texted, "Thinking of you. Hope you're doing well. Call me if you have the chance. Sara." She hit send and rose to get some water. On her way back to the chaise lounge, she suddenly thought of Jason's mom, Annabel.

When Sara first heard of Annabel Sykes, she wasn't much of a fan. Her husband, Harley, the former Sergeant Major, had shunned Jason, his only son, for failing to follow the family tradition of enlisting in the army as an infantryman and trying to become an army ranger. Jason had loved science since he was a boy, and wanted to join the army as an officer, so he elected to go to college first. Simply because of that, the dad refused to speak to him, and the mom defended that decision for most of the last fourteen years.

Jason was shocked by their response, but confidently moved forward on his own. He paid his own way through college and was in the army for eight years, earning a master's in the process before he was honorably discharged as a second lieutenant. It was then he went to work for the Defense Advanced Research Projects Agency, or DARPA and that is where Sara had met him.

When Sara finally met his mom in person just five months ago, she realized Annabel was actually a highly subservient woman trapped in a marriage with an overbearing, tough husband and had little say in what really happened with anything except food preparation. Sara actually felt sorry for her, but given all that had happened since, she and Sara were closer now.

Annabel answered Sara's call. "Sara, I've been thinking of you. Thank you so much for calling."

"Ciao, Annabel. How are you? I just texted Jason on the special app and thought of you. How are things?"

"Okay, I guess. When did you last talk to him?"

"About four weeks ago when I was in Iceland… He was having a rough time."

"I know. Sadly, nothing has changed. Harley had been here in Idaho after bringing Rachael home, but he returned to Germany last week, which worries me. He would only go back if it were bad."

"But he would tell you, right?"

"Seriously Sara, this is Harley. He is next to useless when communicating facts that involve emotion. Everything is need-to-know with him, even to me. Until he can deal with it, nothing comes out of his mouth. He can't help it. It's just who he is."

"I guess I don't understand. If nothing has changed, then why does that create an assumption of bad news?"

"You're right, I need to have a more positive attitude. The concern is his seizures. They have gone from daily to hourly and are getting worse. According to Harley, they don't know why and can't seem to stop them."

"I didn't know that. What can they do?"

"I honestly have no idea. I'm a goddamn nobody. Harley is the only person I can get information from."

"But Jason is your son. Can't you talk to him or the doctors?"

"Sara, they don't even know who he is. Harley is only in the loop because they think Jason is one of his recruits. Please recall, they were on a black mission, so at the hospital, Rachael and Jason were unnamed or 'John Does', as they say." The custom of using John Doe as a placeholder name came from a British legal process used as far back as the 14th century called an action of ejectment. Back then, the fictitious parties were named John Doe (the plaintiff) and Richard Roe (the defendant).

Sara replied, "I forgot that part. I'm sorry, I didn't mean to upset you. Is there anything I can do for you?"

"Let's just keep talking. It's all I have," Annabel said softly.

"This is serious isn't it?"

"Yes, love. Very serious." After a few minutes of unrelated talk, Annabel hung up and Sara set down the phone, wishing she had never called.

The John Doe issue was one reason this was all so hard. The raid was not sanctioned by any government. Although many within the SIS and the CIA suspected Bridget Drummond had escaped to the Maldives, only the SIS Director, Giles Taylor, knew she was actually dead. Taylor had helped the raid team by arranging transportation to a US military hospital in Germany where Harley Sykes created the backstory that this soldier was on a black mission and his identity could not be revealed. The longer Jason was in that hospital, the harder it would be to keep a lid on the story. But if it ever got out, they would all be arrested for murder. The murder of Bridget Drummond.

The sleek high-speed train rolled to a stop inside the massive Rome Terminal and Omer Celebi departed his railcar on track twenty-five. Arriving from Bologna, a two and a half hour journey, he was headed to Sapienza University to meet with Sara Ricci at the request of his boss, Dr. Demir Caliskan. Celebi was a lead project manager and had been involved with Project Solaris since its beginning. Hand chosen by Caliskan; Celebi had thinning black hair with a hint of gray on the ends. He wore a lightweight summer suit, and its cut showed his powerful upper body developed by years of physical work. While age had made him thick around the middle, he was still in great shape for a guy in his mid-fifties.

After an expresso, Celebi headed to the taxi queue for the short drive to the university. An electrical engineer by training, he was one of several lead project managers, but given his closeness to Caliskan, he was a notch higher than his peers. His job today was to impress Dr. Ricci and show her why she was needed. He was also aware of her work, and the problems of the prior few years, but he would stay away from all that, if possible—this was to be a positive meeting.

The taxi arrived in front of the physics lab and, using a map of Sapienza University on his phone, he made his way to her office.

He knocked, and from inside, Sara said, "The door is open." As he walked in, she asked, "Ciao, are you Mr. Celebi?"

"Yes, Dr. Ricci," as he held out his hand to shake hers and handed her a business card that showed him as Omer Celebi, Senior Project Manager, Project Solaris. The address on the card was in Istanbul. Sara handed him one of hers, which he placed in his shirt pocket without even glancing at it. She smiled thinking, *perhaps he, too, had read the dossier on her. Great.*

"Thank you for coming to me. With classes just starting, it was hard for me to leave the university."

"This is no problem. Besides being a project manager, I also help with recruitment and was in Bologna, not so far away."

"When did the project officially start?"

Celebi looked up as if to contemplate the precise date. "The genesis of *Potestas Deorum* was fifteen months ago."

"Power of the Gods, that is quite an imagination."

Omer chuckled. "You know Latin. Yes, some members were not aligned with the concept of a god, let alone that the power resulted from god, so Dr. Zhou relented, and they simply called it Solaris."

"So, of or pertaining to the sun. I met Dr. Caliskan, but not Dr. Zhou. I didn't realize he was a scientist?"

"He is not, Dr. Ricci. He is a psychologist."

Surprised, she replied, "And he and Dr. Caliskan share the helm of the Solak Group?"

"Yes. Dr. Caliskan started Solak and was its leader for five years before he met Dr. Zhou and invited him to co-chair. Today, they spearhead issues together and separately."

"And what is Project Solaris, Mr. Celebi?"

"Please call me Omer."

"Only if you call me Sara?"

Celebi continued, "Of course, Sara. If I may, it is best to share the bigger picture of the Solak Group mindset, so Project Solaris makes sense within the entirety of the problem. Our world is transforming. Aided by humankind, global warming is happening much faster than efforts to reduce it. At the conclusion of a past United Nations Climate Change Conference, COP22, scientists believed they could cap the increase to 1.5 Celsius by the year 2100. The participants of the Paris Agreement then accepted this as a challenge. However, the growth of renewable energies, such as solar, wind, wave and geothermal, are not fast enough to offset population increases, deforestation and advancement of power consuming products. In fact, the International Renewable Energy Agency's latest global outlook says the world needs to generate over five terawatts, or five trillion watts, of renewable energy by 2030 just to stay where we are now in terms of damage related to our thinning ozone layer."

"Omer, Dr. Caliskan shared the trending CO_2 levels, which made me do some additional research. I thought the Dola Amendments to the Kyoto Protocol and the Paris Agreement had worldwide support backed by binding targets? I take it the Solak Group does not believe the commitment is really there?"

"We simply believe based on the last several years of reality, that those are perhaps more words than action. After two years of relative neutrality following the Paris Agreement, global atmospheric CO_2 concentrations rose last year and are now at the highest level ever recorded. The continuation of such milestones must now include large-scale projects to slow the creation of greenhouse gases, like Astro-electricity, and deal with the levels already there through Solar Geoengineering."

"I thought Solar Geoengineering was dangerous?"

"Most people are not aware that Solar Geoengineering has two categories, carbon geoengineering, also called carbon dioxide removal (CDR) and solar geoengineering, also called solar radiation management (SRM). CDR would remove CO_2 from the atmosphere through deforestation reduction mandates, carbon sink projects, biomass projects, carbon vacuums and many, many other initiatives still being designed. Of the CO_2 that is absorbed by nature, oceans absorb the most, although the rising temperature of the water is affecting the absorption rate. CDR would try to boost the flora side of the absorption equation."

"So, it is SRM that might be dangerous?"

"Perhaps. SRM is more controversial as it does not reduce the CO_2 already there. It reduces the amount of solar radiation that hits our ozone layer. It would place stratospheric aerosols via high altitude planes above the ozone layer to shade the incoming radiation much like natural airborne dust does today. There are three primary concerns. One is that the lasting effects of this are unknown. Two, it only addresses the symptom, not the problem. Third, it could disrupt the weather of the entire planet. Imagine if you tried to reduce solar radiation, but instead, altered the weather in specific regions. As an example, India freezes, and the 'breadbasket' regions of the world become too hot or too cold to produce food."

"Wars and chaos take over."

"Precisely. For this reason, the Solak Group is only looking at CDR initiatives."

"But Project Solaris is about using solar radiation as power not CDR."

"Yes, true. For the Solak Group, CDR may define future projects. Project Solaris is about Astro-electricity to reduce the use of fossil fuels right now."

"Okay, I understand, but explain the big picture of how this would work."

"Our concept is to create a network of solar satellites that collect solar radiation twenty-four/seven and beam it back to earth using lasers or microwaves. Depending on the most efficient altitude, this array could be a handful of large satellites or thousands of small ones. Possibly even a large wind sail. On our successful proof of concept, we would then give the technology to the UN Climate Change Conference gratis, hoping they will do two things. First, create a larger system to ween the top ten CO_2 producers away from fossil fuels. Second, create a UN Climate Change Space Force to own and police this power for the benefit of the reducing future greenhouse gas emissions."

"Omer, the technology side of the equation is real, as the United States and Japan already have similar programs in the works. The drawback has always been economics, although commercial space programs have created smaller satellites and significantly reduced launch costs, so yes, it may be possible. But a UN Climate Change Space Force?"

"Yes, that may be too much for the asking, but think back, Sara. It is not a coincidence that the prime locations of fossil fuels reserves have shown increased instability over the last seventy-five years as the world became more dependent on these resources. We agree the technology can happen, but we also believe that space will then become the next frontier of abuse and instability. Conceptually, a body like the UN could be a viable solution."

"Well, I cannot help you there. What exactly does the Solak Group think I can do?" Sara inquired.

"In your early trials of coatings for your PhD thesis, you used methyl ammonium lead (MAL) iodide and several others as a potential tool to capture radiation. Although those surfaces could not handle the high incoming power of your thesis experiments, they might prove superior in our solar radiation application. The second point is to consider use of your Ricci Gamma Ray Conversion Dish as a power source. Dr. Caliskan is suggesting that you work with two of the groups as a paid advisor."

When Sara concluded her PhD dissertation, it included an invention of her own that appeared to capture gamma rays, and she named it the Ricci Gamma Ray Conversion Dish after her great-great-grandfather, Gilberti Ricci.

"How many groups are there?"

"Project Solaris has five key programs. The primary science programs are the Energy Collection and Beaming committees. These are supported by finance, ownership, and maintenance. You would be on the Energy Collection committee, but also assist the Beaming committee."

"Well, as you describe it, this is very interesting and the scientist in me wants to understand and perhaps contribute."

"But..."

"I need to better understand the Solak Group, its players, and their intentions."

"Sara, we do not know each other, and I am only vaguely aware of your rather unique circumstances. I understand such fears, but also know this. You became a PhD for a reason. You are too gifted to not reach out and test your potential. I can only speak for the Solak Group, but can assure you, their intentions are good."

Sara smiled and realized she had made him defensive. She paused for a moment before she replied, "I'm sure that is the case." She stood and walked to a small credenza to get a drink from her water flask and continued. "But Omer, can you really speak for the entire membership?"

Celebi had been engaged and smiling, but now frowned as he realized she would not join them. He stood and held out his hand and replied, "No I cannot, but they only contribute funds. It is only Dr. Caliskan and Dr. Zhou who turn ideas into action. I sense I'm unable to persuade you, Dr. Ricci, and for that, I am sorry. It would have been nice to work with you."

Sara was still standing and had not responded. Celebi turned toward the door. As he reached for the handle, Sara said, "Omer. I didn't say no. I simply don't trust the Solak Group as yet. Give me a few days to think of how to consider this given that and my responsibilities to the university. Fair?"

"That is fair, Sara. Thank you." Celebi smiled as he walked out.

9

Sapienza University, Rome, Italy

O ver the next week, Sara discussed the Solak Group opportunity with those around her to generate additional confidence, and so far, no one was concerned. They knew of Jason's worsening condition and regardless, thought that this was a perfect assignment for her and a much needed distraction.

Sara was out on the terrace toying with the business card from Omer Celebi in one hand, and a wonderful glass of 2015 Justin Isosceles, a Bordeaux styled blend in the other. In the background was the haunting sound of *Wicked Game* by Chris Isaak.

It had taken her three months to get to this point, but there was no denying it. She was here and wouldn't be a victim any longer. She would pray for Jason and would be there for him as soon as his health and doctors allowed her, but meanwhile… it was time to move on. Sara rang Celebi who answered, "Dr. Ricci…"

"Omer, please. It is Sara, just Sara," as she broke into a grin and accepted the position.

D r. Zhou had spoken to Caliskan and was aware that Sara would join them as an advisor. As was typical of their hiring process and relationship, Caliskan would meet with her again, but only if Zhou also accepted her. Such a process took time, but it insured a loyal team and trust within the co-leaders. Zhou felt it best to meet Sara in person and arranged dinner with her at an outdoor restaurant at the top of the Spanish Steps in Rome. He liked the small ristorante, Trinità de' Monti, and knew it was convenient for her.

After arriving in Italy, a private car brought him to the restaurant. On arrival, he met with the maître de and selected a table inside rather than outdoors on the ancient cobblestones at the request of his security team. His security detail was always there, but you would never see them. Zhou never brought attention to himself.

Sara had worn a dress and even put on a small amount of make-up as she climbed out of the taxi and walked towards the hostess at the outdoor kiosk. She was immediately taken inside to Zhou, who was now standing, and greeted her in Italian. "Dr. Ricci, it is an honor to meet you."

Sara smiled and said back in Mandarin, "The pleasure is mine, Dr. Zhou." He held her chair as she sat and came around to his chair, which was facing out to the street, and smiled.

"You have traveled a great distance to accommodate me. Thank you. Is this part of my interview?"

In perfect English, he replied, "I was in Turkey, so this was no inconvenience at all. As for the concept of an interview, Dr. Caliskan and I try to balance each other. We are both gifted, but in very different ways. He has chosen you and I accept this without reservation. His focus however is on the details of the project. My interest is in the people themselves and how they interact with others. I simply want to know who you are."

She laughed and said, "Well, of course, I am Sara Ricci," as she jokingly reached out as if to shake his hand again.

He chuckled at her literal response. "Yes, you are." He motioned for the maître de who poured her a glass of the 1997 Greppo Riserva from the Brunello di Montalcino region of Tuscany he had chosen for her, and they both took a sip. "Dr. Ricci, I understand you have reservations about the Solak Group."

"I can only assume that you have read the same dossier as Dr. Caliskan and therefore know the answer."

"Of course. But I would prefer to hear it from you."

Sara, knowing he was a psychologist, saw this as a test, but it was a fair request. "Dr. Zhou, I have been a student of science my entire life. Mine has been and continues to be a world of facts and figures. Some have suggested my emotional intelligence is rather low, which I can accept. While I never imagined evil would intersect with my science, it did—more than once." She took a sip of her wine. "For reasons I cannot explain, when evil was after me, an inner voice told me I would be fine, and I brushed it off and charged on. I was actually angry that someone was messing with my PhD efforts. But that changed when those around me were hurt. Part of that is my guilt. I pulled them into this, and because of that, they were injured. Another part is that ultimately, I seem to have chosen these paths, which is a different way of saying maybe I like the excitement. Maybe I even seemed to ignore the danger or possibility of danger. It has taken me a while to get my head around the fact that this may be who I really am?"

"Might I call you Sara?" Zhou replied.

"Yes, of course."

"Sara, you most certainly did not choose danger. You chose science. Others simply used that to place you and those around you in danger. You are, or perhaps were, naïve to the ways of the world, but given your isolation to educational institutions, that makes sense. But now you know that this world contains both good and evil."

"Yes, and that was my concern over the Solak Group."

"But that is no longer the case?" Zhou said, picking up on her past tense.

"I have many friends, some in high places, and did my investigation of you, Dr. Caliskan, and your respective groups. You appear to be legitimate."

"Because we are."

"Might I ask you a question?"

"Of course."

"The Solak Group appears to be a global federation of very important people, all from different countries. This selection criterion seems designed by you and Dr. Caliskan? Is that true?"

Zhou stiffened. "Sara, it is fair that you did research on us, but I am not comfortable that you and your associates have researched the Solak Group in this manner. The only way to get such information is to do so illegally."

"I only asked for the information. I did not direct how it was done, but fair is fair. Your organization deployed similar methods given you and Dr. Caliskan know things about my past that I know the CIA and SIS have purposely kept secret." As she said this, she never took her eyes off him.

Zhou paused, knowing she was correct. "I'll allow the question, but in doing so, I would ask that you be careful. The members of the Solak Group are, by nature of their positions and wealth, powerful people who wish to stay private for many reasons." He paused before he added, "Not every member is from a unique place, but the Solak Group, by design is trying to present a mindset of all humankind. In our world there is no

China dominate strategy. There is no Turkish dominate strategy and so on. To avoid bias, we are therefore selective about who takes part in the group."

"Thank you. I understand."

"Sara, it is highly probable that in your lifetime, your science will meet evil again. Your mind is capable of breakthrough thinking, which creates application stimulation. Evil lurks there. You know this."

"I do." Sara glanced down at her hands, folded now on her lap. "Dr. Zhou, as someone recently reminded me, I got my PhD for a reason. I won't let anyone suppress that."

Zhou didn't comment. He simply smiled, had a bite of his meal, and spoke of things that had nothing to do with the project or the Solak Group.

After they had departed, Zhou called Caliskan from his secure cell phone. He explained the tone of the conversation and that she had used contacts to research them before adding, "I understand why she would do this, but it is concerning."

"Shen, this is no concern. The computers trying to determine this information are related to a company called Fortitude Security in Montana. The owner is former US military and has helped Sara in the past. There is not much for them to find, even on the dark web, but we'll monitor them. What did you think of her?"

Zhou thought his words before replying, "I must admit, I had assumed a woman of concern, but found her to be quite spirited and very direct. Based on her own words, she feels guilty about the harm to her friends and loved ones because they were hurt on her behalf. That is not a psychosis. That is simply empathy. I would allow her."

"Excellent."

10

Although Sara had been told there would be limited travel, that was not entirely true. Dr. Caliskan himself had called and politely asked if Sara could meet with the rest of the team in Switzerland. The Energy Collection and Beaming teams were there, and both leaders knew Sara was now part of the team. For her participation, she would receive a generous salary and a royalty agreement should they use her invention for power.

The location of the meeting sounded stunning. A former health institute for the rich and famous, it had gone into receivership during the global financial crisis. Dr. Caliskan had purchased it privately for cents on the dollar and Caliskan Holdings, the Solak Group and Zhou's Sunset Foundation used it for the various groups to gather, brainstorm, or to create more detailed plans.

Sara had taken the Frecciarosea 1000 fast train to Milan Central and then boarded the Eurocity train to Montreux. The journey took six hours, but Sara used the time to get her mind back to the game.

As the train pulled into Montreux, a marvelous city on the eastern shores of Lake Geneva, the image, while spectacular, was very much like Limone sul Garda. This was the place she and Jason had tried to hide from Bridget Drummond. It was also the last time someone tried to kill her and the last time she had seen Jason face-to-face. As her mind took the current image and brought up the past, her breathing became rapid, and she tried to calm herself. By the time the train had stopped, she was flushed as her fellow passengers watched her in worry. She was having a mild panic attack.

Sara quickly exited the first-class car and headed to the front of the station. Her heart was still racing when she noticed a driver holding a tablet with her name on it. She approached him and said somewhat out of breath, "I am Sara Ricci."

The driver noticed she was flushed and pale. "Dr. Ricci, are you okay? May I get you some water?"

"I am fine. Thank you, I just need some air. Please give me a minute." The driver went to the rear of the car and pulled out a water, anyway. Sara was actually thankful and after a few large sips, she calmed, restored her breathing, and they proceeded toward the institute. The drive there may have been lovely, but Sara was looking down as the worried driver watched her in his mirror and soon, they had pulled up to the beautifully manicured grounds of the institute.

Sara looked up as they drove to the front entrance. Each of the two stories that comprised the overall structure was at least thirty feet in height. Those front buildings disappeared back into the hillside, with an enormous expanse of grass in front and covering the roofs of the structure.

The driver said, "Impressive, yes?"

"Wow, I'll say. What a place." The car came to stop and soon Sara was ushered into the lobby. She felt better but thought she should lie down for a bit when Omar Celebi came around the corner. He saw her and burst into a smile, "Dr. Ricci, you are here. This is wonderful."

"Ah, Omer, it is great to see you. At least I know one person," as she shook his hand.

"Dr. Ricci... I mean Sara, are you well? You look flushed. Your hands are clammy."

"I'm sorry, but I had a bit of panic when I arrived. Montreux reminded me of Limone sul Garda, a place with bad memories for me, and I momentarily had a flashback. I'm okay."

"Sara, I can cover for you if you need some time?"

"Thank you, but that won't be necessary. I can do this. Baby steps, as they say."

"Very well. Refresh and meet me in the Sunset room at five o'clock. The signs will get you there, and we can have a drink and meet the team in an informal setting. Perhaps we can have dinner with the two project leaders."

Sara was reluctant, but left this to him. "Please arrange whatever you think is best. I'll see you at five." She had an hour to calm herself.

Sara attempted to doze for a few minutes, but was restless, so she showered in colder than normal water and changed into a light-yellow chiffon pants suit. She put on a white sash and grabbed a white shawl just in case it cooled. The sun was coming down and the remaining light off the lake brought out shadows as she walked carefully, following the signs to the Sunset Room, which she assumed was named after Dr. Zhou's foundation. Regretting her decision to wear heals, she walked into the room.

Although not likely reality, her perception was that the entire room had just stopped to stare at her. Sara blinked as Omer rushed up with a glass of champagne and handed it to her. "You look radiant, but also like you really need a drink."

"Thanks, Omer. Champagne is wonderful, but I'm going to need something much stronger," as she headed to the bar, Celebi in tow.

After trading the champagne for a lemon drop martini, Celebi took her from person to person and introduced her. He soon noted without words that almost all the men glanced at her longingly while the women had formed two camps. Those that were happy and perhaps even impressed to have met her, and those that were immediately jealous of her. He could only imagine how difficult it must be for her to be taken seriously as a scientist. Sara switched back to wine, her nerves back in check as the immersion into science soon made her forget about any anxieties.

Twenty minutes later, Omer guided her out of the room onto a patio that offered partial water views from this height. He walked with her towards a rotund young man in a loose fitting, light-colored suit. The young man turned as they approached, and Omer said, "Dr. Chenglei Huang, I would like you to meet Dr. Sara Ricci from Rome." Omer turned to Sara and said, "Dr. Huang is the leader of the Beaming committees."

Sara shook his hand and asked in Mandarin, "Dr. Huang, you look familiar. Have we met before?"

He smiled and said back in English, "Yes. Dr. Ricci, you and I spoke about my thesis on collimated beams when I was a student at Tsinghua University. I am so sorry our paper caused you any harm. It is ironic that we now work together."

"Of course, I thought your name was familiar. So nice to meet you in person and actually, you did me a huge favor, as it would have been far worse to move forward and then find out later. It will be exciting to hear of your ideas for this application."

Three years earlier, at the beginning of her PhD research phase, MIT had accepted Sara's original project plan to consider if microwaves could beam energy to or from earth. The Tsinghua team, led by Dr. Huang had created an experiment on the very idea Sara had attempted to prove and sadly, it proved it would not work. She had been forced to start over.

"Well, thank you, Dr. Ricci. It is an honor to meet you, and I look forward to working with you." They shook hands again as Omer then guided Sara towards the other end of the patio.

Soon after, they walked up to an older woman, perhaps taller than even Sara. She had very short blond hair and deep blue eyes that stood out to her pale complexion. Dressed in a royal blue pantsuit, she held herself well and noted them coming towards her. As they did, Omer said, "Dr. Julian Hendricks, I would like you to meet Dr. Sara Ricci from Rome." Omer turned to Sara and said, "Dr. Hendricks is the leader of the Energy Collection committees."

Julian Hendricks thrust out her hand, clearly pleased. "Oh, Dr. Ricci, how nice to meet you. Thank you so much for accepting the offer to work with us. I am aware you were Dr. Caliskan's first choice for my role and hope I can live up to his expectation and yours."

Sara, surprised by such humility, responded in kind. "Dr. Hendricks, it is wonderful to meet you and I know we'll have fun working together. I'm happy to help, although I believe Dr. Caliskan has overrated my capabilities with panel perovskites." [1]

"We're equally interested in your gamma ray conversion invention." Henricks replied.

"We have much to look into there as well given the likelihood you'll be in a geosynchronous orbit. How do you know of my invention?"

Hendricks paused and said, "I'll save that story for another time. If you are free for dinner, it would be nice to talk more openly."

"I am free, of course," wondering what that meant.

"Just us girls then." She looked at Omer, who realized he was not invited, and simply shrugged his shoulders as they

---

[1] Pronounced, *pear-off-skite*, it is a mineral, composed of calcium titanium oxide. The term is also used to describe any group of compounds, natural or man-made, that share the same cubic atomic structure, where there are two ions, A and B, often of very different sizes, and a separate ion, X, usually an oxide, which bonds to both ions.

walked away. When they were out of earshot, Sara asked, "What do you think she meant by... talk more openly?"

"Dr. Henricks is aware of my relationship with Dr. Caliskan and like most everyone here believes anything I hear will be told to him."

"And will you?"

"Not at all. I know what is important."

Sara laughed and replied, "I'm sure you do."

"Sara, I'm not a spy, but I am committed to Caliskan and this project. Lack of communication and egos create mental models that can cause things to happen that would not have normally happened. I only use my influence to avoid this."

"Omer, I understand and thought nothing otherwise." They soon parted, and Sara went back to her room to prepare for dinner with Dr. Hendricks.

They met in a small private room an hour later, and Sara had changed once again and ditched the high heels for more sensible shoes. When she arrived, Dr. Hendricks was seated.

"Hello again." Sara said with some affection.

"Dr. Ricci, might I call you Sara?"

"Yes, please."

They ordered dinner and another drink when Sara asked, "Julian, you mentioned speaking openly. Do you not trust Mr. Celebi?"

"It is not a matter of trust. Omer works for the Solak Group, and I think he is the best program manager they have. As a scientist, however, I hear many things. Without facts, they mean little, but as attribute data, when you hear similar versions of the same story, once you cancel out the obscure, the rest is likely true. In Omer's case, he once worked for Caliskan Holdings, the family business of our founder, managing projects in the billions of dollars with thousands of vendors and thousands of connections. It is said he had an altercation of sorts with one of Dr. Caliskan's brothers over a woman. The brother fired him, but Dr. Caliskan knew of his brilliance and brought him to the Solak Group rather than create ill will within his family by trying to defend him."

"So, Omer is indebted to Dr. Caliskan?"

"Yes, I think so. He seems to honor this by placing his entire self on his projects. He cares deeply for Dr. Caliskan and the project, although some disagree."

"Meaning some think he is just a spy?"

"Precisely."

"Very well. What is it we cannot discuss around Mr. Celebi?"

"Sara, this is difficult, but when I heard you were coming to join us, I must say I was taken aback. I'll turn sixty-two this June and Project Solaris is likely my last meaning hurrah as a scientist. I know a little of your story, but simply cannot believe my fate."

"Julian, I'm not following. Perhaps it is best if you simply say what you need to say."

Frustrated, Hendricks shook her head and blurted out, "Sara, before I came to the Solak Group, I worked directly for Sophia Antonion, the Managing Director of MDE Aerospace, one of the Drummond companies."

"When were you there?" Sara replied calmly, not overreacting at the sound of the name of the corporation that had almost killed her more than once.

"I worked there at the same time you were working with Sophia. You and I met briefly in the hallway outside her office. In any case, the moment word came down regarding the alleged crimes by Maximillian Drummond and his security staff, I resigned, as did many others. Sophia was devastated, but understood. I think she wanted to leave as well, but was too guilty to abandon the company when it needed leadership."

"I was very close to working with Aerospace and Defense to help with my funding. As I suspect you know, MDE Commodities supplied the rare earth metals for my dish design, which is how I came to know Sophia."

"She adored you and was very upset when you went alone."

"Well, Maximillian's crimes are not alleged. They were very real, and I know as much as anyone."

"But you trusted her."

"Yes. Even when the dust settled, your intelligence agency, the SIS, said that the independent businesses were legitimate. So, you worked directly for her?"

"Yes, that is how I knew of your invention."

"Did you know Sophia well?"

"Yes, very. We were actually... quite close." Those words lingered longer than she likely intended, and Sara thought perhaps Dr. Hendricks and Sophia were an item.

Sara changed gears quickly and asked, "So, you were concerned I might not work with you because you worked at MDE?"

"Yes, to be honest."

"There is no reason to worry. What became of her and the corporation?"

"After Maximillian's death, the stock plummeted, but stabilized once Bridget took over. All was going so well I considered going back, and the stock almost regained its losses. Then, on the massive criminal investigation that followed on Bridget's arrest, her prison break, and then disappearance, the value of the company dropped over fifty percent in less than a week. It has done a little better since and an investment company in London is trying to purchase the remains, but it is a legal nightmare. Because Bridget has not been declared legally dead, some feel the board has no legal right to sell because it was tantamount to ignoring her shares, which are considerable. In the end, Sophia and Boris are both still there and might even do business with us on Project Solaris."

"Julian, I have been through the ringer by the Drummond family and their security forces, but never thought the divisional leaders were my enemy. I remain with that belief. Thank you for being honest and telling me this upfront."

Dr. Hendricks looked at Sara with the widest eyes. "Thank you. I have been concerned about our first meeting."

"No need for that. I won't let you down. Let's eat, I'm starving."

Sara returned from Switzerland refreshed and energetic. Armed with her new friends, Julian Hendricks and Chenglei Huang, she enjoyed the interaction and felt an immediate attraction to the project, although there was no mistaking. The hard work had just begun.

In her flat, she put that thought aside and made a cup of expresso before she began work on the upcoming week's teaching assignment. She had been gone a week and owed Dr. Ferrera dearly for finding a substitute on such short notice. She would meet with him in the morning.

Coffee in hand, she called her dad in Milan. "Hey Dad, how are you?"

"My special girl, you are back from Switzerland?"

"Yes, it was great to meet the team."

"And there were no issues?"

"No, all was fine. How are you?"

"I am good… Was there something specific, Sara?"

"What? Oh, I get it. Chiara is there?"

"Yes."

"I won't keep you, Dad, enjoy. Save some of your excellent wine for me."

"Always. Love you." As the phone clicked off. Sara realized she was going to have to accept that her dad was a catch, and someone had jumped in line. She smiled and hoped he was happy as she looked back at her computer and the assignment that was upcoming.

The room was full as Sara came to the lectern. She looked out at the students, smiled, and started the fourth week of the class. "Thank you for being kind to the substitute professor. I really appreciate the time off. So, by now..."

From the back of the room, a student interrupted. "So, what project are you working on?" Taken aback, Sara looked around the room as all eyes were on her. "Thank you. I appreciate your interest, but not all things can be revealed. Shall we continue?"

"How about a hint? Does it involve nanobots?" a new girl said from the back left.

"No, not this time."

"Is it in space?" Someone else shouted.

"Thank you very much for the interest, but I'm afraid I cannot answer questions. It is much too early, but I promise, once I can discuss this, I'll give you some very exciting news and a practical use of the very subjects you will learn this semester. Shall we continue?" Hearing only the whines of discontent, she proceeded. "As I started to say, by now you understand Coulomb's law whereby like charges repel and unlike charges attract. The greater the charge, the stronger the force. What happens when the charges are far away?"

The student who first asked about her project answered, "The farther away, the weaker the force."

"Yes, as you might expect, right?" Sara replied. "But that only works for particles or atoms that are not moving. If they move, what has happened?" Nobody raised their hand or commented, which only meant no one had sought a little extra credit to move beyond the material required for the week. "Okay, no overachievers today. Fine. It is because when particles and atoms move, it produces a new field. What might that be?"

"Magnetism," a girl up front said with an uptick on the last syllable, meaning she was guessing.

"Exactly, good guess. Today's class is about things that move, meaning that we are introducing the field of *Magnetism* to our knowledge of *Force*." For the next fifty minutes, Sara worked with them to understand.

When the class was over, she went back to her office and immediately started work on the concept of interjecting her thesis project into a power source for the Project Solaris satellite when Amy Keningburg, a Biologist PhD candidate who had helped Sara on the previous nanobot project with Jason, walked into her office unannounced. "Hi Sara. I just wanted to say hi."

"Amy, how are you?" Sara said, as she looked up from her computer, rose, and gave her a hug.

"I'm good. I didn't mean to bug you. It's just you are one of my few friends and... I missed you."

Sara stayed standing. "Amy, I'm truly sorry for not coming over to see you. It was just too much because we worked on the project together and if I saw you, I would think of him. And I just couldn't." She was referring to Jason.

"I know. I'm so sorry. I didn't mean to be so selfish."

"Amy, you're not. This has nothing to do with you. It's me. I've been able to talk to him a few times although I'm really concerned for him."

Amy nodded and asked, "Is his memory coming back?"

"No, and now he is having hourly seizures. The medical staff is highly concerned, which offers little comfort."

Amy knew enough to understand and changed subjects. "How did things go with that company you worked for in Iceland?"

"Good, I mean, great even. It took longer than expected, but we have a good theory on the rise in magnetism in the permafrost. When I was there, I was approached regarding another assignment."

"And?"

"I declined then, but have since reconsidered. It is with the Solak Group out of Turkey. Have you heard of them?"

"I came across the name when I was working on my master's thesis, but know little about them. Where is the assignment based?"

"Space."

"What?"

"Space, as in outer space."

"You're going into space?" Her faced dropped.

"No. I'm just helping from here, but it will be an enormous effort."

"What is the project, if you can say?"

"I likely can't, but I will."

"How about sharing some wine at my place in an hour?"

"Sounds good. I'll bring the wine."

"I was hoping you would. You always have good stuff. I have food." As Amy headed off, Sara packed up.

An hour later, Sara was knocking on Amy's door, less than a kilometer from Sara's flat. They shared some antipasto, and a small plate of *carni e formaggi*, meat and cheese, before sitting down on her sofa with a bottle of 2015 Sassetti Livio Pertimali a bold Sangiovese from Tuscany. In the background, *Perfect Symphony* with Andrea Bocelli and Ed Sheeran reverberated pleasantly off of the terra cotta stone floor and Sara brought Amy up to speed on Project Solaris.

"So, talk to me about how your invention could work in this application." Amy asked, holding her glass with high approval.

"Well, it's complicated. Every hour, more solar energy reaches earth than humans could use in an entire year. The term 'Space' is legally defined as sixty-two miles above sea level in a place called the Kármán line named after Theodore von Kármán. He predicted this was the point at which air no longer existed, meaning that in aerodynamics, a plane, for instance, could only rely on inertia to move forward rather than lift." Sara took a bite of meat and continued. "When I proved my PhD thesis, the premise was that a satellite, positioned within Low Earth's Orbit (LEO), would circle the earth sixteen times every twenty-four hours depending on the altitude within LEO. As you know, the higher the satellite, the longer it takes to circumnavigate earth, so higher means fewer rotations."

"For your invention, you need lower, right?"

"Yes. In theory, my Ricci Gamma Ray Conversion Dish armed with sixteen opportunities, could convert enough to power a small, non-scientific satellite."

"So why do you sound like it's a problem?" As Amy took a sip of wine.

"I have two gigantic problems. First, I did not have the funding to use actual gamma rays, but mimicked a gamma ray by using an x-ray machine at a higher output setting, so there is a knowledge gap there. The second problem is that to get solar radiation in the manner Project Solaris is requesting, LEO elevations aren't high enough. They really need to be in a Geosynchronous Earth Orbit (GEO)."

"If I recall, GEO matches earth's rotation, so that's just once around per day and you were expecting LEO, which is up to sixteen times a day."

"Correct! My invention might not receive any gammas in just one rotation." Sara walked over to a dry erase board and grabbed a pen, quickly drawing the earth and the two orbits used by satellites.

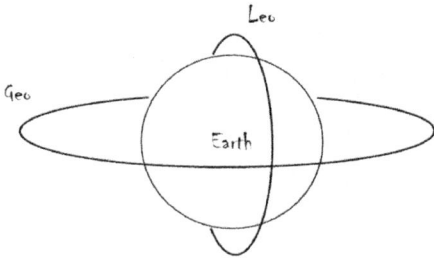

Amy nodded and said, "But there are thousands of satellites in space now. Surely there are other ways to power them."

"Oh, very true. I don't think it has a strong negative effect on the project, but if I could get the Ricci Gamma Ray

Conversion Dish to work, the array would have emergency backup power. And I would get a royalty for every central collection satellite they put into orbit."

"You bitch. It's bad enough you're smart and beautiful, but rich too? It's not fair to us average girls. How can I go about becoming your sister?" Amy said, laughing.

Sara laughed. "Don't worry. I honestly don't know if this is going to work."

"How high is GEO?"

"Roughly twenty-two-thousand miles above sea level where there are no clouds, no atmosphere, no day, and no night. Just twenty-four/seven of solar power." Sara said, smiling, as she took a sip of her wine. It really was good.

Landstuhl Regional Medical Center at Wilson Barracks, in
Landstuhl, Germany, is the only US military hospital outside
the United States still in operation. Sitting between the 62 and
L465 highways, it is less than seventy miles from Luxemburg at
the northwest edge of the Palatinate forest, and it was here that
Jason Sykes found himself under care, although at this moment,
he wasn't aware of that.

Following their mission, Jason and the team were secretly
extracted by the SIS and flown here. There are no records of
any such flight. This decision was made as they flew over the
North Sea when the events of the raid were conveyed to the
Director of the SIS, Giles Taylor. Once he heard the details, he
knew his hands were tied and denied them landing rights within
the UK. The death of Bridget Drummond, and the injury of
two Americans, neither under orders from their government,
would have to remain a deep secret.

Nobody but those directly involved would understand this.
If it ever got out, the media, and likely the law, would see this as
nothing more than an American group of former military

personnel confronting, and then killing, the evil CEO of a Scottish public company while in her retreat on Swedish soil. Scandal doesn't get much bigger than that. As a result, Jason had been in a secure part of the hospital for over three months, yet nobody knew his name or his mission.

Earlier the previous day, Dr. Bruce Chambal, the lead surgeon who had first operated on him to reduce the swelling in his brain, stood in his room talking to the staff neurologist, Dr. Umar Aamir. "We simply have to manage these seizures."

"I agree, but he is not responding to the anticonvulsant medication." Based on the increased severity of seizures, Jason had been incapable of conversation or basic movements for the last three weeks. Medicine was keeping him still, although too much was just as bad as too little. They could not find a balance. Aamir continued, "I'm afraid his temporal lobe was damaged by the impact."

"Temporal Lobe Epilepsy?" Dr. Chambal asked.

"No, although the initial impact created an unusual amount of energy that was discharged across his brain when the bullet hit. Given the suspected damage to the temporal lobe, there was and still may be a disruption to the supply of oxygen to his brain."

"So even if we brought him back he might not respond to treatments."

"That is my thinking, although his scans do not suggest obvious brain damage as of a few days ago." Dr. Aamir put down the chart and said, "I think we should try neuro-rehabilitation."

"As in transcranial stimulation?" Chambal asked.

"Yes, but rather than using magnetics, I would like to stimulate the motor cortex with transcranial direct current."

"What therapy were you thinking?"

"I would use tDCS therapy. A weak direct current up to two milliamperes for ten to thirty minutes per session, using a saline-soaked, sponge-surrounded rubber electrode. I would do this daily for five days."

Dr. Chambal looked over at Dr. Aamir and said quietly, "Anything is better than this. I'll explain it to the Sergeant Major." Chambal walked out into the scrub room and removed his gloves and mask before entering a corridor leading to a small waiting area. This area was restricted, and creature comforts were limited, as no civilian visitors were ever allowed there.

He entered the room and brought Sergeant Major Harley Sykes up to date. Sykes knew he should discuss with his wife Annabel, but time mattered, so he simply nodded and said good luck to Dr. Chambal.

In that moment, a world of regret passed before Harley's eyes, and he teared without letting Chambal see him. Harley Sykes had treated his son no differently than his father would have treated him, but it was obvious now that didn't make it right. He needed the boy to pull through; they had unfinished business.

A week later, Sara was headed back to her house after a late night at the office and pulled up her wrap to ease the coldness soaking into her shoulders. She was vigilant and alert, no longer taking the environment around her for granted. It had been a little more than a year since she had been abducted from almost this same area, and not only was she more observant, the can of pepper spray in her left hand was her first defense. The Beretta 9mm Nano in her hobo bag, thanks to Richard Chase, was her last resort, and she had been trained on how to use it.

As she approached her flat, she stopped just short of the building. Her flat, which was the second half of the entire third floor, was lit up and the blinds were open. Sara knew full well the lights had been off and blinds closed prior to going out.

What the hell was going on? Standing still, she thought, who to call? Thinking the worst and in no mood for a confrontation, she pulled her phone out of her bag to call the police.

She dialed 999 but stopped herself before hitting send. Why would a burglar turn on all the lights and open the blinds?

She chuckled and on a hunch, called her dad. He answered quickly.

"Sara, my special girl, where are you? I am here at your house."

Laughing now, she shook her head and said, "I'm outside, Dad. I thought someone broke in."

"No, no. I'm sorry, it's just me. I should have called you. Please come up." Sara put away the phone, opened the door below, and walked up to her terrace flat. She unlocked the door and walked in, giving him a hug. As she did, she immediately noticed he seemed a little off.

"Dad, what's wrong? Are you okay?"

"Yes. Please come sit with me. Would you like a glass of wine? I opened a bottle of your nice wine; I hope you don't mind. You know this is one of my favorites."

"Not at all. As you have taught me, good wine is meant to be enjoyed. I'll get a glass." Sara really didn't want another glass of wine, but suspected there was a problem with Chiara, her dad's new love interest. Why else would he be here?

Out on the terrace, Sara grabbed a blanket and sat with her glass, looking at her dad and asked, "So what gives Dad? Trouble in paradise?"

He looked at her affectionately but replied seriously, "Ah, no my dear... I spoke with Mr. Sykes today from Germany."

"What? Jason's dad called you. Why?"

"I suspect he has a difficult time talking to women." He set his glass down and came over and sat next to her. "Sara, my special girl... they are going to give Jason one last therapy to control his seizures. They will try some kind of electrical stimulation on his brain for five days."

"And if this doesn't work?"

"They think perhaps the seizures may have robbed the front of his brain of oxygen and that he might never recover, or if he does, there could be permanent damage."

"Dad, permanent damage as in brain dead? Or permanent damage as in diminished brain function?"

"I don't know. I suspect based on how Mr. Sykes sounded, it is very serious either way."

"Can I see him?"

"No, not yet. We'll know more in five days. Mr. Sykes said to call his wife, Annabel, for more nuanced information."

Sara simply nodded her head as she looked down, wondering what she should do, and silently hugged her dad. Giovanni, perhaps longing for the opportunity but hating the reason just held her and kissed the top of her head thinking, *her hair smells like flowers, just like her mother.*

Sara arrived in Montreux via train and a hired car brought her to the institute where she was taken directly to her room. It was a very nice accommodation, reflecting some status amongst the team, although she had barely noticed. She was torn between the news of Jason and having to work, but there was nothing she could do. She quickly unpacked, freshened up, and went downstairs to have a glass of wine as she looked out to the Lake Geneva from the magnificent terrace.

Arriving two days before everyone else, she needed time to herself. Time to think, reflect, and possibly challenge herself to answer questions flashing through her mind.

The bartender, happy to have a customer, any customer, suggested the Domaine Jean-Louis Chave Hermitage 2016, but as he poured her glass, it was obvious she was not in the mood to talk, and he wisely stayed silent.

As for the wine, he was not wrong. Sara sampled the nose of the Syrah from Hermitage along the northern Rhône south of Lyon in France. It was simply wonderful, as she looked out at the water, loving the solitude of that moment. The glass enclosed fireplace in front of her offered enough heat to ward off a serious chill and she suddenly thought how odd it was that water and fire could be both be so mesmerizing but, at times, dreadfully destructive. Such was her mood.

Sara woke early the next morning and had a cup of Nespresso in her room at the Institute. After she had readied herself, she went downstairs for breakfast, and Julian Hendricks was already there. Apparently, work would start early today.

Sara walked towards her and said, "Good morning, Julian. You arrived early."

"Oh, hi Sara." She rose and gave Sara a genuine hug. "I had hoped to be here last night, but had difficulty getting into Montreux. I heard about Jason. I'm so sorry. We can postpone this if needed."

"Thank you, but no. We are behind as it is, and there is nothing I can do for him but wait, so it's best to carry on." Sara ordered fresh fruit, granola, and Greek yogurt while they exchanged a few pleasantries. An hour later, the two were alone in the conference room surrounded by several white boards and Dr. Hendricks had laid out the basic concept.

"Are you sure you're okay to move forward?"

"Yes, please." Sara replied softly.

"Okay. Before we discuss the collection method, we have to consider the deployment methods, which are regular satellites or nanosatellites, also known as the CubeSat program. Are you familiar?"

"Yes. It was an option for my thesis. As I recall, this is a program developed by two California professors to produce nanosatellites in the mid-1990s. They are tiny cubes, roughly four inches square and depending on the science can be expanded into multiples, as many as eighteen. They usually cost thousands versus millions and allow researchers to test theories in space at a university or small company level. Over three thousand were launched last year alone."

"All true. The issue at hand is the type of collection method determines the size of the satellite needed to carry it. Over the last year, three options emerged. The first is a large solar sail. Second is a large grid constructed in space to hold large solar panels. The last is a series of nanosatellites, each containing a solar module that launch, and then join in space as an array without assembly by human hand."

"I take it the Solar Sail option is the least expensive." Sara replied.

"Yes, and here are the preliminary studies of the three scenarios," as she handed Sara three bound reports. Going through them briefly, Sara said nothing, waiting for Julian to tell her their direction. "We have modeled each. As far as the sail idea, thankfully, the LightSail2, launched by the Planetary Society, is still in orbit after several years. That single CubeSat, about the size of a loaf of bread, has a solar sail about twenty square feet. It is currently in LEO at an altitude of 425 miles and has been successfully absorbing photons from the sun and using this power to keep the CubeSat from being pulled back to earth because of atmospheric drag."

"But our version would be significantly larger." Sara added.

"Yes. We would have to use a powerful conventional satellite but send it into GEO. The sail would have to be almost 100 times larger to generate the necessary power."

"How robust is it?"

"That is the biggest concern. First, how do we unfurl something that large without human or robotic help? Second, the sail membrane is likely to get damaged by space debris over time."

Sara set down the report on the Solar Sail and picked up the build-in-space option and as she read, looked up. "Wow, this is billions of dollars for far less energy than a nuclear power plant."

"True, but this has its advantages. There is a lot of energy, it is safe, and it's quite robust. This would have to use a laser since a microwave-based collector and receiving antenna would be massive in order to beam one-hundred gigawatts annually. But as you noted, it is unlikely to get funded at that price."

Sara picked up the third report and said, "So this option is basically a bunch of nanosatellites, launched all at once with a conventional satellite in the center which contains the aperture of the laser or microwave antenna. When the satellites arrive in GEO, they would be programed to link into one unit surrounding the aperture unit."

"Yes. I still await your testing on the type of solar panels themselves."

"We'll have something soon. How big of an array are you suggesting for our final phase?"

"The math says we need forty square meters. That is over fifteen hundred satellites, each with a one-meter solar panel. They would be surrounded by a four, three-meter square collection/aperture units."

"But this first test, Phase I is roughly three meters square, right?"

"Yes. Phase I uses much smaller nanosatellites, each with a one-third-meter solar cell."

"So, sounds like you're committed to the nanosatellites."

"Yes, it is likely the most promising, and Caliskan thinks he can sell the cost."

"Okay, I'll work with the team tomorrow to fill in any gaps in the testing and computer simulations. I'll head over now and see who is there. I know some have already arrived." With that, Sara stood and walked toward the stairs to take her up to the conference rooms. It was going to be a long few days.

Sara was reading her notes from her thesis testing days later when a text came in on the special app that Richard Chase had installed on her phone. This message was from Jason's dad, Harley. It was short and sweet. "Call this number now."

The number was in Germany, and Sara was momentarily apprehensive, as the last person in the world she really wanted to talk to was Jason's father. But for him to reach out, it must be important. She picked up her phone and called. The phone answered, and she said, "Hello?" wanting for the gruff Harley Sykes to pick up.

14

Montreux, Switzerland

"Hey… robot girl." Jason said softly, as Sara fought to catch her breath.

It took several minutes for her to regain her composure. "Jason! Oh my god, I can't believe I'm talking to you." Not even sure what to say she mumbled, "How do you feel?"

"Ah… I'm not sure. They say that I have been in bad shape, but this latest treatment seems to have helped. I don't think I've had any seizures in a few days."

"What are the doctors saying? You sound tired, but surprisingly normal."

"Thanks. They aren't saying much, but I think I am better than they expected me to be. I still have problems remembering and seem to go from moments of absolute clarity to feeling as though I'm traveling through a thick fog. I think that related to the medication."

"You don't even like to take aspirin, so that is likely it. It is so great to hear your voice."

"They say I may have some issues with overall brain function, but to be honest, other than feeling tired and the memory thing, I notice nothing different."

"Getting rid of the seizures was a big deal."

"I have been out so didn't really notice but... Hey, my dad just came in and they are telling him I have to get off the phone. It's good to hear your voice. Dad says to call my mom. Not sure why?"

"Jason, do whatever they tell you to do. You don't have to be tough."

"Well, I don't feel tough, that's for sure." And the call simply ended. Sara wasn't sure what to make of it. *Perhaps Harley smuggled the phone into his room. Would Jason even remember they had just spoken?*

15

Tsinghua University, Beijing, China

All Nippon Airlines flight 6152 landed in Beijing Capital International Airport and despite her business class seat, Sara exited the plane exhausted and headed to customs with her small carry-on bag. Once cleared, she exited the enormous baggage claim area and entered the receiving terminal where Dr. Huang was holding a sign with her name. There were perhaps a hundred similar signs, and more people than she had ever seen in one place. She was thankful to have noticed him.

Despite his status, Dr. Huang had driven himself, and it was just a thirty-minute drive from the airport to Tsinghua University. He had graduated the year before Sara, but held an office there and the university was using the Solak project as a program for master's students. Sara quickly wondered why Sapienza had not considered the same. It was a great opportunity in real-life applications. As they neared the university, Sara was silently regretting the morning arrival, meaning they would go straight into meetings.

On arrival, Dr. Huang introduced her to key staff before they headed to a larger conference room where Huang introduced her to the larger audience, which made up his entire team. There were at least seventy people in the room, all wearing bright white lab coats. Maybe twenty were seated at a large oval table with two open spots. The rest of the team was standing along the outside walls. Huang sat at the head of the table and motioned for Sara to sit next to him. In English he said, "Dr. Ricci, welcome to Tsinghua University and my first-rate team. We are honored to host your visit." As he moved his arm in a motion to address the entire room.

In Mandarin, Sara replied to the eager group, "I am honored to be here with so many accomplished scientists and look forward to our relations over the next few days." The team cheered as Huang said, "Dr. Ricci…"

"Please call me Sara, thank you."

"Of course, Sara." He smiled as he liked this name despite the breach in protocol. Within Tsinghua, any PhD was always referred to formally. He continued in English, "As you know, regardless of the final design, all solar panels will use a sandwich design. One layer is to absorb protons from the sun, and another to enable the output frequency. In the center of the nanosatellites will be a larger satellite, which is the aperture and beam focusing unit."

"Microwaves or ultraviolent?" Sara replied. She was referring to the electromagnetic spectrum, which told her that microwaves are radiation with longer waves, slower frequency, and little energy. Conversely, ultraviolet waves are part of visible light which are much shorter, much faster, and have far more energy. They are used in industrial lasers. For space, communication, best was a bandwidth similar to microwaves at a modest frequency (speed). Anything less, and the atmosphere absorbs and reflects the signal. Anything more, it is absorbed by oxygen and water vapor at lower levels of altitude below 11,000 feet.

"Dr. Ricci, the teams have studied both, and each has pluses and minuses." He pointed to a young girl and asked, "Miss Ming Yue Wei is the head of the Microwave team. Ming can you please update our esteemed colleague, Dr. Sara Ricci?"

"Yes, of course," and she stood. "Dr. Ricci, for microwaves, we are discussing transmission at wavelengths of about two to twenty centimeters long and a frequency higher than thirty megahertz, but lower than thirty gigahertz. This would provide an uninterrupted transmission of power through rain or clouds with intensities no greater than the sun's most intense rays. It would always work and be safe to use in space and on earth."

Ming paused and took a sip of water, then continued. "The problem is the overall size of such a system. Because of the longer wavelengths, the sending and receiving antennas are massive. For Phase II, the transmission of fifty million watts would need a space-based antenna one kilometer in diameter, and a receiving antenna on earth of over five kilometers in diameter. Although we have a workable solution for Phase I, we are significantly over budget and Phase II has no good solution." She walked over and handed Sara a medium-sized binder, and returned to her seat.

Dr. Huang stood again and said, "Sara, that is the draft final report on the use of microwave technologies and its design costs. Please now let me introduce Mr. Li Jie Xiao. He is the head of our Laser Team. Li, can you please update our esteemed colleague, Dr. Sara Ricci?"

"Thank you, Dr. Huang. Miss Sara, to counteract the enormous system size, we are considering the wavelengths used in lasers, which as you know are atomic, in the order of hundreds of nanometers (billionths of a meter). Here, we can transmit the same energy from Phase II using an aperture of six meters square in space. On earth, the receiving antenna would be approximately twenty-two meters in diameter. Small enough to mount on a heavy truck. Unfortunately, lasers also have drawbacks." Li Jie walked toward Sara and handed her a similar draft report before adding, "Because lasers produce a visible wave of light, they cannot pass readily through haze or cloud cover, so we would have to use adaptive optics on the ground which are costly and create inefficiencies. Because the beam is so powerful, our modeling shows significant heat buildup during transfer of solar energy to laser energy. If you recall, heat cannot dissipate in space because there is no air. Unlike our houses which use insulation and the conduction and convection of the air to keep hot out and cold in, the satellite's design must incorporate a radiation based cooling function that keeps the solar radiation from coming in, and also allows excessive heat inside to escape via infrared radiation. We believe we have solutions for much of this, but there is another concern. As this is a visual frequency, no objects can travel through the beam. With countless satellites, space junk, airplanes, and even birds between GEO and the Earth's surface, a shutoff mechanism will be required to recognize beam interference."

"Thank you. I am aware of the inefficiencies with microwaves, but what is the proposed efficiency with your laser technology?" Sara asked.

"We would use diode-pumped, electrical lasers with efficiencies of just over fifty percent."

"Thank you." Sara set down the report and would review it later as she turned to Dr. Huang and asked, "Dr. Huang, if you had to choose today, which would be your consideration?"

"Sara, I think the laser system. Its drawbacks are outweighed by its cost and size. We hope that your gamma ray collection system can enhance the power needs in the aperture unit, as we'll need more power for cooling."

"Unfortunately, we'll have to see what, if any gammas are even there first, using the exploratory sensors for Phase I. Thank you and the team for this excellent work. I will review and contact you tomorrow." Sara bowed to the room, and they erupted in applause.

Sara had concluded her trip to China with an endorsement for the laser-based system. On her return to Rome, she immediately met with Dr. Ferrera to work through yet another absence. "Dr. Ferrera, how are you?"

"Dr. Ricci, I am fine. It is you I am concerned about. How are you doing with all this travel and the scope of your assignment?"

"I am doing well. It is really groundbreaking work. My apology for the travel. This must make you crazy?"

"Not at all. We expected this and are comfortable. I realize some of your colleagues might see my attitude as preferential, but they are welcome to work on projects of such international exposure." He mused.

"I will try not to abuse this, I promise."

"Carry on Dr. Ricci, we only hope for a successful effort." As he walked away, Sara thought about what he had just said and wondered how long her rock-star status would last if this failed. It probably wouldn't.

Sara stood at the podium in her classroom and silently scanned the nearly full room. She was about to start the lesson when, from the back, a student shouted out, "Dr. Ricci, what are you working on in China?"

Another yelled, "Are you going into space?"

Sara used her hands to signal calm and said, "Thank you for your interest. For now, I am just assisting."

"Assisting who?"

"People that wish to remain anonymous. Thank you for the support, but we have a lesson to get through. I have already passed. Will you...?"

That brought the audience to a pause and Sara laughed before she said, "Okay, everyone, and thank you once again for being kind to the substitute professor. So, we have worked through basics of electromagnetism, including stuff that moves. As a refresher, how do we measure the electric field?"

From the front, an American student answered, "Newtons per Coulomb."

"Can you give the class a quick definition of each?"

"Ah, sure. A Newton (N) is a measure of force, and a Coulomb (C) is a measure of electrical charge and specifically, the force between two stationary electrically charged particles."

"Excellent. Who wants to explain how we measure magnetism?"

"Tesla (T)," said the same young man.

"Yes, and besides the man and the car, what is a Tesla?" The room broke into laugher and some applause.

"It is the measure of Flux Density. I'm pretty sure that one Tesla is a force of one Newton on a charge of one Coulomb with a velocity of one meter per second."

"Very good. That is correct and you get the over-achiever award of the day. When we consider electricity, a circuit is easiest to describe as a series of moving charges that are occasionally deflected by things in their path. But I have a question for you? Are these electrons moving fast?"

An Italian boy in the back answered quickly, "Yes, very fast, I think. Maybe speed of light fast."

"Okay... Anyone else?"

"No. I do not think so." A girl answered quietly, clearly trying not to offend. "I think the electrons are moving slowly, but the wave itself is moving fast."

Sara added, "Okay. Interesting. And why do you think that?"

"I am not sure."

"Anyone?"

Another girl from the back said quickly, "The electrons are not focused. Many repeal each other because they are not the same charge."

Sara beamed, "Correct and well done." With that, they discussed the concept of circuits, amps, field times voltage, potential difference, resistance, and they finished with Ohm's law, which relates to current, voltage, and resistance. The class ended, and Sara waited to field a few questions before heading back to her office to work on Project Solaris.

A week passed before Sara returned to the office of her psychologist, Dr. Facciolo, and presented herself to the receptionist. She had not been back since getting the news that the tDCS therapy may have stopped Jason's seizures. She really did not want to dreg this all up—robot girl had work to do, but also knew she should.

The receptionist took Sara into the room before exiting and closing the door. Dr. Facciolo rose and met Sara, calmly motioning for her to sit. "Sara. Good to see you."

"Good to see you as well. Since we spoke, I called Dr. Zimbrean and have a new job. I've thrown myself into my science and have been traveling a lot."

"Excellent," as she raised her eyes, "And your nonscientific thoughts?"

"I've got some good news. Jason received a neuro-rehabilitation technique that has stopped his seizures. I even talked to him for a few minutes."

"That is wonderful news. Are they aware of any permanent effects?"

"I can't communicate with his doctors, but spoke with his mom. She said so far, there appear to be none. Only his memory loss."

"You must be thrilled?"

"Yes."

"Then why do you seem tense and withdrawn?"

"I'm not."

"You are."

Sara rolled her eyes. "I'm not sure why, but yes, it is stressing me out."

"Let's try this. If Jason were here right now, what would you say to him?"

Sara wasn't expecting the question. She thought for a moment and then blurted out, "Um…That I was sorry. I'm glad he's better, and I would try harder to make it all work."

No sooner had she ended the last word than she started to tear up. For several minutes, she said nothing. Dr. Facciolo remained quiet, forcing Sara to think about what she was feeling. "Sara, do you really feel that way, or is that what you thought you should say?"

"What?" Sara replied, kind of bitchy.

"Sara, it's okay to be robot girl occasionally, but you need to let Sara Ricci out of the bottle. Stop scripting everything and just be honest with yourself."

"Out of a bottle..." Sara said with a tearful laugh, "Some genie I would make."

"I have to imagine you are the genie Jason would wish for."

"Yeah. Until he remembers what a bitch I was to him. How one-sided our relationship was?"

"I doubt that. You just weren't ready. Maybe you still aren't."

"What are you saying?"

"You tell me, Sara."

"Are you saying I don't care for him?"

"Sara, I said nothing like that. You have been through a lot and with Jason medically off limits, you found safety back in your happy place: science. Now that Jason may get better, I sense you are not sure what to do." Sara got angry—Facciolo had hit a nerve.

"That sounds petty." Sara said, as a rebuke.

"But it's true, isn't it?"

Sara nodded, unsure of what to say. "It's not that I don't care for him."

"Sara, you care for him. You like him. He is a good friend, and the two of you have history. He is your protector. I'm just not sure you want an intimate relationship with him or anyone right now."

"Perhaps? But that makes me odd, right? I mean seriously, I've never really cared about guys. But of the few girlfriends I have, they're like boy crazy. What the hell is wrong with me?"

"Sara, nothing is wrong with you, but clearly, Jason's recover is making you stress over the relationship that you had. I'm just not sure why?"

"I think I just feel so guilty for him getting hurt in my defense that if he does still want me, I can't very well say no."

Dr. Facciolo liked where this was going, thinking that was possibly the most honest thing Sara had said yet, so she took a chance. "Why are you afraid to commit to a relationship?"

"I have no idea, but clearly, something is wrong with me if I have no burning desire to have a man in my life."

"I'm not sure that is true. You are an only child, raised by loving and nurturing parents. The male role model in your life, your father Giovanni, is your support blanket, your number one fan, one of the very few people you trust and you, at almost thirty, are his…" Facciolo looked at her notes, "…his special girl. Pretty big shoes for any man to fill."

"What the hell? Are you saying I have daddy issues?"

"No. Your girlfriends need a man in their life for reasons related to their own confidence in themselves and their individual needs. You, as an only child with such supportive parents, are so confident being alone, you don't need or feel you have to have a man in your life. It doesn't mean you shouldn't, it just explains a few reasons you don't."

"Okay, that sounds like me. But Jason likes me. He protects me. He thinks I am special. Why aren't I head over heels to let him in?"

"Perhaps because parents love in unconditional, they ask for nothing in return. The difference may be that Jason wants something in return."

"Sex? This is what I'm stressing over?" Sara said, surprised.

"Sex may intimidate you, but no. I think you are so used to being you, you are struggling with altering your behavior when someone else is there close to you. Being with another person requires some level of give and take and sacrifice. My guess is had you lived with Jason the entire time you were in Seattle; this would no longer bother you."

"But robot girl bolted."

"As I said, you are both changed and please know, this simple phobia is not really the problem. Sara, you came a very long way today. I think that is enough for now.

"What do I say if he calls?"

"There is no timeline here, Sara. No rush. Given he doesn't even remember this part of your life, just be friends and talk to him for now. If there is more to it, it will surface, and you'll deal with it." This all resonated with Sara, and for the first time in a long time, she felt she was understanding.

Sara sat reviewing the solar panel tests before she updated Hendricks by phone. This would let the team complete their reports and findings. Since Huang would send his soon, the Energy Collection group needed to be in sync.

Solar panels themselves are not extremely complex and, surprisingly, uses technologies dating back to the 1830s when the term *photoelectric effect* was first discovered. French physicist Edmond Becquerel discovered certain materials could produce small amounts of electric current when exposed to light and he wrote that the materials themselves seemed to absorb it. Sixty years later, Albert Einstein described the nature of light and termed it the *photovoltaic effect*, which won him a Nobel prize.

The basic ingredients of a solar panel are a front panel that contains a layer of anti-reflective coating. Under that is a semi-conductive material. On the top and bottom of this layer is a contact, and beneath that is a final barrier, usually opaque glass. When sunlight hits the semi-conductive material, those materials absorb the photons of light, and electrons are knocked off the atoms in the semi-conductor material itself, which is typically made from mono or poly crystalized silicon. By attaching electrical conductors to the front and rear contacts (think positive and negative), it forms a circuit, and the electrons are captured as direct electric current (DC). This DC current can then be converted to alternating current (AC) like we use in our homes.

The real science in the last thirty years has been the quest to make this process more efficient, primarily the semi-conductor material. During this time, solar panels have gone from converting just a single percent of the sun's photons into electricity to as high as twenty-one percent today. In laboratories, some results are even higher.

Sara made the phone call and waited for Hendricks' to pick up, which she did. "Hello Sara. How are you?"

"I'm good, Julian. Thanks for asking. I met with Huang and his team, and they will submit tomorrow. Their recommendation is the laser."

"Yes, I knew this. I have just finished reading your report on the various panel designs. The panels using semi-conductors made from man-made MAL iodide and MAL halide showed much promise."

"True. Just know that while these perovskites are easily made, their drawback is a much-much shorter life expectancy than traditionally crystalized silicone."

"What is the expected life?"

"Modeling suggests perhaps a year."

"For a proof of concept, this is not a problem, but we'll have to address this for Phase II."

"Okay, I'll order the Phase I panels."

"Great. I need to submit the report tomorrow morning. Do you have the gamma ray sensors?"

"Yes. They are ready to ship from Versilant. Have you chosen the manufacturer of the satellites?"

"Yes. I went to three companies, Boeing, Galant Industries, and MDE Aerospace. Boeing was high bid. Galant and MDE were very close, but Dr. Caliskan did not feel comfortable with MDE, so Galant was given the award. I have some reservations, but they are a good company."

"Why was Dr. Caliskan worried about MDE?"

"I don't know, nor did I ask. I accepted his approach without question to assure I was not adding my bias. That said, I am positive MDE would have been superior to Galant."

"We'll do the best we can with what we have. I'll let Versilant Nanotechnologies know to ship the gamma ray sensors to Galant once we get approval."

"Sounds good. Do you have plans for the Christmas holiday?"

"Yes. I'm going to Milan to visit my dad and his new girlfriend, Chiara. What about you?"

"I don't much care for Christmas, but will spend time with my ex-husband. Christmas day will find me baking with perhaps a good book or two in between."

"You are welcome to join me in Milan."

"Thank you, but I enjoy the solitude. See you after the holiday." And she closed the video.

18

Sara boarded the Intercity fast train from Rome to Milan for some time with her dad during the holidays. This would be the third Christmas since the passing of her mom, and the first with the new girlfriend, Chiara Bulgari. Interesting was the only word that came to Sara's mind as she imagined their time together.

Within the comfort of the first-class car, Sara made the best of the four-hour journey by reading a novel. This was rare for her, but she needed a mental break and forced herself into it with a promise to not meander. The book, *The House of Ilya* by Richard Leslie Brock was a well-written account of a man's journey into what he desired versus what was ordained. Perhaps not what she normally read; it was exactly what she needed now and soon lost all track of time.

As the train slowed coming into Milan Terminal, she snapped out of the spell the story had put her under, packed her things, and took a taxi to her childhood home, a wonderful terrace flat in the old city's center. She paid the driver, grabbed her backpack and her single bag, and went up to the fifth floor. Although she had a key, she stopped herself and knocked, thinking, *wow, this is their place now, I guess?*

Her dad, Giovanni, opened the door with a surprise. "My special girl, since when do you knock?" as he gave her a hug and grabbed her bag. He took it to her room and Sara walked in boldly and decided to get this over with, and went to find Chiara. She only had to travel to the kitchen where Chiara, looking radiant even with an apron on, looked up from chopping and said, "Hello Sara. It is so nice to see you again. Might I get you a glass of wine?"

"Thank you Chiara, please continue. I know my way around." Sara went towards the bar area as Chiara smiled and went back to chopping. As Sara rounded the corner, she did a double take. The bar, which for ten-plus years was really just a large cart on wheels, was gone. In its place was a very large floor to ceiling wine refrigerator and two floral sitting chairs on either side, each with a small ottoman and a side table. Sara looked about but saw no stemware and reluctantly went back into the kitchen. Without a word, Chiara pointed to the end cabinet with a smile and said, "We keep the wine glasses there now."

Sara nodded, grabbed a glass, and noted an open bottle on the coffee table out on the terrace. She looked at Chiara and asked, "May I?" looking at the bottle.

"Of course, my dear. And if that is not to your liking, please open another. Wine never goes to waste here." As she went back to chop, Sara thought this was truly going to be a very long week indeed, and quickly exited to the terrace and poured some wine and sat. The sounds of Milan, the smells of a city cooking and the wonderful breeze here on the terrace. She forgot how much she loved it here.

A few minutes passed, and she wondered where her dad had headed off to. The entire flat was just one-hundred-eighty square meters, so pretty hard to hide. As soon as Chiara came out onto the terrace, removing her apron as she glided forward, Sara understood. Dad had holed up somewhere so they could girl talk. *Really, Dad, really so soon?*

Chiara, holding her own glass, came over and sat down. "Sara, perhaps we can talk first. I know this is difficult for you."

"Honestly, Chiara, it is not. I'm thrilled Dad has found someone who makes him happy. I miss my mom and always will, but I also look forward to getting to know you."

"You are kind, Sara, but I don't want this to be weird for you or your father. He is in the bedroom, terrified."

"What? Why?"

"I suspect he is unsure of your reaction. He adores you, and although I trust you know this, you occupy his mind constantly. He wonders what you are doing and if you'll approve of almost anything he does. I must tell you; it can be difficult. Many times, I feel as though I am the third wheel."

Sara did not expect the conversation to involve her, and stopped to reconsider what she was going to say. "Chiara, only my dad can explain his actions. I love him and know that I filled a place in his heart when my mom passed, but I promise you, he is a kind man. In time, you'll fill that space completely. It's completely okay. I never want him to be lonely."

"Thank you for that and we'll see, as the saying goes. And how are you? You have had quite a time of it. Here I am in law enforcement, and you have seen far more action than me."

"I'm fine. I'm always fine."

"Is that your way of saying I do not wish to talk about it?"

"No. It has taken me a while to realize this, but there is really nothing to discuss. Things happened which I cannot control but I understand that now and have moved on through my science. When Dad comes out, I can fill you both in. My new project is very exciting." Chiara noted how she perked up when the conversation was about work and let the topic drop.

"I'll go pull Giovanni out of the bedroom. I'm excited to hear of your work."

The next hour was pleasant as Sara brought them both up to speed on the project, including the attempt to create a UN Climate Change Space Force. They had a nice debate over that. Chiara alternated her time there and in the kitchen, and at one point, Sara asked if she could help. Chiara asked if she could set the table, which Sara did, although nothing was where it had been. Plates, utensils, and even the mats were all in a different place now.

"Wow, nothing is in the same place?" Sara said jokingly.

"Do you cook, Sara?"

"Some. My mom was not a traditional Italian woman, so I only picked up what she did. You seem to be a true chef."

"Cooking is my version of your science. I cook to relieve stress and allow myself to unwind. Things moved to make the kitchen more efficient. Spices and utensils are things that need to be close to the stove. Dishes, mats, and silverware are needed close to the table. I hope you don't mind."

"Not at all. I just never imagined such precision. You learned to cook from your mom?"

Chiara looked down and said sadly, "No. My parents were killed when I was six. I was raised by my grandparents for a time, but lost them both when I was eleven. I lived with my aunt after that and learned most of my cooking skills from her."

"That is a great deal of loss in a short time for a child."

"Yes, but rather than fear death, I learned to respect it. It is not traumatic for me anymore."

"You are from the south, yes?" Sara asked, noting an accent.

"Ah... you have a good ear. Yes, I was born in Naples and raised in Torre del Greco before moving to my aunt in Parco Virgiliano."

"You must miss the ocean." Sara replied as all these locations were on the Tyrrhenian Sea.

"It has been a change, but I have been in Rome or Milan for almost twenty years."

"I have wanted to ask you, what led you to the Art Squad of the Carabinieri?" Sara was referring to the Comando Carabinieri Tutela Patrimonio Culturale (TPC), often called the Carabinieri Art Squad. The TPC is an arm of the Carabinieri, the national gendarmerie of Italy. It is part of the Italian Ministry of Cultural Heritage and Activities and Tourism and safeguards and protects national heritage, including the recovery of stolen works of art.

Holding her wineglass, she turned toward Sara. "My parents were quite wealthy, and my father had considerable art. When they were killed, a trust had been created for me, which allowed me never to work if I choose. When I turned eighteen, I could finally see the details of the entire estate, both present and what it had been. That was when I discovered the missing paintings. They were minor pieces but painted by the likes of Giotto, Titian, Botticelli, and even a Raphael. And they were all gone. I am quite stubborn, and it really pissed me off, so I vowed to find them and get them back. I trained myself and within three years, I had located five of the nine paintings. My own relatives and my parents' solicitors had stolen them. As a private citizen, I couldn't do much about it, but the Art Squad could, and I gave them my detailed investigative work. The paintings were recovered and given back to the estate, and they were all arrested. Righting such wrongs became a passion, and the Art Squad offered me a job."

"What became of the paintings you could not locate?"

Chiara smiled and replied, "The journey continues. One never gives up. I more or less know how they were removed, but they have changed hands more than once and the trail has gone cold, as they say. I will get them… someday. But enough about this, let's eat." Sara and Chiara transferred the food to the table, and they enjoyed the fine meal and enjoyable wine.

Later in the week, Chiara had gone into her office and Sara and her dad took a walk through old town Milan.

"So, you like Chiara? You are not unhappy with me?" He asked.

"Dad, I love you, and she seems great. I know we are close and always have been, but you have to stop thinking about what I would approve of or disapprove of. That's my way of saying don't blow this."

"She said this?"

"No, but I am a woman and a scientist."

"I was so worried. This does not mean I do not love Annini."

"Dad, I would never think that, and I'm happy you're moving on."

Sara was on the terrace a day later when her phone rang, and it was the cell number of Jason's father and she momentarily panicked. Why would he call her? "Hello Mr. Sykes?"

"I usually go by Jason, but formality works. Hi Sara, just teasing. You thought it was my dad, right?"

"Yes, I did. How are you?"

"Each day gets better. So far, so good."

"Is your dad there now?"

"No, he stepped out, but let me use his phone. It's weird, he is being nice."

"I meant to ask you last time. How is Rachael?"

"What? What happened to Rachael?"

Sara had not expected that, but it made sense he might not remember. "Oh, it's nothing. I just wondered if she was okay?"

"I haven't seen or talked to her in years, so no idea. How do you know my sister?"

Sara sidestepped. "Jason, do you recall the work we did for Dann De Vires on the nanobots?"

"I know I left DARPA to work with Dann at Versilant, but I don't recall actually being there. You were there?"

"Yes, I helped you with the locomotion of the nanobots we made with a company in Canada called Cadieux MT. You led the team at Versilant."

"Wow, no wonder they're worried about me. I don't recall any of that. But how could you work with Versilant? Aren't you still working on your dissertation?"

"I took a leave of absence for two months to help you before I went back and finished. I'm officially Dr. Ricci."

"Oh, wow. I missed it. I'm so sorry, and you're living in Seattle?"

"No. I was there with you for a few months but still live in Rome. I'm with my dad in Milan right now and for what it's worth, you and the Versilant team watched my dissertation on FaceTime. You guys even sang Alice Cooper's 'Schools Out' when I passed. It was great."

"Well, good for you, Dr. Ricci. That's great news. Seriously, I'm proud of you. So, dad just came in. He's giving me phone numbers to call people that know me, to help me remember, so it's best if I call a few more. I'll call again Okay?"

"Sure Jason. That would be great. Good luck." Sara hit end and saddened. Giovanni, having overheard the conversation, put his hand on her shoulder. Sara looked at him. "He doesn't remember any of it?"

"My special girl, I'm going to bed, but perhaps in the few days you are here, you might talk to Chiara. She is better at words of wisdom." Sara nodded and gave him a hug, but had no intention of talking to Chiara about Jason.

19

Copthorne, West Sussex, England

The rain was mild but constant as the cold wind added its layer of discomfort to the drafty and damp old house where Dr. Hendricks lived alone. No longer married and without children, she had taken possession of the house during a brief divorce settlement—a house previously owned by her ex-mother-in-law. With the prospect of house hunting amid a sellers' market in Copthorne, she was elated to receive it, but one year later, she understood why her ex was so willing to part with it. It was a total piece of crap. Old and neglected, she was finally getting used to the fact that most everything worked improperly and had spent over fifty thousand euros on basic repairs so far. The consensus was it would require twice that amount to make the house worry free. Relatively, worry free.

Julian grabbed her afternoon tea and went to the make-shift office in the living room. It was only here the internet connection worked well enough to hold a Zoom call, which she was about to have with Sara in Milan. She connected and waited for her to join. It was just minutes before her sunny face appeared and a minute later, her audio came on.

"Hello Julian, Merry Christmas."

"Same to you, Sara. You look wonderful and relaxed."

"I see by the video, you're in the money pit."

"Yes. Cold and damp, but at least the internet is working for a change." They both laughed. "So, I just spoke to Dr. Caliskan. He meets with the group next week and expects some pushback on the launch budget."

"They were already committed weren't they?"

"You would think, but no. They approved the design and study Phase 0 only, not the later phases. Some members view this as a mistake."

"Mistake, why? The science is real?"

"I think the issue is over the use of the power. The group is divided. Most follow the charter about lowering fossil fuel use, so the largest culprits should get the power. Others have a more humanitarian mindset and want to bring power to those that least have access to it."

"But this is just a proof of concept."

"Yes, and that point has been stressed. It doesn't mean all have accepted the direction. The feeling has been that as the trials go, so might the UN proposal."

"I guess I can understand that. And once he gets approval, you'll place the purchase orders?"

"Yes. Do you have any objections?"

"None. I'm ready."

"Very well, I'll call you, so you issue the orders to Versilant, and I will issue to Galant."

"Will do. Wow, it's getting real."

"It certainly is."

From his fourth-floor retreat, Cristiano Marcon sat facing Izabel, discussing the detailed findings from his team. Izabel had just poured an Aperol Spritz, and Marcon, a glass of Casa Valduga Villa Lobos Cabernet Sauvignon. Outside, it was raining heavily as it did this time of year, although the temperature was a moderate 77 degrees.

The topic of conversation was an intelligence report regarding Shen Zhou. Although he wished to instill no bias in the team, he knew the goal was to teach Zhou a lesson more than recover the money. Having allowed Izabel to read it, her dry comment was in line with his own thinking. "Well, this Zhou is much more than a farmer. His foundation makes very calculated decisions and rarely more than a few hundred million at a time. He is not a risk taker and never invests more than he is willing to lose."

"Yes, he is not at all what I perceived him to be. That said, he screwed Omelchenko so this business must be concluded."

"Can your hackers simply get access to his money?"

"The Russian doesn't think relieving him of 20 percent of his wealth is a true punishment. Zhou refused him entrance into their special club, the Solak Group, and also short-changed him. He wants to harm him in a public way. You know, shame him."

"What about this Solak Group itself?"

"Possibly. They are planning two phases of this Project Solaris meant to engage the UN into backing a full-blown project in the future. It involves just millions now and maybe as much as a billion for the Phase II trial, My issue there is this is not Zhou's money. It comes from the group. How is that a deterrent?"

"To me, this whole Zhou thing shows the heavy hand of the Chinese government. I'm not so sure that Zhou orchestrated this. Perhaps he was forced by his own government to act?"

"Possible, but it does not matter to Omelchenko."

"You know, there is some concern that this Project Solaris represents weapon capability. As reported, the Phase I power is not enough to be weapon worthy, but Phase II is."

"To what end?" Marcon asked.

"The Solak Group is based in Turkey. Perhaps this is all a rouse for Turkey to get a weapon in space right under our noses."

"You have a devious mind, Izabel."

"I know," was her reply as she fondled her Spritz and swirled it to chill the remaining contents. Marcon stood and walked over to the landing that overlooked the sea, "We want to hurt Zhou without hurting Caliskan and so far, I have not focused on the Solak Group but perhaps there is a way to hurt Zhou and simply involve the Solak Group."

"Do tell?"

"Not yet. I need to discuss this with my Russian friend. I'll tell you this, I can use the Turkey weapon idea to our advantage."

"So, you are leaving me again?"

"Yes, my love, but only for one evening."

"Please be safe. He scares me."

"Yes, well, truth be told, he scares me a little, too."

The private jet landed softly at the Sochi International Airport and taxied to the jet services terminal. The airport was quite large after expansion and modernization for the 2014 winter Olympics and was located just a few miles from Sochi proper. It was also close to a small dacha owned by Sergei Omelchenko. As expected, security was in full force, as Marcon deplaned. Walking down the air-stairs of the jet, he noted several former Spetsnaz, Russian Special Forces, armed with AK-74U assault rifles overseeing a black Mercedes G-550 SUV. It idled in the frigid cold air, with the rear passenger door ajar, a subtle way of saying this is where you will sit.

He walked to it and entered, noting the three armed men inside, saying nothing as the SUV took off. They headed down A147 highway and turned left the moment they had crossed over the Matsesta River. The unpaved road, covered in snow and ice, had been made wider since he was last here. After several kilometers, they pulled into a compound where large steel walls, four meters high had been painted like foliage. A few more minutes passed when they arrived at the traditional dacha, a small home, perhaps one-hundred-ten square meters square feet, in the middle of the vast woods. It was not possible to see the close to five-hundred square meter bunker built into the ground beneath it. In the world of Omelchenko, nothing was ever as it appeared.

Marcon was taken with efficiency through a metal detector and then to a loft where Omelchenko sat reading as he entered the landing and glanced over. "Cristiano, thank you for coming. You have a plan, yes?"

"Yes, Sergei." Marcon went on and described the manner in which Zhou protected himself and his money, but also laid the groundwork for his plan of retribution.

Omelchenko had not spoken during the briefing, but when Marcon ended, he replied, "Yes, I like this plan. And you can pull this off."

"Yes, my network can handle this."

"Very well, let us drink," as he snapped his fingers that sent an aide running to get the two glasses and Vodka already prepared.

*2*1

Dr. Demir Caliskan walked with purpose toward the UN assembly building from the hired car that had brought him here from White Plains. That was where a Bombardier Global 7500 owned and operated by his family business, Caliskan Holdings, had touched down two hours before. He passed by the large bronze sculpture by Carl Fredrik Reuterswärd. The self-titled piece, *Non-Violence*, depicts a pistol whose barrel has been tied into a knot that Reuterswärd, friend to John Lennon and Yoko Ono, created following Lennon's senseless death in 1984. *Clever design*, he thought.

Taking care to avoid ice, he entered the visitor's center. It had taken over a year to get a meeting scheduled here, a place so rich with history and conflict. Caliskan's vision was to bring all the heads of space, current and former, from the ten highest annual CO_2 emission countries. That small group produced seventy percent of all annual emissions and held fifty percent of the world's population. He wanted them in one room to debate the concept of using the energy from Project Solaris to reduce their dependance on fossil fuels and also to create a monitoring agency within the UN Framework Convention on Climate Change to oversee space-based energy-related activities.

During the 1990s, most developed nations had created a space force, or at least a space tsar, in varied forms of formality and power. Other than the United States, all have since merged theirs into the agency that best reviled their desires and not surprisingly, most became a branch of the military. Using that as a backdrop, there are several treaties regarding space itself, and one specifically applied to this group.

In 1967, the US, UK and USSR, created the Outer Space Treaty based on the declaration of legal principles governing the activities of states in the exploration and use of outer space complied by the UN assembly in 1962. It has since added twenty-three additional signatories and eighty-four other countries are parties to it. Amongst other concerns, it prohibits nuclear or other weapons of mass destruction from being deployed in space. Another fun fact, astronauts are legally considered envoys of humankind.

It was worth note that the top ten emitters of annual CO_2 on Caliskan's list, of which China was number one and the United States number two, were all signatories or parties to this treaty. The lone exception was Iran.

He exited his floor and headed for a large circular conference room he had been offered. A guard was present at the door where a second set of scanners and security had been established. He passed through and entered the room. It was smaller than he imagined, but it had presence and would serve his purpose. Several delegates were already there, and he met with each. If everyone showed up, he would have an audience of thirty-seven, including himself.

The seats had been prearranged with Caliskan at the center of the U-shaped semi-circle. It took another hour before the room was fully seated, and only three seats were vacant. A better turnout than he imaged.

The room darkened on his command and a montage of images filled the wall sized screen depicting the birth of energy as we know it and showing the change toward renewables namely, Solar, Wind and Geothermal energy. This was followed by graphs and information showing the rate of energy available to the rate of energy required projected out to the year 2100. The last image was the current statistics regarding global warming. The house lights came on softly, although the images remained.

"Ladies and Gentlemen, on behalf of humankind and your host this evening, the Solak Group, I welcome you to New York and this preliminary meeting regarding the harvesting of energy from space." There were several mummers in the audience, which Caliskan expected. "I realize this topic has polarizing views, and I am not here to sell you anything. I am here to ask for your help because whether you agree, energies from space will contribute to our future energy needs as we shift away from fossil fuels. At some point, the question will have to be addressed. Given the treaties in place, have we fully identified how we, the nations of earth, will manage this, police this, or even own this?"

The voices were louder now, but he ignored it and continued. "Perhaps a regurgitation of facts is in order to set this stage. The trends I am going to share are now unambiguous." The room went darker, and the first statistic became brighter.

"Industrialization has increased average airborne CO_2 levels to unprecedented numbers. In fact, almost every year within the 21st century has been the highest level in 800,000 years only to be outdone by the following year. Our world now creates thirty-six billion metric tons of CO_2 each year, a nine-fold increase since 1935, and the countries represented in this room, the top ten, create seventy percent of that. Sadly, the ecosystems of the earth can absorb less than sixty percent, forcing the remaining twelve billion metric tons to rise into our atmosphere." The screen changed again.

"As a result, average ocean temperature has risen one Celsius since 1800 or one-point-eight degrees Fahrenheit. Sixteen of the hottest years of average air temperature in our history have occurred after the year 2000. That and other factors have caused sea ice to diminish thirteen percent per decade over the last four decades. For reference, in 1984 there were seven million square kilometers of sea ice. There is now four-point-six million. It is not a surprise then that the Antarctic and Greenland ice mass has shrunk over two-thousand billion tons in the 21st century, which has subsequently risen the average sea levels one-hundred millimeters. Four inches for our American friends." Some in the room chuckled, and he continued. "Left unchecked, it will rise almost a full meter by the end of this century." The screen showed the coastal areas of the world in red that would be under water. Hundreds of millions of people were affected.

Next were images of storms, heat waves, drought and hurricanes, as he concluded, "I don't have to tell you that record heat, record rain, and a plethora of natural disasters now occur with regularity. Billion dollar claims from natural disasters once made the news. Now they represent daily events around the world. And this is just the beginning. That, ladies and gentlemen is the milieu for this meeting." The lights came on. Uncontested, Caliskan continued.

"Despite these facts, while the world may no longer deny the consequences of global warming, we are falling behind in our efforts to avoid it. The UN Convention on Climate Change Committee determined that any temperature increase over one-point-five Celsius by the year 2100 will be detrimental to human life. The Paris Agreement of 2015 included this challenge. But within the few years since it was adopted, the shift to renewable energy while robust is not keeping up with our exhaust of greenhouse gases and almost all modeling suggests we won't even be able to cap this at two Celsius. The smartest minds in the world say we have less than a fifty/fifty chance. Please note that all excess CO_2 placed into our atmosphere comes from fossil fuels, fires, and deforestation. We must find a better way to both reduce the annual emissions and also reduce what is already there." Caliskan stopped and had a drink of water as the images changed again to the various concepts of change.

"In time, our world will have to complete and implement various forms of Solar Geoengineering, which includes carbon geoengineering, or carbon dioxide removal (CDR) and possibly even solar geoengineering, or solar radiation management (SRM) if it can be done safely. I am not here to argue or defend such projects."

The lights dimmed again, and Project Solaris filled the wall. "This, my friends is Project Solaris. We have undertaken this to show the world that there is enough energy in space to satisfy the world's energy needs every day. As a matter of scientific fact, one twenty-four-hour period of accumulated energy from space fills the energy needs for the entire planet earth for an entire year." Caliskan went through the basis of the initial phases, concluding with, "... Phase II, will occur in seven months and will beam fifty million watts each day or four-hundred-fifty million kilowatt hours of energy over a single year. On successful completion of Phase II, the Solak Group will give this technology to the UN Climate Change Committee gratis in hopes they will promote a larger initiative of the same technology with you, the countries creating the most emissions. It will require twenty-four such systems and produce eleven billion kilowatt hours per year. That is enough energy to power one million homes and is the equivalent of two nuclear power plants, but without the health risks and half the cost. Additional details are in your prospectus. Imagine if they built five times that many? That's five million homes. What about ten times? That's ten million homes?"

The image on the walls showed in computer simulation how the P-POD system is carried into space using a Falcon Heavy rocket. This was followed by how the nanosatellites attach around the aperture and then, how the sun's rays are converted to energy and last how they are beamed to earth. Caliskan noted all faces were on the screen, most in awe. The screen froze on the image of the beam to earth and the house lights came back on.

"Ladies and Gentlemen, Project Solaris, will happen with or without your support, but please consider this. Geopolitics of the late 20th and 21st century have largely been related to fossil fuels, specifically, coal, gasoline and natural gas. Our models suggest the shift away from fossil fuels and search for fresh water will define the geopolitics for the rest of this century. The difference now is that failure could have grave consequences for humankind itself."

Caliskan allowed those words to be considered if the attendee had sufficient mind to do so before concluding his opening remarks. "In your prospectus, the Solak Group is also proposing to create a UN Climate Change Space Force and ultimately, that is why I have asked you here. We need a mechanism to guard energy in space from evil. As I have mentioned, my preference is to make this part of the UN Framework Convention on Climate Change, as rules and protocols are already in place. Might I hear your thoughts?"

It was into the evening before all voices had been heard and whatever Caliskan thought might have happened; he was not entirely prepared for the reality. This group of individuals, as talented as they might be, had wasted the entire opportunity. He now suspected some couldn't even find their way out of the room if the exits had not been marked.

With few exceptions, each wanted to grandstand, reaffirm their government's propaganda, or worse, bash the person who had just spoken based solely on the country they represented. Such childish behaviors were going to challenge him.

Caliskan, although highly frustrated, calmed himself and with resolve, closed the meeting with kind words and hopes they could dwell on what they heard and continue the dialogue at a later time.

He also added that his government, Turkey would ask for a resolution on behalf of Project Solaris. Caliskan did not need a UN resolution to launch either phase, but he needed one to propose the actual space based solar power concept to the UN, hoping in a few years, they would own this and fund the larger array system for the world to use.

22

Kennedy Space Center, Merritt Island

The Sun was bright in a cloudless sky across much of the Florida panhandle. There on the cape was a gentle breeze aiding the ambient temperature to just under seventy degrees—picture perfect weather for a space launch. The Cape Canaveral United States Space Force Station, the militarized site, sat to the east, where the Banana river separated it from Merritt Island, home to the Kennedy Space Center. This was the launch area most were familiar with.

Both sites have a long and distinguished history in the America space program, from the Titan, Delta, Atlas, and Saturn rockets of the 60s and 70s, to the Space Shuttle and Minotaur rockets of the 80s and 90s. By the new millennium, commercial space programs had begun the shift from NASA to private companies, albeit with funding from NASA. From the early days of private commercial space programs with the launch of Falcon I, modern times include the Falcon 9, Falcon Heavy, New Sheppard, Electron, Antares, Artemis, and StarLink. The success of these programs has focused NASA primarily on science and the outer reaches of the heavens rather that commercial tasks such as satellite launches. The result is a significant decrease in cost per launch of millions. As much as forty percent by one account.

Project Solaris intended to launch the entire group of Phase I nanosatellites all at once, and there were two approved locations to launch the rocket. One was here, and the other was the Vanderburg Air Force base in California. Because of the launch to GEO, Florida was the preferred location and much of the Project Solaris team was here either working at the mobile launch center or on the mobile receiving antenna that would receive the beam from space if all went well. Sara and the two team leaders were there, while Zhou and Caliskan were observing via a video link.

Weeks before, the nanosatellites produced by Galant Industries had been loaded into the P-POD system, which was now concealed under the nose cone of the rocket. For two days, the teams had been checking, rechecking, and assuring a planned launch at 1:00 p.m. that afternoon. As the time approached, tension was building when the mission commander gave the all systems go signal and the countdown began… Five, Four, Three, Two, ignition and liftoff…

Sara realized she had been holding her breath and exhaled loudly as the rocket lifted off the pad slowly and then shot away. The vapor trail was soon all one could see as the launch team went through the various stages of the control. All was working to plan.

Hours passed before various monitors told the room the rocket had entered the geosynchronous transfer orbit (GTO). From here, it was common to deploy satellites under the rocket power and then use satellite boosters to take them into GEO itself. But that took power and up to forty-eight hours for the satellites to follow the elliptical movement out of GTO into GEO. The nanosatellites simply did not have that kind of booster power given they still had to find their mate and then orient into the right position to beam. As a result, they would take the Falcon 9 into GEO itself and release. Once there, flight control and the Solaris team would program the satellites to join.

It took an hour for the P-POD system to deploy the satellites, and approval was given to join them together. The Project Solaris team programmed ten nanosatellites to join into an array, end over end, before each of those ten were joined to the one next to it with the collector/aperture in the center. This process took several hours, but it wasn't long before they received a signal that some nanosatellites could not connect.

The look on the face of Project Manager Omer Celebi was one of concern and frustration. It wasn't like they could just reach up and fix it. After three attempts, nine of the ninety-four satellites would not join and were sent into the background, away from the main array, which was now a three meter square solar panel with a few holes where the defective satellites should have been. The team then used the small thrusters to move the entire panel into position.

When complete, the system immediately started to collet radiation from the sun and fill the collector, which was connected to the aperture of the laser. The team gave each other cautious high-fives in celebration.

Sara and Julian were pleased that the system was working, but not happy they had lost ten percent of their available solar energy. Omer promised a thorough investigation, and as they spoke, Sara noticed a team member doing nothing but taking in the room near the door. In the hours they had been there, she had watched him several times with this same observation. Given the lack of action on his part and his visual nervousness, he looked up to something, and she suspected whatever it was, it wasn't good.

Sara motioned to Celebi, "Omer, I'm sorry to interrupt, but who is that young man?"

Omer stopped mid-sentence and glanced over. "I'm not sure of his name. He is a grad student. Why?" Sara reiterated her concern, and both were now looking at him. When the student turned and caught both of their eyes staring at him, his face showed panic and concern. He knew he had been made.

Within seconds, Celebi started toward him, and the student immediately exited the door and left the mission control trailer. Omer ran to the door, going out after him as various team members wondered what the heck was going on. Outside, he thought he saw the student turn a corner and ran in that direction while he used his comm device to alert security. He was running toward several large buildings when security arrived, and he gave them a general description of the student. Not wanting to miss the action he let security take over and returned to the command center winded.

As he walked back in, he looked at Sara and shrugged his shoulders as if to say, *no idea where he went*. The team was still monitoring the collection units and Omer was quickly pulled back into task, thinking little of the odd exchange.

Sara was looking at her monitors when her phone buzzed in silent mode. She looked at the caller ID and it was Annabel Sykes, Jason's mom. Sara should have let it go, considering, but took the call as she walked into a small side room. "Annabel, I am at the launch site, can I call you back or is this an emergency?"

"No emergency. I guess it can wait. I just needed to talk to you."

"Annabel, hold on. Let me see how much time I have." Sara said, sensing a problem as she hit pause and went out and asked Omer who said she had time. Sara tucked back into the room and said, "I have a few minutes. What's up?"

"I heard you spoke to him." Referring to Jason.

"I did for a few minutes. Have you also?"

"Yes, he wondered why, since in his mind, we haven't spoken for years."

"I know. He recalls nothing about Seattle, not even the work."

"Sara, I know you have an amazing life ahead of you, but please don't give up on him?"

"What? Why would you say that?"

"Sara, I am a miserable woman who fell for an Army relic. But I am still a woman, and it is not lost on me that your relationship with Jason was just getting started. When he comes around, we're all going to have to work at this. I guess I'm just hoping you will, too."

"Annabel, it is difficult for me to admit, but the concept of love, romance, and desire is quite foreign to me. You are not wrong in sensing our relationship was new, challenged, and perhaps even one-sided. I honestly don't know what will happen. We'll just have to find out."

"Sara, I'm sorry to share my worries. I just know you make him happy, and if he pulls through this, I want him to be happy. I doubt he'll ever let me try." She cried.

"Baby steps Annabel. When Jason spoke of you he was never bitter. He was just resigned to no longer worry about it. That means at one time he was worried about it, so he cared. Ironically, he is more likely to reconnect to you than your husband, but you'll have to help him understand your side of this. I got the impression he expected this from his dad, but not you. To hear him say it, his own mom abandoned him."

"If I had sided with him, I would have shared the same fate. I had no career, no money. My goodness, that sounds so selfish, now. He is my son."

"Annabel, you'll be able to work through this. I have to go, but we'll talk soon."

23

Geosynchronous Earth Orbit

It was late in the evening when system control said that the collector had received full power from the array of solar panels and could beam. The array in space was quite small and therefore, when the collection units reached capacity, the solar panels shut themselves down to protect the system from overheating. Sara and Hendricks had moved away from the action as Dr. Huang came forward to get his team in place. The receiving antenna was three kilometers away for safety reasons. If all worked as planned, about three-point-one million watts would beam into the megapack battery system under it.

Sara had been working with an engineer to see if her gamma ray sensors that were on each satellite had located any remnants of energy from TGF activity lower in the atmosphere. Early indication was that several sensors had triggered meaning gamma rays were at least present.

After an hour to assure all systems were a go, Huang ordered the beam to power up. Unfortunately, their small video feed was attached to one nanosatellite that didn't connect, so the video feed was from behind the array, resulting in a poor image.

Relying on the monitors, Huang gave the command, and the nervous technician sent the radio signal to beam, which took about the radio waves several minutes to travel the distance.

Sara was so engrossed in her own data collection she jumped when the room let out a collective gasp and she immediately looked up at the monitors, which were now all blank. All data was gone. The screens were just a series of menus with no live data in any of the fields. Huang was yelling at his team as Hendricks quickly disconnected the room's video feed at Dr. Zhou's request.

For a few tense minutes, the team was frantically typing commands, but nothing changed. Had they lost the connection? Was the beam interfering with the signals?

Huang confirmed nothing had been received, meaning the beam had not activated even for a moment. Since the laser beam was visible light, they should be able to see it with the naked eye, but the camera feed to the receiving antenna showed nothing. The night sky was jet black.

Hendricks was on the phone with Caliskan and Zhou, trying to relay what was happening when a control manager entered the trailer and motioned for Hendricks to come to a wall phone. She did and answered, holding her cell in her other hand where Caliskan and Zhou awaited any news. Sara watched her face go white as Hendricks nodded and slowly placed the phone back on its cradle. She looked across the room and said solemnly, "Team, that was Space Forces Command. They are confirming an explosion at the location of our array. All is lost."

It was nearly two o'clock in the morning as the team leaders sat in their hotel lobby trying to understand what had gone wrong. They had promised Caliskan an update in the morning. Celebi, Hendricks, and Sara had discussed the first failure, the nine units that would not join. Had this created a short circuit? Celebi created a quick plan to have the backup satellites not in space inspected. His thesis was that the pins and receiving holes that allowed the units to connect were made incorrectly. The design team had made these of chromium, which was a heavy dense metal normally not used due to weight, but it could withstand the vast change in hot or cold with minimal expansion or contraction. He suspected tolerances had not been initially met as the reason the units would not join.

Meanwhile, Huang had brainstormed with his team by phone, but could not provide a reason for the explosion. Yes, there was energy, but it wasn't combustible in theory. He could only suspect that the failure mode was heat. This although the cooling systems were working fine leading up to the point of system loss.

It was then that Celebi mentioned the possibility of sabotage. He mentioned the student Sara had noticed and his disappearance some twelve hours before. They would mention this to Caliskan. On that, the team slowly rose and headed to the elevators tired and dejected.

The following day, the Project Solaris leaders were summoned to Montreux where they would be expected to determine what happened. The exception was Omer Celebi who stayed in Florida with the backup satellites and would hire a local company to inspect the units to specification. He had alerted Galant Industries to the problem, but not to his post-inspection.

Dr. Huang worked with his team to analyze the stored data up to the point of the system loss for anything related to a short circuit or any alarm in temperature. They poured through hours of data and twelve hours later concluded there was never a point of critical heat and that the radiant based cooling system had worked flawlessly. They also could not locate any spike in current to suggest a short. But they weren't empty handed.

At the exact moment the aperture had received the signal to initial beam, there was a spike in transient voltage. This was expected, and the powerful collector unit contained many critical diodes to rectify this. Huang called Celebi and asked him to verify the make and model of the diodes in the single backup collector they had.

The next afternoon, Celebi confirmed two important items. For the nanosatellites, they had five spare units. Two of the five had incorrect tolerances in the machined pins or mating holes. Although the units could be assembled at ambient temperature, at extreme hot or extreme cold, this would not be the case. For their lone spare collector/aperture unit, it contained diodes by the company specified, but were a different part number which were inferior.

Huang and Hendricks updated Caliskan who eventually negotiated a settlement with Galant Industries. He was not happy this had failed and would issue a press release, but he was also relieved that the idea of sabotage appeared unlikely.

Sara had meanwhile given the name of the young Brazilian student to Richard Chase and asked if he could do a background check on him. It wasn't six hours later when Chase called. Sara left the room to take the call. "Richard that was fast. What did you find?"

"I had a friend in Interpol check and your boy, Diego Rivera is in fact a master's student at Universidade Estadual de Campinas (UNICAMP) in Brazil. He has no criminal record; however, he is an idealist and has been connected to several protests relating to renewable energy. There are a few activist outlets on school campuses in Brazil and it is rumored that a

Brazilian entrepreneur, Cristiano Marcon, funds them. This Marcon is CEO of Povos Engeria, one of the largest petrol station owners in Brazil. According to Interpol, although Marcon is the legitimate head of several businesses, he is thought to be involved in organized crime, especially in Latin America and Russia. Not sure if that helps, but it's all we have."

"Thanks. I'll pass this along just in case." After hanging up, Sara called Celebi who would update Caliskan later that evening.

The Solak Group issued a press release the next day explaining the failure of the system and the likely causes without mentioning Galant Industries by name. They planned to reconstruct Phase I with corrections before moving forward with Phase II. There was little discussion and little fanfare, as the project was only being followed in scientific circles.

As they concluded, Caliskan mentioned to Zhou his relief that the project had not been sabotaged, but he also told Zhou about the disappearance of the Brazilian student, Diego Rivera, who might have been a plant to get information on the project possibly related to his past with activist groups. They would reevaluate the teams to assure they had missed no other surprises.

24

Levent, Istanbul, Turkey

The large digital wall clock showed thirty-three minutes past ten inside the grand conference room on the 53rd floor of the Istanbul Voltaire building. The room was two-thirds full as members of the Solak Group filed in greeting each other, some for the first time, others as veterans. The group met twice a year, and attendance was strongly suggested. Although members could send an alternate, that person must actually vote on the members' behalf. For security reasons, no video sharing was allowed.

This meeting was timed to coincide with the Phase I launch and its recent failure would be part of the agenda.

Caliskan had not yet entered the room and was watching the members through an anteroom to the right, which housed a large round conference table with concentric wings surrounding the center. It could seat one hundred and twenty. Security had been tight, because of the possibility that Phase I had been sabotaged. As the time approached eleven, Zhou and Caliskan entered and took their places.

Zhou called the meeting to order. "Ladies and Gentlemen, thank you for coming. On today's agenda are six items. First, we have four new member recommendations. In front of you is a dossier on each. We will vote after lunch. Second, Phase 0 of Project Solaris is complete, and an executive summary has been given to you, and there is no additional action required. Phase 0 created the basis for Phase I, which, as you know, failed, and we'll discuss what our investigation revealed. That will be followed by a vote to repeat Phase I at a discounted price because of vendor performance and last, to approve the approximate cost of Phase II as we know it today. Dr. Caliskan will explain. Our last agenda item will be a discussion on the Nile basin project, but we'll not vote on this until our next session at the earliest. Are there questions?"

The room was silent, so he continued and went through the bio of each new member who had been recommended.

Zhou then closed the blinds with the flick of a switch, and the center of the room became a holographic screen as Caliskan went through a pictorial description of the launch of Phase I and the ultimate loss of their array. He gave the findings of their research as to causation and his settlement with Galant Industries. They would rebuild the Phase I satellites at their cost, saving the group twenty-two million euros. Given the failure, they felt it was too much risk to advance to Phase II without the success of a Phase I trial, and he requested forty million euros to reattempt the trial. "Are there questions?"

A member from Bulgaria asked, "What is the estimated cost of Phase II?"

"Based on our best estimate, it is six-hundred-sixty million euros or six-point-four million per member."

A newer member asked, "What if Phase I fails again?"

"Should we have a second failure, which I doubt knowing now how it happened, we would place the project on hold pending an investigation. Dr. Zhou and I would fund the cost of the investigation and present our findings to this body to determine the next steps."

"If this vote is not unanimous, I see no reason to move forward." Said another member.

Zhou stood now and said calmly, "Ladies and Gentlemen, we are over a year into this effort and yes we had a setback, but great things are not achieved without risk. Should the vote achieve majority, monies lost by any member that does not fund the Phase re-launch will be paid by the Sunset Foundation to avoid any increase on the remaining members. It is only fair to remind everyone that refusal to pay once a majority is reached bans that member from the group." Nods circulated.

"Thank you, Dr. Zhou. That is a generous offer and one I hope will not be needed. Questions?" Caliskan asked.

The room was silent, but some were stirring, and a few members murmured there were other ways to seek power, and perhaps this was too expensive. Caliskan ignored them since they did not address the assembly and simply asked for the vote. The vote was electronic, and the results were shown on the wall next to the digital clock. It took fifteen minutes, but the final was ninety-one yes and thirteen no. Caliskan spoke. "We have a majority. Are there any members who wish to dispute payment?"

In terms of a group dynamic, this was always the point that the room waited for, to see who opted out. Some secretly had side bets, as they considered who had the stomach for it and who might not. With thirteen negative votes, would all thirteen not pay and be banned? All eyes were on the digital printout as the number one flashed, then two, before it finally stopped at five. Shen Zhou stood and said, "The five disdaining members will be shown to the exit, and I will pay these dissident funds. Thank you."

Caliskan took control and went to the statistics of Phase II. Again, he used the projection system to create the image. He closed by saying, "As was already described, the estimated cost for Phase II is six-hundred-sixty million euros. In order to begin procurement, I wish to bring this to vote as well. Are there any objections or questions?"

An American stood and asked, "If there should be a second failure and the project review suggests that Project Solaris not move forward, will monies from this vote be lost or refunded?"

"A good question. In the rare scenario you just mentioned, all unspent monies would be refunded to all members on the vote that cancels the project. Any monies spent would become part of the formal review process. If the review shows a failure of project management, Dr. Zhou and I will reimburse the membership in full. If the fault is deemed an act of nature, or its legal term, force majeure, the money would be lost."

There were no more questions, so Caliskan asked if the Phase II expenses could be called to vote. Again, the results were shown on the wall. It took over twenty-five minutes for this larger call to action. The final was ninety-seven yes, and a single vote for no. Caliskan spoke. "We have a majority. Are there any members who wish to dispute payment?" The digital counter showed zero for five minutes before it flashed to one.

Shen Zhou stood and said, "We will now break for lunch. The single disdaining member will be shown out. Thank you." As the group rose, Zhou placed his hand over his mouth and spoke to Caliskan. "I hope they vote for the new members. This is our largest defection at any single meeting." Caliskan simply nodded his head.

25

D r. Ferrera glanced at his aging Lenovo tablet computer while sitting and having a cup of expresso in his small but pretentious office. The subject on the small screen was the failed attempt of Project Solaris. The press release alluded to the causation by supplier failure, which would be remedied as they prepared for a relaunch in less than three months.

This news wasn't entirely unexpected, but a failure is a failure, and Ferrera was trying to gauge the reaction from the university administration. He liked Sara and enjoyed the relationship they had together, but he was the one that had pulled strings to get her an assignment here and certainly had given her favorable treatment for several months, some of which had resulted in complaints by other staff, many tenured and much senior to her. It was bad enough that there were rumors of a sexual nature regarding his intent, which was nonsense but, it also meant any negative reaction to the university because of her, would fall to him, and him alone.

For now, he surmised all was fine and prepared to discuss this, as she was on her way over to his office. Sara walked up the stairs and asked the assistant if she could have a word with him. She said yes as she rose and walked her in before backing out and closing the door. She had been expected.

"Sara, welcome back. How was it?"

Sara wasn't sure what he knew and thought it best to just get it over with. "The launch went well, but we had difficulty pairing the units. Ten percent would not join, although we immediately starting collected the energy, which was wonderful. When the team instructed the aperture to beam, however, the entire array exploded."

"Most disappointing. Do they know what happened?"

"Yes, the units didn't pair because of a manufacturing defect, and the beam didn't work because the supplier used an incorrect diode. At the threat of being held libel, the manufacturer agreed to remake the units at cost, and the Group gained approval to relaunch yesterday. We have a second chance."

"I am surprised the manufacturer wasn't publicly roasted."

"They would have been had they not agreed to the terms of settlement from Dr. Caliskan."

"And your invention. Did it work?"

"This array was too small to house my invention, so we only sent up sensors to tell us if gamma rays were present. I have at least ten hours of data and by all measures, the gammas are there. We'll test for them again on the relaunch, and if they're still present, we'll place four dishes on the center satellites in Phase II. The number of gammas in GEO is quite low, so this will only serve as potential backup power. There is not enough to act as primary power."

"Well, I hope for your sake and the university, they use the dish. It would make for great publicity. Speaking of which, we would expect you to write a paper on the findings. The more your name is published the better visibility for us both."

"I know. You only like me for my representation to the university," she laughed.

"That is not true, but your written work is an important part of the accomplishment and your own career."

"I know. We'll publish three papers as a group of which I will be named. Separately, I'll author my own paper related to my invention."

"Excellent. As I said last year, you are the rock-star of physics here and an inspiration to countless new female scientists. Are you aware Dr. Ricci, that of the one-hundred-thirty students in your class, over six-hundred applied? Of those, two-thirds were women. That is unprecedented and attributed to your youth, your surname, and your unique story. It is rare for Sapienza to garner such positive news from an only mildly published and un-tenured professor. I hope you don't see our interest as inappropriate."

"Not at all, Dr. Ferrera. I get how the game works. It's just a lot of pressure to not fail so soon out of the gate."

"I can imagine, but we have complete faith in you. Failure happens. It is what you do with it that matters, and you have done well. Keep it going, as they say."

As Sara walked back to her office, she realized that while everything he said was true, he still looked at this as a pathway for her to become a tenured professor. She wasn't sure if that was what she even wanted.

The following morning, Sara was making an expresso when her cell phone rang. It was Jason. "Good morning. How are you feeling?" She said happily.

"Good, still no seizures. Because of that, they have removed most of my medication, so at least I'm not a zombie all day."

"That's great to hear. I can actually hear it in your voice. Are you close to going to a normal hospital?"

"I talked to my dad, and he says I need to stay here until I can return to the States. If I have this right, they think I am a recruit being sponsored by him. We were on some secret mission when I got shot."

Sara understood, perhaps better than Jason, given his mental lapses. "I hope that is soon."

"Me too. Hey, I recall you had some big work thing coming up. Did I miss it?"

Sara explained the launch and the failure quickly and with little detail to make it easier for him to understand, which he did before she mentioned the second launch. "In a few months, we'll try again."

"Sounds like you're busy."

"You know me."

"I know, robot girl." He laughed.

"Has anyone mentioned when you can return home?"

"They are saying two weeks if my condition stays as is."

"Will you head back to Seattle?"

"No. my dad said I might need to spend some time with my sister Rachael at Fort Benning. I'm not sure why. Must be part of the cover he is using."

"I think that is right. You know Rachael was there with you and your dad."

"He alluded to that, but it seems strange. Honestly, I wasn't sure it was even true."

"It is. Richard Chase was there also with three others. I don't know exactly what happened, but while the mission was a success, you were shot when you jumped to save Rachael."

"Sara, what were we doing there? I know I'm not in the army anymore."

"This wasn't about the army. The mission was to apprehend Bridget Drummond."

"The sister to Maximillian? I remember her. She was a real bitch, but why? We're not the police?"

"No, and that is the reason for the cover story. She tried to kill me three separate times, and you twice, but was arrested. She escaped from the prison in Nova Scotia and then fled. She was planning to hide at an island retreat in the Maldives where they do not have extradition to the UK. If you hadn't stopped her, she would have gone into hiding just waiting for another chance. I hope I'm not in trouble for telling you."

"Sara, my current memory is fine, so thanks, and this really helps. I won't say anything to anyone, but it's really strange to hear this and have no recollection of it."

"That must be difficult." Sara said, thinking of them in Seattle, not the mission.

"It is. Anyway, I'll let you know what happens next."

"Please do."

"Don't work too hard?"

"Me, never. Call me if anything changes."

"Will do." They hung up, and to Sara it was a moment of reflection. The conversation they had was reminiscent of when they first met at MIT. She sat on the terrace trying to picture him, not in a hospital bed, but when they first met.

26

Kennedy Space Center, Merritt Island

The Falcon 9 rocket sat on its pad two and a half months later. The modern gleaming white edifice was a feat of engineering genius surrounded by commercial efficiency. Using several small rockets instead of one massive one, the various booster towers were also reusable after being salvaged, saving millions and keeping huge pieces of space junk out of the upper atmosphere. For this relaunch, Galant Industries and the Solak Team had done a good job rebuilding the nanosatellites, and Project Manager Celebi had inspected each one, often working sixteen hours a day to accomplish the task. He saw this as the price paid to move the project forward. Another failure would likely end Project Solaris, and perhaps his career.

From the launch center, the team was again in control and for this relaunch, Zhou and Caliskan were there also, as both felt their reputations were on the line. Of course, the team leaders were there, as was Sara. They were forced to scrub the launch the day before because of the wind, but today was calm. The launch window came into view and the mission commander gave the all systems go call and the countdown began. Sara was calmer this time around, as she knew what to expect, and the rocket lifted off the pad without concern.

It was five hours before the monitors indicted the rocket had entered GEO. An hour later, the P-POD system had unloaded the nanosatellites and approval was given for them to join. The team programmed them accordingly. They would join into an array, end over end, before each of those ten were joined to the one next to it with the collector/aperture in the center. The process went faster this time, and there were no stray satellites. All joined, and the team had its first small, but needed celebration.

In just minutes, the system started to collet radiation from the sun and fill the collector, and the team was more generous in their celebration.

Five hours later, system control said that the collector had received full power from the array of solar panels and the panels were shut down. They were ready to beam. Dr. Hendricks and Sara vacated the controls and Dr. Huang came forward, his team already in place. He was nervous and the tension in his body was quite obvious, but they had checked and double checked the process so many times; he was inwardly confident. He looked over at Zhou and Caliskan, nodded nervously, and gave the command to beam.

As before, the same truck mounted receiving antenna was parked three kilometers away. All eyes were on the screens, including a camera looking at the receiving antenna when the glow of the visible beam illuminated. It took less than sixteen minutes for the roughly three-point-eight million watts to arrive and store into the megapack. The beam had interrupted itself over fifteen times, because something had entered its path, but it successfully reconnected as soon as it could.

The team erupted and even Dr. Zhou, who displayed almost no outward emotions, smiled, and gave high fives to several of the team. It had been a success, and Caliskan immediately sent out a previously written press release. He had written two, one for success... and one for failure.

For her part, Sara sat in the corner with two technicians and observed the gamma ray sensor data. It was very close to the first trial, maybe even a bit improved, which confirmed the gammas were there and mathematically could offer some secondary power.

Two months later, Caliskan was back in the UN building and back in the same room as before. He had hoped to use the success of the Phase I launch to pave the way for a more positive decision regarding the UN Climate Change Space Force. The audience was largely in place, although where he had an audience of thirty-four the first time, only twenty-five were present now. The Americans had not even bothered to cancel. They were just absent, but perhaps it was for the best as their new President had recently pulled them out of the Paris Agreement.

He motioned for the meeting to begin and as the house lights dimmed; he used the presentation from the Solak Group meeting to show the project and highlight the success of finding, capturing, and beaming almost four million watts to earth. They had beamed regularly for five days to prove the repetition of the concept before it was stopped momentarily. In time, they would have to move the receiving antenna off the grounds of the Kennedy Space Center in order to continue.

As the lights brightened, it was pretty clear how the room was divided. The scientific minds were giddy and asking for details, which Caliskan happily gave. Those with a strong military bent were concerned, indifferent, or bored.

Thankfully, without the Americans in the room, the meeting was far more interactive than months before. A young man from the UK asked, "Dr. Caliskan, if the UN took such a step even though this is highly unlikely, who would own the 24 systems you propose?"

"Unknown, but possibly the UN itself. Alternately, it has been the view of the Solak Group that one or more systems should be owned by countries that create the highest CO_2

emissions. Alternately, the systems could be owned by the highest GDP nations, much as UN dues are calculated today."

For several hours, the discussion went on, and while better than the first meeting, it was nowhere near any form of action.

27

Rublyovka, Russia

The weather had turned sour, as it often did this time of year. Snow from previous months was largely gone, bringing wet and horrid conditions to earthen roads and a dampness to the air, which settled into the bones of Sergei Omelchenko. This drab gray sky was cold, but not cold enough to remove the excessive moisture from the air. Sitting in his study in front of a slow burning fire, he poked at the large orange wood logs burning in the fireplace. The hard wood produced a fragrant aroma and very high heat. You couldn't start a fire with it, but once a hotbed of coals was available, it was a treat.

Omelchenko set aside the forged steel fire poker and sat down. He glanced at a lengthy contract, but skipped it to read the update from Cristiano Marcon regarding the Project Solaris from the Solak Group. Thanks to his previous role in the former Russian Space Forces, Omelchenko had several contacts within the newly forced Russian Aerospace Forces and was keen to watch the next steps of this project.

His contacts thought this was possibly a weapon for Turkey itself although that was untrue, and a rumor Marcon had started on the dark web as part of the plan to shame Zhou.

Project Solaris had some tailwind, thanks to the recent success, but Marcon had lost his inside man and was trying to get another. For now, Omelchenko would trust this to Marcon and on the successful trial of Phase I, but he also wondered if this was perhaps an opportunity for his own corporation, Geoentergetics.

Was his anger at Zhou keeping him from seeing a golden opportunity? Should he possess this technology? It could not be any more difficult to get, considering what he was doing to ruin it?

It was just past six in the evening when Sara arrived at the
Institute and immediately walked into Julian Hendricks who
had just come in from the airport. The entire team was here to
get started on the many details that would be required for Phase
II, the much larger and riskier conclusion to Project Solaris.

After a brief dinner with Dr. Huang and a celebratory glass
of wine, they met with the sub-team leaders to recount the
Phase II general features. This array would use the same
nanosatellites, but they would be larger, approximately 3-times
the size used in Phase I, each outfitted with a solar array one
meter square. When the array was fully deployed, the total solar
panel area would be forty meters square. This number of
nanosatellites, almost sixteen hundred, would require eight
separate launches on the Falcon Heavy rocket: a logistical
nightmare.

From an anteroom off of the main area where the teams
were, Sara joined with Huang and Hendricks. Huang spoke
first. "I received an odd call from a member of the Chinese

government. They have heard rumors that Project Solaris is a precursor for a weapon."

Sara looked at Julian in horror and said, "A weapon for whom?"

"They say Turkey." Huang replied.

Hendricks spoke, "That makes no sense. I suspect it is just disinformation to taint the concept of a UN Climate Change Space Force."

"Well, of its design, it is not a weapon of any kind so I do not view this as a concern but we should all be aware of such thoughts so we can address them within the teams or the outside world we contact with." Said Huang.

Julian replied, "Dr. Huang, you are not wrong, but it's sad to see things like this taking away from the achievement itself."

"I agree." Sara added.

Hendricks changed the subject and asked Sara about her invention. "Sara, I saw the purchase orders issued to Versilant for the four small dishes of your design. So, this will power the larger center units?"

"No, there is only enough available power to be used as a backup to the initial battery power." Dr. Huang nodded.

"Okay, I was instructed by Dr. Caliskan to issue you funds per your royalty agreement."

Sara replied, "We have revised the agreement since it cannot provide main power."

"Yes, I saw that, and the cost per system was significantly reduced. I think you personally could have negotiated much more." Julian said matter of fact.

"It is more than generous. I am quite satisfied to even have my first commercial application."

"Good for you, Sara," she replied.

In Barcelona, Spain, Zhou and Caliskan sat in the private lounge of an air services company as their Gulfstream G7 was being fueled. Zhou had been on a call and looked now over at Caliskan and said, "These rumors of a weapon are a distraction."

"I agree." As he contemplated the origin of the rumor. "We may wish to issue a press release to put this in check. It could overshadow the entire basis of the project."

"We also need to verify the origin. Our usual sources will look into this and follow it back from your meetings at the UN building. I am convinced it started before that, meaning someone is trying to redirect the message of our positive launch."

"The UN meetings?" Caliskan asked, puzzled.

"When you mentioned who would own the UN system, them, you mentioned the GDP based system. That was used to establish this might be tied to Turkey itself."

"Are you serious?"

"Demir, I'm almost always serious."

"Very well, keep me informed."

"I will."

Sara left the Institute in Switzerland and headed for Vincenza, an industrial region in northern Italy. She had rented a car and drove to a supplier there as a favor of Dr. Hendricks. When Sara concluded her business, she planned to stop in Milan to see her dad and Chiara and wearily arrived at their terrace flat around seven that same night. She walked up to the fifth floor with her small bag and again; knocked out of respect.

Chiara herself answered the door and gave Sara a hug and kiss. "Ciao, Sara. You look beautiful and full of life. We have so enjoyed following your success."

"Thank you Chiara, but it is truly a team effort, and the heavy lifting has just begun." As she said this, her dad, dressed in the most fashionable clothes Sara had ever seen on him, walked over and gave her a huge hug. Sara thought he looked so happy. *Was that cologne he was wearing? Dad never used cologne.*

"My special girl, it is so good for you to stop by. How long can you stay?" He asked.

"Just until tomorrow, I have to get back." She couldn't resist saying, "Don't you look fancy?"

"Chiara says I am a gentleman now and must dress the part. I do this for her." This was not a stretch. A few hundred years before, a person who was not of royal blood became a gentleman once they no longer had to work. This allowed them to spend their time philosophically, giving mind to subjects not possible when one focused on making a living.

Sara smiled. "Well, you look great. You both do. What is that wonderful smell coming from the kitchen Chiara?"

"In your honor, tonight we have Osso Bucco, braised lamb shanks. It is a specialty of mine." She went off to prepare as Sara and Giovanni went out onto the terrace and he poured her a glass of wine. After an amazing dinner, they sat at the table, and Sara filled them in on the project and some of the politics. They were quite informed, so Chiara had been correct. They had been following the news.

Sara asked Chiara about the Carabinieri Art Squad and specifically how it all works, and Chiara was happy to answer. "The original intent of its formulation in 1969 was driven in part by Italy's vast collection of antiquities created by the Renaissance. A secondary contributor was the theft of fine arts from the Jews at the beginning and during the war throughout Europe. Many precious pieces were taken from here, but many were also brought here during Mussolini's quest to align with the Germans. That said, the squad focuses on archaeology, antique dealing, fakes, and contemporary art. In more recent times, art is being used to launder money by terrorist groups, criminal organizations, and billionaires."

"Launder money?" Sara asked.

"Yes. Please recall that art is a unique transaction, unlike any other. There are virtually no regulatory requirements for art sales even at prices of one-hundred million euros. Most sales are in cash and there is no registration required to move it into or out of the county. It is one of the few markets in the world that has no market price. It is simply what the buyer will bear. Last, it offers anonymity. Who has not seen an auction with a buyer represented only by an associate holding a phone?"

"So, how do you launder money with art?"

"Most involve multiple parties, involved with several transactions, and most likely in two or more different countries. Many times, this art is taken and placed in special holding areas where it can be sold many times over and never physically leave its storage. By the time this process is done, there is no trail back to the original money."

"So, multiple criminals use the same art and buy and sell it to favor all parties involved."

"Yes, this happens all the time. Let's say you want to park Russian Rubles which you gained illicitly into an investment which you intend to convert to British Pounds. You can buy the art, or have a front man steal the art from a private collection. Regardless, you purchase it from the owner or art thief with the illicit cash. The cash is now converted to art, and the art gets sold and resold many times. It is now an appreciating asset and often converts currency during its journey."

"So, you represent those that lost the art to begin with?"

"Yes, usually an estate, a trust, or an insurance company."

"So, how do you even know it's happening?" Sara asked, fully engaged in the subject.

"There are a handful of lost old works such as *Poppy Flowers* by Van Gogh, *Diana and Callisto* by Rubens, *A Mythological Scene with a Young Bacchus* by Jordaens, *Nativity with St. Francis and St. Lawrence* by Caravaggio and my favorite, *The Storm of the Sea of Galilee* by Rembrandt. All lost or stolen in the last half century. Very few credible sightings and then, suddenly, starting sixteen months ago, many sightings. The art is on the move, as we say, but we don't yet understand why."

"Simply amazing," was all Sara could say.

"Simply dangerous is what I say," Giovanni said as Chiara's eyes rolled back, and her head shook.

"Giovanni, this is me. Take it or leave it," she snapped.

"I take it, of course, but why must the two beautiful women in my life always subject themselves to danger? This makes a heart attack for poor Giovanni. Even nice clothes to satisfy my gentleman status will not save this." He pointed to his heart under the new cashmere sweater to the laughter of Chiara and Sara.

Sara was traveling once again, this time to Seattle to work with the Versilant team on her invention, the Ricci Gamma Ray Conversion Dish. She had somewhat dreaded this trip, as it would be unavoidable to be there and not have Jason at the forefront. After all, these were all his friends, but she had a job to do, and possibly a nice payday attached. If this worked, the salary and royalties would exceed what she had earned in the last four years, and she desperately needed some financial independence. Up to now, being smart had not paid exceptionally well.

The Delta flight from Rome finally landed in Seattle-Tacoma airport, after a three-hour layover in New York. Susan De Vires, wife of the Versilant CEO and founder, Dann De Vires had offered to pick her up, but Sara rented a car, hoping for some independence. This was going to be emotional, and she needed a breakaway, or at least that is what robot girl was telling her to do.

She pulled into the lot at Versilant Nanotechnologies, took a deep breath, and headed in. The moment she set foot in the lobby, the rear door immediately opened and Dann, Susan, and much of the team came out to great her. Unexpected and comforting, through smiles and tears she hugged and shook hands on her way out into the factory.

Once there, the design team took her to see the completed titanium frame of the dish to her invention. Sitting nearby were the ribs that made up the dish with half of the tungsten carbide skin attached.

The crux of her dish design was two-fold. First was the unique parabolic shape she had made using sketches from her great-great-grandfather, Gilberti Ricci. The second was the coating itself, which was developed through a series of trial-and-error recipes. Sara and friends had tried to locate materials, including rare earth metals, that held high atomic values and density to stop the gamma rays from passing right through the dish itself. That is what gamma rays do, and the fact that she could stop and convert any of them was a first.

The coating they would place on the dish was a collection of rare earth metals that were specially ground into a dust, then mixed in a certain way and applied to the dish under high heat. The entire process was a well-kept secret, and each phase of the process was a potential for failure. Created and perfected by Cerium Scientific Compounds (CSC), De Vires had been a partial owner when he had suggested CSC to Sara two years earlier, but the events that took place here last year had placed the company in his and Susan's control.

Dann walked out and approached Sara. "So, it is coming along. We should have the coating done in three weeks, and Galant Industries will have all four units before the end of the month. It must be exciting for you to see your invention applied to a commercial use."

"It is, and thanks for taking on the project. I hope there are many more of these in the future. We have a lot riding on this Phase II project."

"I can only imagine. This Solak Group you work with is quite secretive. It is hard to follow your project."

"They claim it is to focus on the science, but I think the reality is the collection of members don't want to be known."

"You sure know how to pick them."

"So, I've been told. The thing is it's not about me, it's about exploitation of the science. A person recently said that because I work in breakthrough sciences, that is where evil lurks. I don't want it this way, but I accept the possibility and just hope nobody gets hurt."

"Well, the Versilant and the CSC teams are glad to be part of your world. You are a god to some of these kids here just out of school. To me, that is quite an amazing honor."

"It is, and thanks for sharing that with me."

"You must be excited that Jason is now in Georgia with his sister, Rachael."

"I knew he was there, but have only talked a little with him. He has been through so much."

If Dann caught her dour tone, he didn't show it, but responded as she expected, "Well, last year was difficult for us all." Sara nodded, and the rest of the day went by quickly and included a trip to CSC, but as the evening neared, Sara politely declined an offer to have dinner with the De Vires, citing she had work to do. Truth was, she didn't want to be forced into a position to have to talk about everything that had happened.

When she finally left Versilant just after five that evening, the skies were dark with rain clouds and perhaps it was a conscious error, perhaps it was just a mistake, but instead of turning right out of the parking lot, which would have taken her back to her hotel, she turned left as a light rain started. It was just a few miles when she realized she had erred and pulled over to turn around. As she did, she looked out and between the windshield wipers; she saw it. She froze and pulled forward and to the side of the road.

Still raining, she exited the car, leaving her jacket and umbrella on the seat, and walked down to the corner, where a small, tiny house sat with a partial view of Lake Washington. Painted red with a white trim, the house did not appear to be occupied as she stood and admired it before she went to the right of the house to a log that had been cut and made onto a bench. She sat down and grew melancholy, while she unconscionably ran her finger into the carved names of *Sara +* *Jason* on the end of the bench.

When Sara had arrived in Seattle a year before, assisting Jason and the Versilant team on the nanobot project, she felt compelled to protect herself from getting too close to him. She had never had a relationship with any man but her father and wasn't sure if that moment was the right time to start.

She had lived with Jason that first week, which was nice at first, but as Dr. Facciolo had suggested, Sara wasn't used to sharing space with anyone let alone a man. After a brief argument, she rented this little, tiny house and came to love every inch of its two-hundred-eighty square feet.

And it was here in a cold rain, on this same bench, that Jason could have yelled at her, could have berated her for her outburst at an important meeting, but he didn't. Instead, he had left work, purchased a nice bottle of wine, and came here where she had been sitting in the cold rain for hours unsure what to do. She recalled her thoughts. *Just be friends? Give in to him? Run back to Milan?*

When Jason had arrived, she was freezing. He said nothing, but carried her inside and prepared her for a warm shower. He took off her soaking wet clothes and made no advance, although she was sure he wanted to. That was the moment she regretted being in Seattle. He really cared for her, and she had been avoiding him in all ways but at work.

The rain was coming down harder now, and dusk had turned into night although Sara had yet to move. Still on the bench, she realized if at that moment, a year before, had she just gone back to Italy, he never would have been shot. All the ugliness would have been avoided.

The temperature had dropped at least ten degrees, but she remained there, her mind bringing up all the thoughts she had compartmentalized deep in her brain, hoping to avoid. But slowly, robot girl was being weakened by the cold; it was too much all at once.

Several minutes passed when a gruff voice appeared. "Miss, you can't be here. This is private land. Run along now and get out of this cold."

Sara heard the words but didn't reply. A flashlight was coming her way and a dark shape bobbled towards her, repeating the message, when suddenly the pitch of the voice changed. "What the hell? Sara, is that you?"

Sara looked up in surprise and saw the weathered face of her old landlord, Betty Martinez. "Betty, I'm... sorry. I just..." she shivered, the spell broken, and the cold swept in.

She was nearly hypothermic.

Betty rushed over and pulled her up. She was a large woman, strong as a horse. "What the hell were you thinking child, come on, into the house." She walked with Sara, but not to her house, but to the vacant tiny house. The door was unlocked, and she went inside and pulled Sara up. Betty headed for the shower and shouted back, "Get your clothes off and put them in a pile! After you warm up, put on a robe. It's in the closet and I'll be back with your dry clothes and some food. Sara, the water is barely lukewarm, but it's going to hurt like hell. Suck it up and every five minutes, make it a little warmer."

"Okay," was all Sara could manage, vaguely remembering Jason doing the same for her.

Betty looked at her naked body, pink with cold, as she headed to the small shower. She shook her head and muttered to herself, "I don't know where you got your PhD, little girl, but it must have been a free prize in a box of damn Cracker Jacks." She kneeled down, grabbed the cold, sopping wet clothes, and went back to the main house.

Sara let the barely warm water pound her skin for fifteen minutes before she dared to increase the temperature. Betty wasn't wrong. It really stung. She was saddened as she relived this déjà vu moment, but at the same time, oddly comforted. Something had clicked in her mind since she arrived here.

When she finally came out of the shower over 30 minutes later, she put her hair up into a towel and pulled on the robe. The heat hadn't been on, so the small space was still cold. She sat on the couch and pulled up a throw blanket. In that moment, it was as if she had never left.

Another thirty minutes passed before Betty came in with her dry clothes and a covered plate. "I haven't gone to the store in a while, so I have little, but this will warm you up." Sara changed and came back to the couch where she eat the homemade beef stew slowly when Betty asked, "So, darling, you going to tell me what this is all about?"

Betty was an old soul, and they used to talk a lot, so Sara told her everything that had happened since she was last there. The look on Betty's face said it all. She had no idea about any of this and immediately felt sorry for her. "Jesus, kid, that is a lifetime of hell in just a few months. Can I call anyone for you?

You are welcome to stay the night here. Hell, you can stay here as long as you want."

"My car is just down the road, and I have a hotel room not too far away."

"It's not like me to butt in, but since you just about did yourself in, I think I'll pull your car up here. You need a nightcap and some sleep, and then you can be off in the morning if you wish." Betty stood without waiting for a response and walked out the door with her umbrella and Sara's rental car keys. She returned five minutes later with Sara's phone, her keys, her jacket, and a bottle of Bailey's Irish Cream and made a half-pot of coffee, which she poured into two large mugs with a healthy amount of liqueur. She handed a cup to Sara. "You okay?"

"Strangely yes. Thank you, Betty. I loved it here and as difficult as it is to be here again, weirdly, it was what I needed."

"Well, it's not rented. I'd love to have you back."

Sara was distant, but replied, "As nice as that would be, Italy is my home."

T he Dark Blue Fiat Bravo screeched around the corner as Chiara Bulgari, driving much faster than traffic or the stated speed, arrived in Monza, a city fifteen kilometers northeast from Milan and the location of her Carabinieri Art Squad office. There was no crisis, no emergency. Chiara just drove fast when she was angry.

She thoroughly despised the gutless Fiat longing for her Alfa Romeo SportWagen she had lost in a work related accident two years before. She loved that car, but this was the only one available. Carabinieri's command had moved away from their mandate to only use Italian made vehicles and newer cars at her level were Subarus or Land Rover Defenders. Bulgari thought it was disrespectful to alter tradition and refused to switch. This left her with a very high mileage, crappy 2007 Fiat, which she intended to drive until it blew up. Given how she drove, that was inevitable.

The little car flew into her parking space, coming very close to hitting a steel pole, meant to protect the building, and she jumped out, grabbing her bag. The small engine made little strange hissing sounds as if it were out of breath and happy for a rest.

Walking with purpose, she headed inside to a few waves and nods, entered her office, going straight for an enormous white board that took the entire wall. On it were color photos of the eight contemporary and old world masters that she had been following. This was how she started every day. Reminding herself of the missing treasures. As she had told Sara, for years there was no mention of these works, and on the board it showed the timeline of such activity. From the 1940s to the 1970s, zero sightings, zero leads. From the 1980s into 2010, less than one sighting per artwork, few actually confirmed. In the last two years, almost three sightings annually. Some more, some less depending on the painting or perhaps more important, the value of the painting. The higher the expected value, the more sightings. These works were clearly on the move and the team under Chiara had taken each sighting, listed its location, and the individual related to the sighting, rumor or otherwise.

Bulgari's boss, Captain Marcello Abruzzo, walked in, smiled, and asked politely, "Bulgari, I read your brief. Is this true about the Brazilian?"

Chiara smiled at Abruzzo, a legend within the Art Squad and a great boss. She turned to the wallboard as she said, "We have twenty-seven sightings of which seventeen are confirmed and verified by more than one source. For three of the eight artworks, each has at least one reference to Izabel Vargas. She is tied in with Cristiano Marcon. He is in the mix, but she is clearly handling the art."

"It is said this Marcon assists Russian oligarchs. He himself has money, but not enough to be directly involved, given some of these are likely to be in the fifty to hundred million euro range. You suspect he is fronting for someone?"

"The pieces are moving quickly, so yes, this has a laundering feel. Marcon is reported to have a dark side, but we have not heard of Vargas before. It all started just sixteen months ago. You mentioned Russia. Any knowledge of which Russians are involved with Marcon?"

"Most rumors involve Sergei Omelchenko, CEO of Geoentergetics, a large Russian energy company."

"I know the name. He has come up several times but never paintings, it's usually antiquities. That said, he is known to park assets in tax shelters like Oktyabrsky and Russky Island. There is also a lot of money conversion by him. Rubles to Euros, Rubles to Pounds, and sometimes, Rubles to Dollars."

"Perhaps he is branching out. Keep me informed, but be careful Bulgari. Marcon is dangerous, but Omelchenko is downright evil."

"They're all evil." As he walked out, Chiara sighed. This was the reason she was driving so fast. Giovanni was pestering her about her dangerous job, and she was angry. After a disastrous and brief marriage, she had enjoyed some wonderful men, but the relationships always ended this way. Same old shit. She worked too much, she cared more about her lost art than them, it wasn't right for a woman to be a cop... *blah, blah, blah. Little fucking whiners.*

What she needed was a real man like James Bond, but what was she saying? She would hate it because he would treat her as a plaything. Chiara Bulgari was nobody's plaything and just wanted to be loved. Doesn't every woman?

Her mind back on business, she picked up the phone called a friend and former member of the French DST, Directorate of Territorial Security that had since disbanded. Louis Moreau was now an agent of Interpol, and she wanted to know what they had on Marcon. He picked up on the third ring. A bored voice snapped, "Moreau."

"Louis, ciao, it is Chiara Bulgari at Comando Carabinieri Tutela Patrimonio Culturale."

"Chiara, always nice to hear your voice. How is the underbelly of-the-art world?"

"Highly stimulated given all the money that's out there. It has been a tough couple of years with no added staffing."

"Yes, the mad, mad world has somehow gotten worse. What can I do for you?"

"I am looking for information on a Brazilian, Cristiano Marcon and his associate, Izabel Vargas. Might you have anything?"

"Popular guy. You're the second call regarding him this month. I can send you what I sent my friend. It's not much. This Marcon is very sharp and hard to tie down."

"I understand if you cannot say, but who else called? Were they from TPC?"

"No. It's an American friend who runs a private security outfit. He was following a lead for a gal he does favors for when Marcon's name came up."

Bulgari recalled Sara mention the student suspected of spying on her project and on a whim said, "Sara Ricci?"

"Yes. Do you know her?" As she smiled.

"Yes, I am dating her father and had dinner with her just a few weeks ago."

"Small world indeed. I have no problem sending you this file, but you'll have to talk with her if there is more to it. It would be unprofessional of me to talk on her behalf."

"I understand, Louis, and thank you. If I get anywhere, I will tell you what I have found."

"Is this about an art theft?"

"More likely laundering with art monies, but it may involve stolen art. It appears Vargas is heading up the sales effort. See you." Chiara hung up amazed that Sara's name was connected to an Interpol agent. For a mild-mannered physicist, she was much more than met the eye and had friends in high places.

Back in Seattle, Sara was in Versilant when Chase called, and she answered right away. "Sara, we did a little more digging and could tie your grad student, Diego Rivera, to three anti-renewable rallies that were rumored to be funded by the Brazilian Cristiano Marcon. He himself is well connected, and we found several ties from him to a Russian billionaire named Sergio Omelchenko. It might mean nothing, but we also came across a business deal between this Omelchenko and the guy in the dossier we did for you, Shen Zhou."

"What kind of deal?" Sara replied, now alarmed.

"Apparently, this Omelchenko invested in Zhou's company during the financial crisis. My guess is the Russian's money was through an agent, not himself so it is doubtful Zhou even knew. They parted ways two years ago. Zhou paid him close to $2 billion for his shares when his government shut down all foreign investment in that sector. Thing is, Zhou then sold the company a year later. My analysts say Omelchenko would have more than doubled his money. I have no idea what that means, but that is where our limited inquiry stopped."

Sara wasn't sure either, but thanked him, wondering if she should tell Dr. Caliskan?

The Project Solaris team was again in Montreux to work out various details as the launch date neared. After a brief lunch, Sara had returned to her room, and as she walked in that direction, Dr. Caliskan was coming toward her. They smiled, shook hands, and after some brief small talk, Sara asked, "Dr. Caliskan, I came across a piece of information that might mean nothing, but felt I should say something. It is about Dr. Zhou."

He smirked and replied, "But you feel you should tell me?"

"I don't know Dr. Zhou as well and thought if it was nothing, you could help intercept this for me rather than alarm him."

"I'm not sure I am comfortable in this role, but what is this news?"

Sara told him about her search for the missing grad student and the possible link to Marcon. She then mentioned the tie of Marcon to Omelchenko and the latest, the link between Omelchenko and Zhou. She stressed the investigator was sure that Omelchenko's identity was likely hidden, but he was rumored to be a terrible guy.

"And you think this is related to Project Solaris, or at least the Solak Group?"

"I'm not sure. The student was here to spy on us, possibly related to his activism in anti-renewable projects. Apparently, this Cristiano Marcon has bankrolled these grass-root rallies in the past. The Russian may have a grudge against Dr. Zhou."

"You never cease to amaze me Dr. Ricci. I'm sure this is nothing, but I appreciate knowing and will determine if this has merit, but let's keep this between us. I am quite serious."

"Of course, Dr. Caliskan. I understand."

Whatever he had intended to do at the moment was placed on immediate hold as he turned and went to the Sunset room to find Zhou. He had played it cool with Sara, but he knew Omelchenko and he was not someone you ever wanted against you. An army of one is how his family saw him although they had done considerable business with him over the years, primarily pipelines.

As he walked into the room, Zhou, with his perceptive ability to judge facial and bodily expressions, asked, "Demir you are troubled."

"Yes. We have to talk." Caliskan closed the door and revealed the entire conversation and especially the link between the likely spy on the launch site and Marcon, and then he brought up the tie to Omelchenko. Zhou said nothing, but his mind was unsettled. Several minutes passed and Caliskan knew better than to interrupt.

Zhou released the tension from his body and spoke. "It is amazing to me that this young woman, supposedly afraid of danger, has contacts in government, police, and Interpol that she uses to understand threats around her. As to the problem, I suspect now that a Hong Kong financier, Nigel Corbyn was likely the front for Omelchenko. I also know he tripled his money on the valuation the Minister of Finance placed on Realtime, but he would have made double that a year later. I will have to assume he thinks I did this purposely. On top of his rejection from the Solak Group, I can imagine there is no love lost for me. Nonetheless, I will meet with him to discuss a remedy. I don't wish harm against us or my foundation."

"Be very careful Shen. My family knows this man, and he is a formidable opponent. If you need anything, let me know and never let your guard down, even for a moment." Caliskan walked away, knowing this was something Zhou would have to process. He just hoped he would confide in him.

As Caliskan walked away, Zhou leaned back and recalled his earlier encounter with Sergei Omelchenko. He had been nominated by a Bulgarian to join the Solak Group just weeks after Zhou came on board. The dossier seemed fabricated, and

Zhou had one made on his own. This Russian met several of the desirable traits as a member, but under the facade, this man was not much more than a criminal, and a ruthless one at that. Zhou remembered the brief call they had after he had refused him.

Omelchenko had called Zhou once he was rejected. "So, your foundation is too good for me?"

"Sir, we mean no disrespect, but you have a reputation for violence and other dealings that we just cannot accept."

"All lies by people who simply want my money."

"Perhaps, but if that is the case, much of the world is involved in this campaign against you."

"Look over your shoulder Dr. Zhou."

"Thank you for proving my point Mr. Omelchenko." As the line went dead.

After the trip to Seattle, Sara was more secure and more grounded regarding the topic of Jason and wondered for a moment what he was up to as she picked up the phone and called his cell, which was now active. It took a few minutes before he answered, "Hey Sara, how are things?"

"Good. I hear you're back in the States."

"Yeah, I got in a month ago. I'm staying with Rachael, and she is helping me remember the whole thing. Wow, a lot happened. I had no idea."

"Is it helping?"

"Hell yes. It is so unsettling to lose like six months of my life and not know why. I feel better. Still on the light side, but I'm eating all I can and getting back in shape. I heard you were in Seattle?"

"Yes, Versilant and CSC are building my invention for the larger satellites. I stopped and saw the tiny house. It brought back a lot of memories."

"Tiny house?"

"Yes, I lived with you for a bit, but needed my space and rented a little house. It was cute and fit me like a glove."

"We lived together?"

"Just for a week, but you drove me to work every day even after I moved and got me hooked on Starbucks."

"I'm a giver." As they both laughed.

"So, how long will you stay in Georgia?"

"A few more weeks. That is why I was talking to Dann. I'm going to reconnect with him and the Versilant team. It might help bring back some memories and I'm going to try to get back now that the doctors cleared me to work."

"That sounds great. Let me know when you're there. I have at least a few more trips planned to Seattle, and we could finally see each other."

"That would be great. I'll call you, okay?"

"Okay, bye."

A month passed and Sara was sitting in her small office at Sapienza, munching on celery sticks and humus as she prepared for a class just a few hours later. She reached over to grab a notebook when the door softly opened and to her surprise, Dr. Zhou entered without a sound. "Dr. Zhou?"

"Hello Dr. Ricci, and my apology for this sudden appearance. I needed to talk to you."

"Okay," Sara replied, unsure what this was all about.

"When we first met, I was alarmed when you used your contacts to investigate the Solak Group, but it would appear you have not stopped. I am here to understand your motives. You are clearly more than just a scientist."

"More than a scientist? What does that mean?"

"Your contacts are using the dark web and hacking into private sources to gain information about me, and I am not used to such an intrusion. Especially by a young woman who just months ago was too scared to join the real world. Was that all just an act?"

"Dr. Zhou, I will not answer such a ridiculous question. You're the psychologist, was I lying?"

"I am no longer sure, but yes, possibly."

"That's bullshit. As I told you, I originally asked about you, the Solak Group, and Dr. Caliskan, as I had every right to. Given my past, I needed to know what I was getting in to. When the grad student, Diego Rivera, ran after Omer and I noticed him during the Phase I launch, I used my contacts to find out who he was. I was concerned, but there was no illicit intent by me or my friends." She wanted to say something about the Russian, but assumed is would only make things worse.

"I will watch you more closely Dr. Ricci. As I said, for one who just months ago was a victim, you are surprisingly well informed in matters you should not be." Without another word, Zhou rose and left the room to a stunned Sara who wasn't sure what the hell had just happened.

Did he really just insinuate she was a spy?

The Citation XL, leased by the Sunset Foundation, landed in Kalispell, Montana, as Zhou prepared to confront the owner of Fortitude Security, Richard Chase. He had not told Sara, as she would no doubt would have alerted him, and Zhou was a firm believer that the truth was best revealed in surprise. He climbed into the hired car and left the airport.

As the car drove through the heavily forested area, it cleared and to the left was a large barn-like structure with several windows, which he assumed was the company itself. The land around it spread out for what appeared to be twenty acres with high ground on the far side, and other than a small lake and clustered trees, the only other visible structure besides the barn was a modest log cabin to the right. The car pulled in and stopped at the front door where a hand carved sign said Fortitude Security and next to it, a sign saying the entire premise was under surveillance and an armed response should be expected.

Zhou climbed out, smiled at the sign, childhood myths of the wild-wild west, and walked into the lobby, and approached the young receptionist. He asked to speak with Richard Chase, and she offered the usual; do you have an appointment? Are you a current or former client? How do you know Mr. Chase? Ending with the purpose of his visit. Zhou understood and answered each question tersely, giving up nothing, but the team had already used facial recognition software to reveal the tall Asian was Dr. Shen Zhou of the Sunset Foundation. A small light appeared on the receptionist's side of the desk, which told her she was welcome to bring Zhou back to Richard's office.

As Zhou walked in Chase stood and held out his hand as he said, "Dr. Zhou, welcome to Kalispell, Montana, and Fortitude Security."

"You expected me. Mr. Chase?"

"No."

"Then how is it you know me?"

Chase huffed with a smile, "I run a security business Mr. Zhou. It is my job to know. Have a seat. What can I do for you?"

Zhou was as always direct and to the point, explaining he needed to understand if the inquiry into him was the doing of Fortitude or Dr. Ricci. Chase replied, "Mr. Zhou, it is not a crime to solicit a profile of any person, including you, and the dark web is not illegal to access. You obviously know of Dr. Ricci, but she is off limits to this conversation."

"Mr. Chase, you have used more than the dark web to get information about me that, and if I chose, could use this information to close your business and place you in prison under the laws of your own country. In combat, you would be formidable, but in business, you would find myself and my resources difficult to beat."

"You're reaching Dr. Zhou, but to your point, is that a threat?"

"No, Mr. Chase. It is a warning. The mere inquiry into a man such as Sergei Omelchenko can get yourself and your entire family killed simply because you might stumble on information you should not have."

"Strange that you would warn me without having heeded your own advice."

Zhou sighed, "Omelchenko funded my business through a banker out of Hong Kong, and I knew nothing of him personally. I have to make peace with this man somehow, but you and your associates must stop any attempts to locate information regarding him or Cristiano Marcon. They most certainly already know you have been looking."

"I understand what you are saying. For the record, Dr. Ricci does not know how we do our investigations, but I have a soft spot for her, so it is me that is directly responsible for the search. She only asked if you were legit and to get the background on a student she suspected was a spy."

"Very well. Thank you for your time, and I will assume we understand each other." There were no additional words as Zhou rose and left. Chase, a lifelong soldier, had faced death so many times, it had been years since he felt the butterflies in his stomach or the rapid sensation of anxiety but today, at the thought of Omelchenko, he had a whole field of butterflies in his stomach and went to find some antiacid.

Zhou climbed into the hired car and returned to his plane. Once he was airborne, he called his team and asked them to arrange a meeting with himself and Omelchenko. He intended to offer him a financial peace offering.

Izabel Vargas pulled into the six-car garage, using her personal code to enter, knowing she was being viewed by three different cameras. She was used to it as she brought the long-wheelbase Range Rover SV Autobiography to a stop. As she exited, an aide approached her, but she waved him off and entered the elevator to the kitchen level. Izabel liked nice things, but was not one to be pampered. The lift opened to the main room, and she walked toward Marcon who was dressed in pressed light gray trousers and a crisp dark gray shirt. He stood to the left in the kitchen with a bottle of sparkling water and nodded to Izabel as they proceeded together to his office on the fourth level.

"What do you have for me?" As he kissed her softly.

She kissed him back and gave him a rare hug. Cristiano was far from the touchy feely type. In fact, he really did not like to be touched at all. He had never had a massage, but she imagined he would like it if he ever got past the soldier in him. The elevator door opened, and they walked into the study with 270-degree views.

"We had Zhou followed halfway around the globe. He first went to the university where a Dr. Sara Ricci works in Italy. She is affiliated with Project Solaris. He was there less than ten minutes where he delivered a private message. One that needed to be done face-to-face. She left her office sometime later but did not seem troubled and went straight to her home close by."

"And then?"

"Zhou flew directly to Fortitude Security in the United States. This is the company our analysts discovered had been looking into you and possibly your Russian friend."

"Do we know why he was there?"

"No, and again he there just a few minutes. He left and was in the air within an hour. The flight plan was China."

"So once again, this was a message he felt he needed to deliver in person."

"Yes."

"Direction or a warning? I am trying to understand if Zhou is using the girl and this security firm to seek information on us."

"We know nothing about the message."

"Have the team find out."

"Understood." Izabel stood, gave Marcon a seductive smile, and walked out of the office. He used Izabel more as a sounding board than an extension of his network, but she was smart, cunning, and got the job done.

Richard Chase was not looking to get tied down, but he had been seeing a woman, Veronica Sutton, off and on for about a year. Technically, Chase was still legally married, although he and his wife in the Philippines had not been together for almost twenty years. Work was the primary reason he rarely dated. The nature of security is feast or famine. You can have no work for days and then get slammed with one or more clients that require hands on attention. Attention that was non-stop for days on end, meaning he had little time for anything else. But Veronica traveled as well, and perhaps that was why their relationship seemed to work.

They had just left the Oak Tavern, a casual bar and grill on the edge of town, and neared his truck when a large van pulled up slowly, blocking their path. Perturbed, Chase grabbed Veronica's hand to walk her around when the side door flew open and two large men jumped out. Each was armed with a silenced Beretta M9A3 pistol.

Veronica yelped and Chase reached to his back when the tallest of the two said, "No Mr. Chase. That would be a deadly mistake. Please enter the van."

Stalling, Chase replied, "You seem to know me, but I don't know you."

"The van please."

"Just me. The woman stays." Chase replied with authority.

"I'm afraid not. Both of you enter the van now, or we will assist you."

"Richard, what is going on?" Veronica pleaded.

"Let's find out. I'm sure this can be sorted out quickly." As he guided her to the van.

"Richard, they have guns pointed at us. Are you fucking crazy?"

"No, my dear. These men are professionals. Their guns will stay silent as long as we cooperate." He was still holding her hand and reached out, helping her up into the van, and followed. The two followed and closed the door as they jumped in and the van left. They took Chase's gun and searched him, removing a throwing knife to Veronica's horror, as both held aim at them as the sole means of restraint. The rear of the van was compartmentalized from the front and the windows were painted black and there was no way to see out.

Chase knew it was pointless to ask questions and was silent as he comforted Veronica who was scared out of her mind. Some forty minutes later, they turned off the highway and went slowly up a dirt road. Chase had taken care to note every turn and based on the sounds of the tires, more or less knew exactly where they were, but said nothing.

The van stopped, and before Chase could react, he and Veronica were blindfolded. Chase, still holding her, heard the door slide open and allowed the men to guide them out.

They were brought inside, and the blindfolds were removed. Inside what was a log cabin, Chase noted all windows were covered. One of Marcon's top lieutenants, a huge man came forward and motioned for Veronica to sit, and offered her a bottle of water. She took the water and sat when he then asked Chase to follow him.

"Where I go she goes."

"Mr. Chase, she is not party to this conversation. She will stay here, and no harm will come to her. Please, this way."

"Only if she comes with me."

"Please avoid escalation. Just do as I ask."

Chase burned his eyes at the man and said softly, "Someday you and I will meet again."

He actually chuckled and said, "Yes, of course. I look forward to that?" as he motioned for him to enter the room next door. Chase nodded to Veronica and told her all would be okay, and walked into the room as the door immediately shut. Chase expected the room to contain the reason for the trip here, but no one else was in the room as the man sat down and asked,

"I would like to know the reason for Dr. Shen Zhou's visit to your business."

Surprised this is what it was all about, Chase replied. "I cannot discuss client business."

"And Dr. Zhou is a client of Fortitude Security?"

"Perhaps?"

"Mr. Chase, this is a simple inquiry. Please dispense with these games. I have no orders to harm you or the woman, but will do whatever is necessary to get the information I seek. Why did he visit you?"

"He came to tell me to stop looking into his affairs and gave me a warning about a Russian that he suspects is after him."

"Is this related to the dark web searches you have been doing on behalf of Zhou and others?"

"Yes. I was hired to research the Solak Group on behalf of a client. We came across information related to Zhou, a Brazilian business owner named Marcon, and found connections between him and the Russian and then the Russian and Zhou. This information was given to my client, and perhaps that is how the information found its way to Zhou."

"Regarding the Russian, Zhou is not wrong. So, you do not work for Zhou, and he is not your client. Your client is the young girl?"

"If you know this why go to all this trouble? You could have just stopped at Fortitude and asked me?"

"Mr. Chase, you would have no incentive to tell me the truth if this had been done formally. I am simply supplying information. But information leads to action and the wrong information can bring unwanted and unnecessary consequences. That will be all. You will be taken back to your vehicle. I might add, let this go. It was a simple transaction, and nobody was harmed."

"With all due respect, you disrupted my date, abducted us, and held us at gunpoint. For a guy like me, that is hard to forgive."

"And for a guy like me, this politeness sucks. I would just as soon kill you and your date. You may choose your fate, Mr. Chase."

Chase understood in the world of thugs there was a pecking order. This guy was at the top and Chase wanted to stay alive, so he nodded an affirmative.

The large man silently motioned to his men and within an hour, the two were back at the restaurant parking lot and heading towards his truck. Once inside, Chase immediately called the local sheriff, a friend, and told him to meet them at his cabin next to Fortitude.

A cream colored Subaru pulled into the decomposed granite circular drive. It slowed and the sole occupant parked and walked past the garage and to the porch of a log cabin that Chase and his son Nathen had built some seven years before. Sherriff Billy Jenkins casually looked around as walked to the front door. He didn't knock, he just walked in and seeing Chase and Veronica at the bar, walked directly to it. Both were drinking Ballentine old fashions, signaling a certain level of seriousness. Chase, a casual beer drinker, rarely drank spirits. "One of those for me?" Jenkins asked.

Chase pointed to the lone glass and said, "Help yourself. You'll need it after this," and proceeded to give him the story.

"Chase, if it wasn't for you, this would be a pretty damn boring job. Glad you're both safe. So, you think you know where they took you?" He asked as he admired the high ceilings and the handmade antler chandelier above.

"Yes. I'd like to head out before the sun comes up. I doubt there is anything to find, but at least need to look." They looked over a detailed topographic map, and Chase pinpointed the location.

"Okay, I'll get a chopper and some guys. We'll meet you at the airport at zero-four-thirty." He glanced at Veronica who was stoic and visibly shaken. "Miss, are you okay? That had to give you a scare."

"I'm okay. Thank you. I don't understand why you have to go find them. Isn't it clear these are bad guys?"

"Yes mam but see, so are we. You just didn't know it. This is what we do." Veronica Sutton had heard enough, shook her head in disbelief and with her drink, headed to the bedroom, slamming the door shut.

Jenkins looked over at Chase and said, "Guess we won't see much of her after this."

"Yea, that was my assumption as well. Damn, I really liked this one."

33

In the morning's darkness, Chase slid silently off the bed where Veronica had miraculously spent the night, despite the abduction and his resolve to go back to the location in the morning. Coffee had been made via a timer, and Chase poured it into his travel mug and walked out the door. He did not leave a note, as he had clearly stated when he was leaving. He assumed Veronica was asleep, but she wasn't. She was awake and heard every sound. She didn't understand this, but prayed he came back in one piece. He was apparently not who she imagined him to be, but she liked him. You felt safe around Richard Chase, and now she knew why. He was fearless.

Chase jumped in his perfectly restored 1970 GMC truck and made the short drive to Kalispell airport where Sherriff Jenkins stood with two others. Chase knew them and thanked them for their help as they climbed into the helicopter and the pilot started his pre-check. Thankful to get a full cup of coffee into him before the clear sign was given, Chase readied himself as the Bell 206 Jet ranger shook and prepared to lift off. The craft calmed once they were free of the earth and headed to the coordinates that Chase had sent Jenkins, a location off state route 93 in Rollins, a small town south of Kalispell on the shores of Flathead Lake.

It was difficult to see the ground as the sun had not yet risen, but as they neared the town, the pilot veered west to a large clearing on Big Lodge Lane. As Chase looked down, it seemed right. He gave a thumb up to the pilot and they hovered before coming down in a clearing a few hundred feet from the cabin. The door opened, and they filed out one by one, each holding a Heckler & Koch G36 in an aggressive and armed position. They neared the house in the dark, although the sun had started to rise behind the mountains of the Flathead National forest. There were no cars. Chase was in the lead and having not seen the cabin from the outside, still wasn't positive. The windows were free of blinds or shutters, or the blankets he had seen when he was inside. He silently walked up to the porch and tried the door. It was locked.

He motioned to the others, and each spread out. They regrouped when the search revealed nothing. Chase used a pick to enter, weapon out. Once inside, there was no doubt. This was the place. The location where Veronica sat was before him and the door to the side room was as he remembered.

The team entered the house, and all were trained in how to analyze a location, but found nothing. No apparent DNA evidence in the bathroom, no furniture out of place, and in the office where Chase was questioned, nothing.

The sun had peaked over the valley now, enough to see, and they walked outside, less worried. Sherriff Jenkins looked at Chase. "You sure this is the place?"

"Yes, the inside is identical, and the location fits."

"Well, just saying, there aren't even tire tracks. Who the fuck cleans up a site that well? You want me to get the team out here?" He was referring to forensics.

"No use, Billy, these guys do this for a living. It would be a waste of resources." Chase headed back to the chopper thinking, *What the hell have I gotten myself into?*

Cristiano Marcon was in Moscow on unrelated business when he got the update from his team and rang Omelchenko to get an audience. As was his style, he did so face-to-face and was allowed access to the entrance of Rublyovka and then to the residence. His car was searched, as was he, and a soldier drove with him to the front steps. Marcon was taken inside and after a slight wait, was taken to see Omelchenko. He did not rise when Marcon entered. He just asked, "So how are you, Cristiano?"

"Good, my friend and you?"

"The same. So many environmental threats. They have grounded half of our projects. I miss the old days when we could just pay them or kill them." He looked over at his head of security, Dima Ivanov, and said, "Dima, please leave us."

Dima arose, his eyes on Marcon with hatred, before he left the room. Omelchenko noted the look and said, "What news do you have for me?"

"Zhou does not appear to be looking into you. The search was a leftover from a young PhD who hired the Montana firm to look into Caliskan, Zhou and the Solak foundation before she joined them. They were thorough and have done work with her before and found the link between Zhou and you. You were the largest shareholder."

"So, Zhou's visits to them were a warning?"

"Yes. Basically, he was telling them to stop looking into his and your affairs."

"And this PhD is someone special? I mean who hires a security company to vet a potential employer?"

"We checked into her as well. This young woman has an interesting past. She was at the heart of the woes involving Maximillian and Bridget Drummond last year."

"Well, that would explain that. Does she run this Solak Group project?"

"No, it is run by two other PhDs, a Dr. Huang and a Dr. Hendricks."

"So, Zhou fears me?"

"Yes, and he said to the security man he was aware of the aftertaste the sale of his company made and he's going to make things right for you."

"Yes, his people are trying to arrange a meeting."

"Will you meet him?"

"Not yet. I'll make him sweat a bit. I dislike him for several reasons. How are your plans coming to punish him?"

Marcon gave him the details and asked for his tacit approval. "I agree. Proceed." Omelchenko replied.

"Very well. Will there be anything else?"

"No, and thank you, Cristiano. You are a good man. And Izabel, is she still with us?"

"Yes. She remains a loyal aide."

"Be careful. Women make interesting enemies."

"Always," As he rose and walked out, *wondering exactly what he meant by that comment.*

34

Montreux, Switzerland

The team met in Switzerland one last time to go over the many details of the upcoming Phase II launch. Walking down to the conference area to meet with the team, Sara already knew much of the hardware was complete, including her gamma-ray dishes and the nanosatellites. The receiving antenna with the megapack battery was less than a month away from completion. Meeting with Huang first, she asked, "So, I hear the collectors are complete."

"Yes, we have all four, and they have been inspected, re-tested, and sent to the launch site to fit into the payload capsule. I believe they also have some nanosatellites."

"And there are eight launches total?"

"Yes, two per day, with three days between launches."

"Were you able to incorporate the several security projects we discussed?"

Huang looked around to assure nobody was near and said softly, "Yes, we have a firm set of controls," smiling.

"Excellent." Sara replied. He nodded and excused himself to work on something else. Sara went off to find Julian, and after a few hours, they went into town for dinner. A treat as they rarely left the Institute.

It was an hour into an enjoyable and ridiculously expensive meal when Dr. Hendricks excused herself to the lady's room. Sara, happy to sip the excellent, 2016 Stag's Leap Cabernet Artemis in solitude sat at the table thinking of their conversation. The server came and went, and after ten minutes, Sara noted Julian's absence seemed excessive. She told the server they were not yet leaving, but she needed to check on her friend and entered the restroom. "Julian, are you okay?" No response. Sara kneeled down, but both stalls were empty. She glanced at the window, which was shut. "Julian?" No reply.

Sara went back to the table thinking perhaps she missed her, or she had taken a call and causally looked about, but nothing. Twenty minutes passed before Sara became very concerned. Sara had called Hendricks' cell, but there was no answer, and based on the almost immediate prompt to voicemail, she thought the phone might be turned off. Strange.

Sara waited twenty more minutes before she called Caliskan to tell him what had happened. He told Sara to stay where she was and an aide from the institute would locate her and bring her back to safety. He would have a team search for Dr. Henricks, and Sara was now officially concerned.

Twenty-four hours later, there was no news. Her cell phone wasn't just off, the SIM card had been removed. Dr. Julian Hendricks had disappeared, and likely against her will.

The old Rocar TV-41 panel van, its faded red paint almost indistinguishable from rust, slowed as it reached the front gate of ReboVolt. Specializing in residential electrical panels, the company was largely deserted at this time of night. Sitting in the van's rear was a restrained Dr. Hendricks who had been drugged for the original car journey to a small airfield in Lausanne, Switzerland, where a private plane had brought her to Cluj and now this short ride to ReboVolt.

She would remember none of this, but once within the compound, they helped her to a small suite and laid her down. It was over two hours later when she stirred and awoke, startled. *Where am I? Why am I lying down?* Hendricks had no idea, and she tried to put the events of the night together and soon realized there was a gap of perhaps a dozen hours as she glanced at her watch. She had no idea where she was or how she got here as she looked around the room and assumed incorrectly that she was in a hotel room. Had someone given her GHB or Rohypnol, the date rape drugs? She instinctively brought her hands to her body, but she was fully clothed.

Julian sat up; her head was spinning. She laid back down, trying to orient herself. She rose again and noted there were no windows, and it was then she saw the door. Missing was a handle to get out from this side. She got herself up and slowly walked towards it. Knowing this was abnormal, she resigned herself that something was very wrong and used the bathroom. As she was coming back into the main room, the door opened, and a woman came in carrying a tray of food, water, and juice. Julian peppered her with questions. "Who are you? Where am I? Please help me?"

The woman said nothing. She simply put down the food and motioned towards it as she expertly backed to the door and the moment it clicked and cracked open, she was out, and the door was closed. Julian was now officially scared out of her mind.

Two days passed with no change in this routine. She was fed twice per day, protein winning over carbohydrates but ample portions and a nice red wine to accompany the evening meals. Hendricks was very smart, but not of the criminal world, and would never have thought she was being watched. On the wall was a piece of art that looked like polished lacquered wood, and behind that was a small room. In the room were Marcon, Yuri Antonov, the Managing Director at ReboVolt, and his head of security, a nasty woman named Antanasia Albescu. A few minutes passed when Albescu left and entered Hendricks' room. Still dazed, Julian looked at the exotic woman, thinking this was clearly not a maid or one of the hired help. Albescu sat on the couch facing Hendricks, saying nothing to intimidate her. After several minutes, Hendricks gave in. "Who are you? Why am I here?"

Albescu was a trained engineer and began to ask questions regarding Project Solaris. Hendricks, unsure what this was about said nothing or offered vague answers. It was clear this woman was a scientist herself and possibly dangerous. She just had that look.

Through the glass, Antonov watched with amusement. It was lucky for Dr. Hendricks that Albescu had been taking her medications and having a good day. Otherwise, she would already be dead.

Sara had stayed in Montreux on high alert. Caliskan had provided extra security, which helped, but Sara remained concerned. What the hell had happened? One minute Julian was there, and one minute later, she was gone. Caliskan had not shared with Sara that a review of the security tapes at the restaurant, although limited, revealed no obvious sign of an abduction. Hendricks was seen on tape heading to the restroom, but there was no view of her being taken out of the building although the Swiss Polizei and Solak security now believed that was exactly what happened. Likely via the rear where cameras usage was scarce.

Although Sara was concerned, the entire team was here, and it wasn't a day before they were coming to Sara for guidance, approval, and related leadership tasks. Sara talked with Caliskan and asked what she should do. He was sympathetic considering the disappearance of Hendricks and asked her to take over under the circumstance. Sara heard the words and typical of her current situation, was mistrustful. Caliskan had wanted her to run this, and she refused. Did he orchestrate this to get her in charge? She shook her head angrily and said to herself, *for Christ's sake girl, get your shit together, the project is almost over.*

As Dr. Caliskan walked away from her, he was agitated and felt the abduction must be related to Project Solaris. He would talk to Zhou when they had a secure opportunity. A failure of the upcoming Phase II trial would be unacceptable and mark the end of their project. It would also gravely damage the reputation of the Solak Group.

For a moment, he considered postponing the trial altogether, but immediately reconsidered. After all, they didn't know for a fact the abduction was related and if it were, what did the opposition, whoever they were, want from her?

Antanasia Albescu was standing, looking at a composed Dr. Hendricks on the sofa. For thirty minutes, she had spoken very little and offered little in terms of useful information. It was time to raise the bar. "Dr. Hendricks, since you refuse to provide meaningful answers, are you familiar with the concepts of torture?"

Startled, Hendricks looked at her and said, "This isn't the movies. You won't hurt me."

"You are a very naïve woman, but to answer your question, you're correct. I was actually thinking of hurting someone else."

"Who?"

"I don't know yet. Who do you care for? Who do you love?"

"What are you saying?"

"Your ex-husband Rex, perhaps? That girlfriend of yours, nobody knows you have. It's Gabriella, right? Or perhaps the cute little scientist who works for you, Dr. Ricci. We have been watching you. It is obvious you have feelings for her, although she is clueless." Julian Hendricks immediately lost her composure. Yes, she was gay, but that was something she kept under wraps for the sake of her career. An old-fashioned response, perhaps.

"What kind of monster are you? You would actually hurt those close to me?"

"Yes, Dr. Hendricks. I would like to hurt you, but I need you, so perhaps now you understand. My patience is wearing thin, and I'm on my very best behavior here. I will return and then you will talk, or I will provide you with some motivation of my choosing. Until then." She walked away, smiling.

"Why are you doing this? This is a good project. A project that, if successful will help humankind."

"I don't recall saying anything about hurting your project. I only asked questions to understand it. When I return, you will help me?" Hendricks wept as this situation was completely outside her ability to comprehend. She hated the thought of letting down her team, but creating a situation where those she loved were harmed because of her? That was worse.

Albescu left the room without another word and went next door where Marcon and Antonov had been observing. She walked in and said, "I will give her an hour to dwell on my words and then we will get down to business."

"How in the world did you know she was a lesbian?" Marcon asked.

"Cristiano," she said, smiling, "You're such a man. You see an attractive woman and just assume she needs only you." She laughed, although he did not.

Sitting in his office with Zhou, Caliskan sipped his tea and asked, "Perhaps we should consider postponing the launch?"

"For what purpose?"

"I realize my ideas about a UN Climate Change Space Force have generated fears within those that see space as a military frontier. Perhaps this is their way of stopping us."

"It is doubtful that the abduction of our scientist is related to this. You have only mouthed a concept. The success or failure of Project Solaris does not add to or take away from that. No, this is about Sergei Omelchenko and his losses from the sale of my company and the fact that I rejected him from the Solak Group. I am sure of this."

"Have his people responded to you?"

"No."

"What will you do?"

"It was my intention to make him whole. I will make one last effort."

"And Project Solaris?"

"I would continue. We will have to be ready for anything, but given the Phase II launch is not even my money, I do not think he would attack it. Although it is possible, he may want the technology for himself."

"Perhaps. I will assure that security is heightened and discuss this with Dr. Huang and Dr. Ricci."

"Any news from the Swiss?"

"No, there are no leads, and we have not heard a word from Dr. Hendricks. I fear for her safety."

"I as well. In a possibly related matter, what are your thoughts regarding this growing thought that Project Solaris is a front for a Turkish Weapon? We laughed it off at first, but the Americans and UK are taking it up in committee meetings. Such a thought is misaligned to everything the Solak Group stands for."

"We have been trying to understand the origin. According to our team, this media campaign started on the dark web weeks before you're meeting at the UN and has been traced to Brazil."

"And is that because Brazil is a UN member, or because that is home to Cristiano Marcon? Friend and enforcer to Omelchenko?" Zhou asked?

"I dared to say it, but since you brought it into the open, yes, perhaps."

"It is just talk, yes?"

"For now. My sources say a US Senator has suggested to hold a special session to deny us the right to use the Kennedy Space Center for the launch."

"Is this possible?"

"They say with just three weeks' time to launch, they doubt a resolution can occur that fast. This Senator is not well liked or trusted, although I have not heard of one that is."

"I have never understood the American political system, but we'll have to pay attention to this as well." With that, Zhou rose to leave. They shook hands before he departed. Caliskan assumed he was heading back to China, but he was not.

Julian Hendricks had not moved from the sofa as she contemplated the next steps. She knew when the nasty woman reappeared, the tone would change, and she feared for her ex-husband, Rex. He had been a good and caring husband until Julian came to grips with who she really was. At first he was angry, but had settled into a good place and accepted her. She loved him for that. And Gabriella, her on again, off again lover of two years did not deserve to be harmed. Julian even feared for Sara. The poor girl had been through so much. Julian could not imagine her actions causing any of them pain or suffering. Her mind was made up, she would talk. She only hoped the team would understand.

When the door opened, Albescu entered. She looked downright mean, but handed Hendricks a bottle of water and sat down across from her. No small talk. She simply repeated the opening questions about Project Solaris and Henricks answered with remorse, but she answered. It was perhaps two hours into this exchange when Hendricks noticed the questions formed a pattern. She said nothing, but within fifteen minutes; she knew. They were trying to understand how to communicate with the array so they could control it. This was not good.

Yuri Antonov had left the observation room knowing that Albescu, as always, had got the scientist to talk. He went down the hall and into a war room where his team was reacting to the information that Henricks was conveying. It was being broadcast into the room, and each team was using the answers to questions they had created for Albescu to ask. They only had a few weeks to pull this off.

Sara paced in her small office having taken a temporary leave to focus on the upcoming launch. She had been working upwards of twelve hours a day, and it was taking its toll. She couldn't sleep the night through and worse, she was having difficulty holding onto thoughts, a rarity for her. Thankfully, the team was responding well, although the disappearance of Julian was a dark cloud over everyone's thoughts.

She glanced at the phone as she had for the last hour. On her mind was Richard Chase and the thought that perhaps his team could help Julian. Sara was hesitant, and had she at all known about Chase's run in with Marcon's men or the meeting with Zhou, she never would have dialed. But she didn't and, feeling desperate to help Julian, she called. "Hello Richard, it is Sara."

"Sara, how are you? Is all well?"

"I'm fine, but there has been a development." As Sara gave him the limited information she had on the disappearance of Dr. Hendricks. "I was wondering if any of your sources knew of this and, if so, what could be done to help her?"

"Sara, I know nothing about this, but I can ask. Let me look into this myself without using my team and get back to you."

"Why do you say this? What has happened?"

Damming her intuition, Chase replied, "Sara, that Russian I told you about is simply not someone Fortitude can deal with. Frankly, he is almost a country by himself."

"Are you worried? Should Dr. Zhou be worried?"

"I am, and suspect he is. He told me he was trying to broker a deal with him to put this concern aside."

"I had no idea. Forget I ever asked and do nothing. Please promise me, Richard. You have done so much for me; I can't have any harm come to you."

"Sara, let me make just one call. I will tell me all I need to know about any attempt to go forward."

"I wish I hadn't called. Please, just drop it." Sara pleaded.

"Just one call and I'll get back to you."

The following morning, Chase promptly called his friend, the former director of the Department of Homeland Security, Jeremy Hicks who answered quickly.

"Chase, you know I'm retired, right?"

"I do, and that is why I'm calling. You being bored or feeling unloved is simply not a good thing." He told Hicks the story and asked, "Have you heard anything?"

"No. I heard about the weapon for Turkey nonsense and of course know of Omelchenko from the past. But the disappearance of a Project Solaris scientist, no. I'm just glad it wasn't Sara."

"I thought the same. Well, if you can, make a few calls for me and let me know if you hear anything. By the way, this Dr. Hendricks is a UK citizen."

Hicks let out a laugh. "Ah. Now I understand why you called."

"Thanks." And Chase hung up, smiling.

Hicks stared at the phone and actually considered the call he was about to make. Chase wasn't wrong. His old college roommate was none other than Giles Tylor, now director of SIS, formally known as MI6. The last time he had called to ask for help was the infamous raid on Bridget Drummond's compound in Sweden. Chase and the team didn't need help with the raid, but they might need help out of the country if they actually captured Drummond, or they themselves became injured. Everything that could happen, happened, and Taylor helped them as promised, but his career would be irreparably harmed if word of this ever got out, and thankfully, the cover story had held. For this reason, Hicks wondered if Taylor would even take his call. A moment later, he had located the coded contact name within his encrypted cell phone and hit send.

Hicks waited, and Taylor came on. "Jeremy, always good at hearing your voice. Can I assume the young scientist is once again in trouble?"

"Good to hear your voice, Giles, but no, not this time. She is however, working on the Solaris project with the Solak Group. One of their lead scientists has gone missing. A UK citizen..."

"Named Dr. Julian Hendricks. Yes, we are aware. How is this related to you?"

"It is not. Sara works for her and, fearing her safety contacted our friend Chase and asked if he could look into her disappearance. Chase declined because he got wind of a connection between the Solak co-founder, Dr. Shen Zhou, and Sergei Omelchenko. Too dangerous, even for a guy like Chase."

"We are also aware of this. Also in the mix is Cristiano Marcon out of Brazil."

"So, you are looking into her disappearance?"

"I officially cannot confirm nor deny this, but the Solaris project and its tie to a possible weapon have many agencies looking into all the players mentioned."

"Do you think either of these guys is behind the disappearance?"

"Jeremy, I cannot discuss this one any more than I just have."

"Very well. Let me know if there are any changes on your end."

"I will and thank you for the call." As Taylor hung up, Hicks smiled. The SIS was looking into this, and they knew something the US did not. He hoped it could help the poor scientist wherever she was.

Back in his office, Taylor made a call to the Foreign and Commonwealth Secretary who would, two days later, discuss Project Solaris and the matter of Dr. Julian Hendricks with the Home Secretary, Jocelyn Holmes. Even though there was not a strong likelihood the American Congress would stop the launch, it was felt that the UK should be on record as supporting the United States to delay the launch until it could be proven the array was not a weapon of mass destruction (WMD). It put the threat on record and, with more eyes on the launch.

Demir Caliskan was at his residence, having more or less kicked the family out for several hours, so he could think. Although not entirely true, he felt they were losing operational control of the project with all the distractions and negative news feed. The new American President had chosen a unique sound bite for any subject he didn't wish to discuss and referred to the question as 'fake news', forcing the listener to question the question rather than the lack of an answer. That quote was now used around the world, and a new standard in how to not answer tough questions. The concept that Project Solaris was a WMD was absurd, but nobody cared about the facts. Twitter had said it was a weapon, so it must be. Anything else was branded as 'fake news'.

Caliskan had made calls for almost an entire day to drum up support and while almost every caller was in his corner, not one would speak publicly, given the reference to Omelchenko. Caliskan was on his own.

Shen Zhou sat stoic in the back seat of a hired car in front of the gates that led into Rublyovka where they had been parked for almost an hour. The entrance was guarded by former military, all with assault rifles. The message was loud and clear. They would do nothing until the VIP resident told them to.

Inside the compound, Omelchenko smiled at the thought that Zhou assumed he could simply fly here and get a meeting with him. His aides had tracked Zhou and knew he was coming hours before he even landed. Omelchenko had told them to make him wait at the entrance for one hour. Once at the residence, he would wait another hour. He would then be brought into the residence and Zhou, or anyone in his position would likely be furious. He would therefore make him wait an additional hour before Omelchenko would hear him out.

The driver turned to Zhou. "Sir, they are allowing us in. Do you wish to proceed?"

"Of course. Why would I leave now?"

"Sir, there is most likely another checkpoint outside the actual residence, and I suspect you will wait there as well."

"It is of no consequence. I must have an audience with this man even if we have to wait ten hours."

"Okay, it's your money." As he calculated his time. The two hundred dollar drive was now closer to one thousand. He drove forward and stopped outside the residence for round two. When they could finally enter, Zhou was surprised that a soldier had driven with them to the house and there were troops in front of them and behind them. This Russian took his security most seriously.

Once inside, Zhou was offered tea, which he accepted. The house was exceptionally cold, and he was left waiting yet again. He knew this game, but didn't care. It was at least an hour later when two large men, guns readily available in their shoulder harnesses, escorted him into an enormous study where Zhou met Omelchenko in person for the first time in his life. Tall like him, the Russian was a large, heavyset man that clearly lived a good life.

Omelchenko said nothing as Zhou approached him and said directly, "Mr. Omelchenko, I have been told that I have wronged you and wish to make you whole. Is this acceptable to you?"

"You have courage Dr. Zhou. No one has ever tried to gain my presence without an invitation." He chuckled.

"I offered several times, but received no reply. Pressure was on me to discuss this with you."

"I can imagine. And how might you make me whole?"

"Two billion dollars in any currency you wish."

"Just because you heard a rumor you crossed me?"

"Sir, I am a but a former farmer. You are a powerful man, and I am trying to avoid confrontation."

"A former farmer with billions of dollars at his disposal. Answer me this question Dr. Zhou. Who convinced the government to expel foreign investment in the telecom sector?"

"I did. My government wished this, and I was chosen to orchestrate the initial move so that others would follow because I was respected in this industry. Had I not, the government would have simply taken my company from me. It has happened here in Russia, so I suspect you understand. I did not know of your investment, and I did not have any say in the valuation."

"But you knew you would sell at some point."

"Yes."

"And was that knowledge part of the government, or your own desire?"

"My desire. I wished to sell the company to start the Sunset Foundation."

"Well, Dr. Zhou, at least you are honest. Thank you, but I must decline your generous offer."

Visibly shaken, Zhou replied, "Can I assume this matter is closed to further discussion?"

"Yes."

"Thank you for your time." With that, Zhou turned and under guard walked out. Despite the rejection, he was not defeated. Omelchenko had just revealed himself. He was going to harm Zhou or his assets. The question was when and how.

39

Sapienza University, Rome, Italy

Sara had never been so tired, or at least she did not recall it.
Her daily work routine was now closer to sixteen hours, and she
was living on biscotti and coffee. Her brown hair had lost its
sheen and if she took the time to weigh herself, she would have
been surprised to note she was eleven pounds thinner. She might
have been concerned, but at the same moment she had never
been more connected to what she was doing.

The university, including Dr. Ferrera and the staff, left her
alone as they had been instructed. Jealousy among the more
senior staff of less notoriety was growing, but no one dared
confront her. She was a bear if interrupted and all sensible
people got the hell out of her way, thinking the obvious. *Was she
that driven? Was she really just a bitch? A prima donna, perhaps?*

Sara was on the computer checking a calculation for a team
member when the phone rang. Annoyed, she glanced and saw
that it was Dr. Caliskan. She reluctantly answered. "Dr.
Caliskan, what might I do for you?" hoping to turn the call into
action and avoid chit-chat.

"Dr. Ricci, I am calling to head off some of the negativity going on within the group, hoping you can understand where this is coming from and frankly help me kick it down a notch."

"And this would be that we are building a WMD?"

"Yes, I wasn't sure if this had reached you."

"It has, some time ago. It is ridiculous. There is nothing in the array capable of being a weapon."

"I share your view of course, but the rumor has attracted a great deal of attention especially in America where one of their more dramatic senators has suggested they cancel the launch as a matter of National Security."

"Can they do that?"

"I assume anything is possible. Thankfully, word has it this is unlikely."

"So, what do we do?"

"We move forward. We feel the scientific gain outweighs the negative publicly."

"So long as we succeed."

"Well, yes, that would help. Despite the absence of Dr. Hendricks, I feel confident in our preparation and see little chance of failure."

"Have you heard anything new about her?"

"No, but I believe the SIS is involved." Sara said nothing, knowing that was probably former DHS director Hicks' doing. Chase had come through yet again.

"I only hope she is safe. I miss her and worry about her."

"Dr. Ricci, if I might ask. Given your history, what do you think is going on? Why would someone abduct her?"

"I think she is alive somewhere being forced to talk about our project. Someone wants this technology for themselves. Or possibly, they want to destroy it."

"I hope you're wrong, but thought the same."

"If asked by the team, what do you suggest I say?"

"The truth. We have nothing to hide."

"Thank you. I'll do my best. See you in a few weeks."

"Yes. See you in Florida."

Zhou and Caliskan were in the Solak headquarters drinking tea when the subject of the launch was discussed once again and Caliskan asked, "So, it is only by the will of the United States that Phase II will be disrupted." Zhou said nothing as he looked down, a rarity for him. Zhou was always present and looked directly into your eyes. Caliskan noted it immediately and asked, "Shen, what is wrong?"

"Nothing Demir, I just did not expect such negativity to our positive project."

"Are you sure that is the entire source of your temperament?"

"Demir, I am sorry, apparently you are learning to see. You are correct. I have deceived you." Zhou paused and explained his meeting with Omelchenko and failing to achieve his objective.

"I cannot believe you met him. That takes courage, I'll give you that. But I think your concern is misplaced. If Omelchenko disrupts Phase II, what does he gain? It was not even your money? Solak Group would have a setback, but not if we can prove sabotage. I know Sergei Omelchenko personally, but he is not a playground bully. He rarely does anything just because he can."

"Demir, my mind says something bad is going to happen, and I have learned to trust my instincts."

"Then we will step up security even tighter and be ready for anything."

"Agreed. I only hope my actions have not brought disgrace to the Solak Group."

Hours before, in New York, the UN National Security Council was underway in the Secretariate room at the UN building. The new President of the United States sat bored. He liked to talk but loathed to listen. This emergency meeting was in response to the American and United Kingdom's recommendation to postpone the launch until the assessment of the proposed weapon of mass destruction was completed. Experts had testified both of the possibility and the unlikelihood that the launch posed any threat. Countries aligned with Turkey said this was fake news. Countries opposed to Turkey said this might be the beginning of WWIII and on it went.

When it was finally time for the US President to speak, it was unclear what he would say. He held a prepared speech, but was unlikely to use it. He stood to an audience of praise, angst, and a general sense of mistrust. Undeterred, he ignored the script and in simple language, railed against those that said this was a weapon with no concrete facts. He talked of several subjects that had nothing to do with global warming, or even the purpose of the special session. At some point, an aide must have motioned him back on script and, looking down at the speech, he ended by saying he would not stop the launch. There was no crisis and no reason to consider it a national security issue.

Most of the room erupted in applause and, while some abstained, some laughed, and some even booed, but there was no rebuttal. The launch of Phase II of Project Solaris was officially on.

40

Cluj, Romania

Most people, especially those who have never faced it, believe that torture, or the concept of torture is solely related to Hollywood depictions of people getting physically harmed, electro-shocked, water-boarded, etc. These may be historical torture techniques, but the reality is much of torture is rarely physiological; it is usually psychological. This was the case for Hendricks who was being treated well, being fed nice meals, and had fine sleeping accommodations. Her evening meals even included wine!

Her hell was two-fold. First, she was being forced to betray her employer, her team, and her friends. Her captors knew this affected her and used it to make her miserable. Second, she was being interrogated by very smart people for hours on end in three different languages. All of which had to be translated. A painful process for any words, let alone a scientific thesis. She was tired, worn out, and they had her questioning herself, her science, and even the validity of the project.

The security head, Albescu had assured her, she would be freed but Hendricks knew in her heart, she would either die here or at the least, never be the same. Perhaps it was best if she died at the hands of her captors. The world would learn what happened, but at least she wouldn't have to face each day as a traitor.

Despite the negative thoughts, it was becoming clear to Hendricks that they were on a deadline, and she knew it was related to the launch. If the original date had not changed, it was just days away. Her captors had all they needed, and conversation now was a mixture of cross-examination and verification. To this point, other than at least a dozen scientists, she had only seen Antanasia Albescu. The guy running the show, Yuri Antonov was never present.

He was, in fact, pushing the team with all his might, as they had just three days to go. The phone next to him rang, and it was Marcon from Brazil. "The US President just refused to delay the launch. We are a go. Your team is ready?"

"We will need another day, but will be ready. Is everything set on the other end?"

"Yes."

"We will proceed until we are told otherwise."

"There will be no delay. Only our friend can stop this. Please make a note of this."

"I understand. And the British woman, Hendricks?"

"Do nothing until after the launch."

"Okay." Antonov hung up and looked through the glass. He would follow orders, but felt that this woman should not be left alive. Perhaps she would have an accident. These things happen.

Launch Center LC-39A was busy as the workers prepared the site. The Falcon Heavy rocket, F9HB5 would launch the following day, weather permitting, and system tests were already underway. The skies were clear, with only high clouds, although the winds were up. In the most aggressive and ambitious launch event in the world's history, two rockets would be launched on the same day. There would be three days between launches to re-stage and prepare, and the process would repeat itself four times. Ambitious, it was an amazing proof of the Space X concept.

The senior Solak team was there at the command center. With less than an hour to go before the countdown, the media was everywhere. Depending on the political alignment of the news agency, reporters were spouting off the science, or that an explosion was likely. One reporter was even wearing a bullet-proof vest with 'Media' written across it certain that he and his cameraman would catch the explosion from their safe vantage point.

But everything on the launch site had been checked repeatedly. The payloads had been loaded under armed security and every single event anywhere near the spacecraft occurred under the eye of multiple observers from Solak, Space X, NASA and even Space Force personnel from Cape Canaveral.

Of course, nobody listened to the mainstream media. This was a social media campaign, and the world knew the truth. This was going to blow up on launch. Everyone on Twitter had said so.

Minutes later, the pulse of the room changed, and all was silent. "Control, this is Launch Commander. You have permission to start the launch sequence."

"Roger Launch Commander. Sequence starting on my count."

The countdown started, and all eyes were on the monitors, the main boosters fired, and the Falcon 9 Heavy erupted in a display unlike Phase I. This rocket was enormous and the entire Launch Control, even built on shock absorbing materials, was vibrating as the mighty craft broke from the tower and slowly proceeded upward. A brief cheer came from the team and before it calmed, the rocket was ten miles in the air.

There was no catastrophic event. Nothing happened, nor would it even when the payload was deployed into GEO. The second craft went off uneventfully several hours later.

The next twelve days were a mixture of pain and joy. Pain because of the rapid launch cycle that had never been executed before and joy because all systems were a go and working as planned.

Zhou and Caliskan sat in a small room to the left of the control center and discussed the next steps. Zhou was speaking to the launch. "The media led people to believe that an attempt of sabotage would occur at the launch, but given the controls in place, that did not happen, nor did we expect it to."

"It makes me wonder however about the other phases of the project."

"You mean an opportunity of failure at joining, collecting, or beaming?"

"Yes."

Sara had just walked by when Caliskan asked, "Sara, do you have a moment?"

"Sure." Caliskan told her what they were thinking about the possibility of a problem elsewhere in the process.

"Would you agree?"

Sara considered the question. "Not really. It makes little sense. Outside of sabotage, there is just nothing there to blow up."

"But if Dr. Hendricks has been taken to understand the Energy Collection system, and not the beam itself, it would leave us to think the array is the target."

Sara gave this thought and said bluntly, "Dr. Caliskan, I am proud of what we accomplished, but there is just nothing that anyone with similar knowledge could not figure out if they wanted to. The only real secret we possess is frankly, how to communicate with the array and I think we have that locked up pretty well."

She excused herself to complete her checks, leaving Zhou and Caliskan with a look of concern. They hadn't even considered communication as a threat.

The large semi-truck moved slowly down a flat and well-graded dirt road. It finally stopped when its custom trailer was in line with two identical ones, three kilometers northwest of Launch Control. Because Phase II power was estimated to be over 50 million watts, the receiving antenna vehicle itself was much larger than the previous trial, and the dish that would unfurl from these three trailers was almost seventy feet in diameter. Each of the three trailers contained a megapack, a massive battery system, to store the incoming power. Looking down on this from space were more than a thousand nanosatellites and four larger collectors waiting for the command to join.

At the same time in London, Giles Taylor discussed the status of the Phase II launch with Alistair Evans. Both were pleased that nothing had happened to the various launches of the Solak Project in the United States. They were however, briefed by the

CIA that another opportunity for sabotage could occur when they were joined although that too was doubtful.

It was then the phone rang. Evans picked up and murmured something before handing the phone to Taylor with a sharp retort, "Would you care to sit in my chair as well?" Apparently, the call was for Taylor in Evan's office.

"No, sir, that will not be necessary." He grabbed the phone and said, "Taylor." He listened intently as his counterpart in MI5 spoke in hushed tones. "And you are sure this information is credible?" He listened further. "Very well. Thank you for the update." He hung up and turned to Evans. "Sir. They have located Dr. Hendricks. She is being held at a manufacturing plant in Romania. We have three separate inquires as confirmation, but as yet, no visual verification."

"What are your intentions?"

"I would like to brief my counterpart in the Romanian Intelligence Service (SRI). It is my intention for a small team of Royal Marines to join with SRI forces and bring Dr. Hendricks home."

"Is the SRI in bed with the owners of the factory?"

"I cannot speak for them all, but my contact is dedicated to his post. He is loyal to the SRI, and I can't imagine him choosing people that were not similarly oriented."

"Very well. Approved, but make sure you bring her home, Director. Alive!

"Yes, sir." And he promptly walked out.

Florida launch command had checked all systems and found no discrepancies before giving approval to join the four collection satellites and then the nanosatellite solar array around them. They gave the command, and all sensed a moment of truth as the small units slowly fired their miniature boosters and moved toward their preordained mate to join as designed. It was over five hours before the entire array had been constructed. The team burst into applause having not lost one satellite. As expected, the nanosatellites used much of their power to join, and the computers said the remaining power levels were between twenty to thirty percent. Sara checked the four Ricci Gamma Ray Conversion Dishes aboard the large collection satellites and was relieved that they had already begun to generate minute amounts of additional power.

Checks of the system continued into the night when just after nine o'clock, they give the signal to receive power from the array. Sara, wearing a Sapienza University jacket at the request of Dr. Ferrera and the approval of Caliskan, stood nervously in the control room as the command was given and the first amounts of solar radiation poured into the collectors. The entire room was being filmed, although only through a disaster would this feed ever make it to prime time.

But the effort was not in vain. Students and scientists around the world were watching as the team offered more high fives and more cheers when command once again signaled all systems were a go.

Thousands of miles away, a large white Dongfeng DFL Cabover truck, dirty with road grime drove slowly down Lihue Road towards downtown Shanghai, pulling an oversized load. The truck and its cargo were larger than a normal truck and trailer, but no one paid attention. In this part of town, and much of China, the roadways were shared by every method of transportation imaginable. It made its way to Yuntai Road before making a sweeping right turn and then immediately turned onto a spur road before the truck jerked and stopped in front of a large building with little character or architectural features. Had anyone been watching, the skill of the driver had been on full display as he accomplished this feat in a vehicle over twenty meters long.

The driver put on the emergency flashers and jumped out of the truck, which was so much larger than him, the appearance was somewhat comical. He walked behind the cab and hit a hydraulic control that brought the large cabin forward to reveal the motor and transmission underneath. He then placed red cones around the truck, signaling caution, and climbed up into the motor compartment. The mighty truck had apparently broken down.

The Romanian city of Cluj sits within the region of Transylvania and is equidistant from Bucharest, Budapest, and Belgrade. Here in this fourth largest city within Romania, six members of the SRI and six members of the Royal Marines had spread out in the shadows surrounding the large manufacturing building. Both team leaders felt the security they saw was largely for show. Many guards, but they did not appear to have significant firepower, and most did not walk or act as highly trained forces.

The highly specialized teams formed six teams of two, matching one SRI to one Royal Marine. The teams would enter at once from all sides and aim for the only area where housing existed. Several were there sleeping according to heat imagery from an SRI drone thirty minutes earlier.

Midnight struck, and the teams were in the compound in less than five minutes having cut into the surrounding fence or scaled walls at the rear of the property. Despite its size, they quickly took the site, given their element of surprise. They received several random but unfocused shots but returned fire, killing three plant security. All went to locate Hendricks.

A Royal Marine had walked down a corridor, checking each room as his SRI teammate provided cover. The marine had just checked four doors when two plant security came around the corner. They yelled and raised their weapons as the SRI soldier fired, but took a head shot and went down. The marine was half inside the door and jumped out shooting but immediately retreated when a dozen more Romanians came around the corner. He would have been dead but for his four teammates that entered the corridor from the opposite direction and overwhelmed the security forces, killing them. In the fifth room, they found Hendricks. As the door flew open, Hendricks, who stared at them in awe, was at first frightened until she saw the Royal Marine insignia and knew then she had been saved. Shaking from this change of events, she said sincerely, "Bloody hell, am I glad to see you?"

"Likewise, mam. We must go." He covered her in a bullet-proof vest and a Kevlar helmet, and they quickly left the way they had come with no additional shots fired and no apparent leadership on site.

Although Hendricks was weakened and having a tough time moving so fast, she sucked it up, thrilled to have been rescued, but saddened by the scene in front of her; SRI and Royal Marines carrying out their wounded or deceased brothers in arms. She, in that moment, knew what Sara had felt. They had died for her, and she didn't even know them.

Kennedy Space Center, Merritt Island

The solar array took twelve hours to gain peak power sufficient to charge the collection arrays. Sara and her team had already backed away from key command stations and moved to monitoring consoles as Dr. Huang brought his team in. They had spent the last four hours validating equipment and except for a slight temperature elevation in the collectors, all was as designed. Huang was confident and looked at Caliskan and Zhou in a clear gesture to suggest he was ready to beam.

Caliskan glanced to the head of the receiving antenna team who made a few checks and signaled they were ready to receive. He then looked over at Huang and asked him to verify the array position. A technician double checked and he, too, signaled that they were in position. There was hardly a sound in the room as everyone there knew this next few minutes would define the project and their fate.

Caliskan nodded back to Huang who then proudly asked the control station to beam, and two technicians keyed in commands. It would take two minutes for the radio frequency communication to reach the antenna on the satellite and then... absolutely nothing happened.

Huang looked at both technicians who looked back at him in shock. What the hell was going on? Zhou immediately killed the camera feed in the control room as Huang ran over to their station and the room erupted into a frenzy. Huang screamed for everyone to calm themselves when one technician, a young woman, said into a microphone that amplified into the room, "Sir, we have lost control of the array. It is no longer responding to our systems."

Whatever anyone had thought might occur, this was an unanticipated challenge. Caliskan came forward, "Repeat."

"Sir, we have lost control of the array. It is no longer responding to our systems. It would appear we have been locked out."

Caliskan yelled without considering the reaction, "Oh God! What have they done?" He stared at Zhou.

The technician, unaware of what was going through the minds of Sara, Huang and Caliskan asked, "Who is 'they' sir?"

"Not important," was Caliskan's reply in defeat. Despite the efforts of Huang and his team, nothing changed on the vast array of monitors regardless of commands being thrown at the solar array itself.

Alongside the small highway off the M9 Motorway, in Volokolamsk, Russia, stood an old building with no signage. A passing car might think it was an auto repair business, and locals knew it as a former welding shop, but it was much more than that.

Underneath the dirty and rusty factory works was a modern, air-conditioned bunker filled with computers and technicians, mostly former employees of Rosecosmos, the Russian aerospace company. From above, the only possible evidence that something different was happening here was an old outbuilding that housed a huge transformer feeding an insane amount of power into the ground under the derelict building.

From their elevated platform, Yuri Antonov stood with Antanasia Albescu and Cristiano Marcon. The team of Russians before them cheered as they successfully had taken control away from the Solaris team halfway around the world and they were now in control of the array. Antonov signaled to a technician who nodded and keyed something into the control terminal. All eyes lifted, and the numbers reflecting the location of the array slowly changed. Antonov asked to another, "And there is sufficient power to complete this?"

"Yes sir. Power in the nanosatellites is limited, but the power units in the collectors, which we do not fully understand are creating enough to reposition to the new coordinates." They continued to monitor the feed.

The truck driver in Shanghai had been working to fix whatever ailed the truck, but it was apparent that he could not. The driver exited the engine compartment and wiped his hands on his pants.

From inside the utilitarian building, few had even paid attention to the truck, but one young analyst, whose cubicle faced the roadway had more or less watched the driver off and on for the last hour. The driver had been talking on the phone and after he hung up, grabbed his bag, and walked away. The analyst thought nothing of it until the driver began to run. Strange, he thought.

Back at Kennedy Space Center and Project Solaris Command, the team could only watch in horror as the array itself moved according to their camera, the only signal they still controlled. Ever so slowly, but there was no mistake. It was moving.

Someone was repositioning the array. Twenty minutes passed before it stopped.

Caliskan and Zhou had retreated to another room and shut the door. They were discussing the reality of their situation. Caliskan asked, "It has to be the Russian, but for what purpose?"

"He wants the power, but this does not make much sense. The power to be generated is an amazing technological feat, but hardly worth a significant amount of money."

"Perhaps it is something else. Where did the array position, too?" Caliskan replied.

Unexpectedly, Zhou jumped up and ran to the control room, and in front of the team, said to a liaison officer for Space X, "Do you have access to any other satellite feeds to determine where the array was moved to?"

"I do not personally, but can get this information." He picked up the phone and called over to Space Base command. He spoke to several people, and it was over ten minutes later when he said to the phone, "All this is confirmed?"

He looked up at Zhou and replied, "It is aimed toward China, sir. Specifically, an area within Shanghai. Space Base is asking what has happened and is sending over a member of the Space Force."

Zhou said, "Fine," or something to that effect, and ran back into the small room. He used the secure line to call the

Sunset Foundation, as his mind quickly assumed the worst. A receptionist picked up and Zhou barked to get the foundation director, Ting Jiang, on the line immediately. Jiang answered as if she had been running, "Dr. Zhou, is there a problem?"

"Ting, please look outside for anything out of place near the building. A van, perhaps a large truck. Look out all four sides of the building now. This is an emergency."

"Dr. Zhou, the there is a large truck on Yuntai Road. It broke down several hours ago."

"Get everyone out of the building now, right now, yourself included. Alert Emergency Services and explain that a large explosion is imminent. I believe the truck is a bomb. Do this on your cell as you are getting everyone out and tell everyone to run as fast as possible down Lihue Road away from Yuntai Road. I repeat, away from Yuntai Road. Go now!"

Zhou hung up, sick with the thought that the single phone call was all he could do despite his money and relative power. Rarely a man of violent thoughts, Zhou was livid that Omelchenko had refused his money, money he did not even deserve all because he intended to destroy the Sunset Foundation and the reputation of the Solak Group. Hundreds, if not thousands, would die.

45

The situation was tense when Zhou finally received word that his foundation had been evacuated and nothing had happened as yet. Police and the fire brigade in Shanghai were attempting to disarm the detonators while in Florida, Sara and Huang frantically considered their options. Suddenly, Sara turned to Zhou and Caliskan and explained. "I think I know why nothing has happened."

All eyes turned toward her, and Zhou said, "Please explain."

"Early in our design phase we were concerned that the communication link was vulnerable. To avoid a single source of failure, Dr. Hendricks and Dr. Huang compartmentalized the software into zones. Imagine that each step has its own login code. I suspect now, they got enough information out of Julian to communicate, but she smartly left out that they needed a separate access code to activate beaming versus collection."

Said Caliskan, "I am happy about this, but we don't have control either."

Huang spoke, "This is true, but we also wrote a back door into the code. It was Miss Sara's idea. They, of course, went through the front door and took control. We can go through the back door and take it back."

"You can do this?" Caliskan asked, looking at Zhou, impressed.

"I can, but what Miss Sara is trying to say is that control has to be given from collection before I can enter the code to open the back door. Think of it as a door must close before I can open another. They took control before we have a chance meaning, they have control, but cannot beam."

"So, where is the code?" Caliskan asked in alarm.

"Julian has it." Sara said in a panic. All faces dropped as she frantically went through her notes to see if she had somehow written it down. The room was silent, as all eyes were on her. She went through every page and looked up and shook her head in frustration. "I'm not sure if this is it but these are the only codes I have." She rushed over to Huang who entered the first code she had. Nothing happened. Huang tried the second code. Again, nothing happened.

The tense scene was broken by the door opening into the control room and a member of the United States Space Force entered. He walked directly to Dr. Caliskan who along with Zhou assumed this was the Space Force responding to the fact that the array had been hacked and repositioned. Instead, the soldier motioned to the wall phone. "Sir, I have a secure call for you. On the line is Conrad Anderson, director of the CIA."

Caliskan walked over and with some trepidation, picked up the phone. "Dr. Caliskan speaking."

"Dr. Caliskan, this is Director Anderson, CIA. Several hours ago, UK and Romanian special forces rescued Dr. Julian Hendricks. According to her statement, which I just received from the SIS Director, she is safe in a secure location but demands to talk to a... Dr. Sara Ricci. Immediately."

Caliskan put his hand over the phone and said to the room, "Team, please listen, but do not react. No yelling, please! Dr. Hendricks has been found and is safe. She needs to talk to Sara, but I demand silence to regain control of our project." He motioned to Sara who rushed over and grabbed the phone. "This is Sara Ricci."

A faint but unmistakable voice replied, "Sara, it's me, Julian."

"Julian, I'm so thrilled to hear your voice."

"Sara, what is happening?"

"They took control and repositioned the array. We believe they intend to destroy a target in China, although nothing has happened now for almost two hours."

"And you know why?"

"Yes, but we need your code for the collection system to allow Dr. Huang to access the back door. They took control before the handoff was completed."

"What?... Oh crap, that makes sense, I forgot that part which we'll also need to fix. Okay, hold on, I have to remember the code." Hendricks paused for a few minutes and then said, "Okay, I think I have it. Tell me when you're ready."

"I'm putting you on a speakerphone. Hold on one second." Sara motioned to a technician who connected. All eyes were on Sara who said aloud, "Ready."

"Lowercase, lima-oscar-alpha. Then, capitalized, Bravo-Mike-Victor. Then, a comma symbol. Next, lowercase whiskey-alpha. Next, numerals 5-7-8-2. Last, lowercase, papa."

"Repeat, loaBMV,wa5782p." Sara said with authority.

"Affirmative."

Sara looked at Huang, and he entered the code into the system.

46

Volokolamsk, Russia

With the Solar array repositioned so the aperture of the laser pointed to the center of the receiving antenna on the trailer parked in front of the Sunset Foundation, the Russian team was ecstatic. The receiving antenna was not large enough to receive the energy the beam would send, but that was not the point. It only had to generate enough heat to ignite the blasting caps under it. The trailer itself was filled with a mixture of ammonia nitrate, nitromethane, diesel fuel and more than a hundred tubes of Tovex, a water-gel explosive. This was enough explosive power to level the entire corner and everything in it, including the building that housed the philanthropic Sunset Foundation. The blast itself would be felt almost thirty-five kilometers away.

Antonov and Marcon were clearly pleased with themselves as Antonov gave the signal to activate the beam. They had watchers on the ground in China to monitor the destruction and would soon call them.

At the Volokolamsk command center, the technician on Antonov's order commanded the beam. They waited the initial two-minutes for the radio waves to arrive at the aperture in space. Their faces, a mixture of pride, nervousness and apprehension, all cringed at the two-minute mark, fully aware of what was about to happen.

But then... nothing happened!

Antonov screamed at the technician who shouted back, "I told it, I told it," before the control director knocked him out of his seat forcefully and took over, reiterating the command. Again, nothing happened. The room was soon filled with raised voices, none of which could hide the fact they were no longer communicating with the array. The control director ordered two technicians to determine the connection, and they quickly verified the RF commands were being sent and they were being received. They just weren't being accepted.

Albescu was on her feet at first, sensing the problem, and now thinking she knew what the problem was. She walked toward Antonov and said, "That bitch."

Antonov spun around to face her, "Explain."

"Hendricks gave us faulty information."

"But we have control. The other side does not."

"We had control of the array, not of the beam. She misled us on purpose. There must be some kind of handoff code. I will get that code and kill her and everyone she fucking knows," as she ran back to the office and grabbed her phone. Antonov loved her anger. It excited him as he took joy in watching her scream into the phone to the poor bastard dumb enough to pick up the phone ReboVolt in Romania. The scene was not lost on Marcon, who had surmised what was happening.

As both he and Antonov watched, Albescu's face went from rage to horror. She screamed into the phone and then suddenly threw the phone with all her might into the glass window that separated the small office from the control room. The glass shattered into a million pieces which peppered those unfortunate to occupy the area in front of the window with chards of glass. None said a word in fear as she walked out, her entire face was contorted in anger. Marcon didn't mind violence, but he despised drama and he yelled, "What the fuck was that all about?"

Intimidated by no one, she stared at him and calmed herself before she said, "SRI and British forces raided ReboVolt, killing seven of our guards, wounded six others and rescued the good Dr. Hendricks two hours ago. They were too afraid to notify us."

"Call the spotter in Shanghai and find out what is happening," barked Marcon.

Albescu hesitated. "There is no need, nothing has happened."

"Do it now," Marcon screamed, and pulled out a gun and aimed it at her head.

"I will make the call, Cristiano, but drawing a weapon on me will bring consequences, even for you."

There was no hesitation as Marcon pulled the trigger with a single shot to the exact center of her forehead. She flew backward, falling off the chair onto the floor in front of the desk. Marcon looked around the room at the screams and faces of panic. Antonov tried to suppress his anger, but said nothing, knowing he would be next. He quickly pulled out his cell and called. He listened for several seconds and hung up.

"The police have shut down the street, and the building has been evacuated. Somehow they knew." He turned to the team in the room. "Get control of that fucking beam now or I will kill you all." All eyes were looking at their monitors while fingers flashed across keys, attempting to regain control. It did not take the coders long to see that there was, in fact, a handoff from the collection phase to the beam phase. It required a code that was 256 bit encrypted. That meant to break the code by force, there was a one in one-hundred-fifteen quattuorvigintillion chance of success, leaving them with no idea where to start.

Back at Solak Space Control, over the fifty voices in the room were seemingly all talking at once. Sara told Julian she would call her back once they were ready to beam. Julian tried to speak, but the room was so loud she couldn't be heard. Sara yelled, "Quiet!" and the room stopped cold.

A tearful Dr. Hendricks said from her heart over the speaker, "Please... please let me stay on the phone. They were going to kill those I love. I tried to resist and did my best to provide this fail-safe, but I'm heartbroken knowing I let the team down. Please forgive me and allow me the opportunity to see this through with you."

Consulting no one, Sara said, "Julian, the team loves you and misses you. You did just great under the circumstance." Sara turned and nodded to Huang who entered his normal release code into the backdoor. The monitors for beaming came back to life, and the team burst into applause before taking a few moments to recheck all controls. They had successfully taken back control and got into the beam control.

Sara asked, "Chenglei, what is the remaining power of the nanosatellites?"

"Twenty percent of them are dead or nearly drained. There is ten to twenty percent power in the remaining units. I'm afraid your invention will become the main power in less than ten minutes."

"Is it enough to reposition?" Sara asked, willing for a positive answer.

"I simply don't know, there is not much there." Huang said softly. Sara solemnly nodded and looked over to Caliskan and Zhou who seemed hopeful.

"We have little choice, please give it the command." Caliskan replied. Sara, listening and watching so intensely, at first didn't recognize the annoying buzz coming from her phone. She glanced at it briefly, saw it was Jason, and let it ring in silent mode. There was no way she could talk now.

Three thousand miles away in Lakewood, a suburb of Seattle, Jason was sitting on the half log bench outside of the tiny house where Sara used to live. He didn't remember her being here, but remembered the little red and white house and called Sara to tell her, but she wasn't answering.

He hung up and figured he would call again as he looked down at the letters 'Sara + Jason' carved into the top of the wood log, wondering how they got there.

47
Volokolamsk, Russia

Cristiano Marcon sat helplessly as the monitors in the control center all blinked off, leaving the team blind to what was happening. No one in the room dared make eye contact with him. He knew they had failed and was rapidly thinking of how he might handle this.

It took but a minute to understand he no longer held the cards, and this entire room was now a liability. Nodding to Antonov, he walked outside. Antonov understood the inference and immediately walked over to a small keypad inside a desk drawer where he keyed in a six-digit numerical sequence and set the timer for ten minutes. With a sigh, he headed to the stairs that went up to the door. Two soldiers in black were facing him as he walked out, closed the door, and quietly locked it from the outside. This was all part of their failure protocol that would leave no trace.

He tensed as he walked towards them unsure of their orders, but given Marcon had departed first, he was sure he knew as he pulled out his weapon, shooting one guard and forcing the other to take cover. Even though he was no longer the man of his youth, he was still fit and trained daily. He ran toward the forest as fast as his legs would propel him, firing back over his shoulder to hold the guard under cover. As soon as he hit the tree line, gunfire came his direction as he attempted to jump over a fallen log. He made it over, but just missed the height by the toe of his right foot, forcing him to corkscrew in the air and land hard on the ground. Winded, he jumped up to run when a bullet grazed his shoulder, and a second one hit his left hamstring. He went down to the ground once again, withering in pain.

Using his good arm, he pushed off despite the pain, intent on doing whatever he had to do to get away. As he rose, four strong arms grabbed him and yanked him backwards, dragging him back toward the building. Still in a seated position, they shoved him next to a steel pole holding up the roof of the welding area and pulled his hands behind his back with the pole in the center and handcuffed him. He resigned his fate. No one failed Sergei Omelchenko.

Staring forward, those inside the bunker were now pounding on a door they could never open, and Antonov's thoughts drifted between the pain in his leg and his secret love, Antanasia Albescu, dead on the floor downstairs. Having never told her of his feelings for her, for a moment, he imagined kissing her when searing heat overcame him, and all went dark. He and the entire team had been vaporized by the detonation of the incendiary bomb that Antonov had armed ten minutes before.

Marcon was several kilometers away, heading to Rublyovka where he would have to deliver the news to Omelchenko. As was his custom, he elected to do it with honor, knowing he would likely be executed by Dima Ivanov.

He made a call to Izabel, and in the few minutes he was allowed. He asked about her and spoke of nonsense from the past. She tried to get him to tell her what was going on, but he refused. As his rental car pulled into the main gate of the subdivision, he said goodbye and disconnected. Izabel had never experienced him like this and was frightened as the phone disconnected. *What in the hell was that about?*

It wasn't another ten minutes before he was in the study of Sergei Omelchenko. Ivanov wasn't there that he could see, but was likely nearby, waiting for his opportunity. Omelchenko knew immediately just by Marcon's facial expression, they had failed, but it was necessary for Marcon to acknowledge this. He asked, "Cristiano, do you have news?"

"We failed. Dr. Hendricks neglected to mention a password protecting a handoff from the collection function to the beaming function. They also had a backdoor into the system, and using this code, they retook the controls. When we tried to rectify this, we learned that SRI and British forces rescued the scientist in Romania. The facility in Volokolamsk has been eradicated, with all personnel, including Antonov and Albescu."

"And ReboVolt?"

"Key personnel were eliminated as a precaution. We'll be back up and running in several months after diplomatic efforts to restart. There is no tie to you or me."

"What should I do about this rare display of failure?"

"That, of course, is your judgment. I have called Izabel and made my piece." Omelchenko was slightly amused that a man like Marcon was momentarily humbled by him. He honestly thought he was going to die.

"Cristiano, you have been one of my most loyal and effective associates. Perhaps we are not true friends, but we respect each other. I can look the other way about this. You are not to fear me."

Almost without words, Marcon gathered his emotions, breathed a sigh of relief and replied, "Thank you, although I consider you a friend, Sergei. It is probable that there will be some heat over this. I would suggest a week or two away from your normal habits."

"Very well. Do you wish to join me on *Vertigo* tomorrow? We can drink an unhealthy amount of vodka and think of a new plan."

"Thank you for the offer, but I wish to see Izabel and reflect on how this all fell apart."

Omelchenko was not pleased with the rebuff but suddenly laughed, wondering if perhaps Marcon had wet himself. Power was intoxicating especially with powerful people. He pressed a button, and an aide walked in with a bottle of vodka and two glasses. "Fine, have a drink with me and then call Izabel and tell her you are on your way home."

48

The team spent an hour to assure the position of the array and the systems within. During that time, Zhou reinstated the video feed. Although thruster power was at critical; they had enough to reposition the entire array and when it ended; the team shouted in pride. Huang called the receiving antenna team who gave the okay to transmit. He looked around the room, nodded to Sara, then Caliskan, and then Zhou. Out of respect, he said to the air above him, "Dr. Hendricks, are you ready?"

The speaker phone answered with a muted cry, "Oh my God, thank you. Yes. Do it."

Zhou asked Huang as he stared at him and Sara. "You are sure they cannot come back in?"

Huang replied, "Not without my release code, which only I have." Pointing a finger to his left temple.

Zhou waved an affirmative gesture. Caliskan did the same. It was time. Huang nodded to the technician, who smiled and immediately keyed in the commands. The beam appeared to work, and they got confirmation when the camera looking at the receiving antenna, sent a video back of the ultraviolet beam. It disconnected several times because of some obstruction over its journey, but within twenty minutes, 52 million watts of solar power had been received into the megapacks. The room erupted in applause.

Fifteen minutes passed as Sara sat elated, but thoroughly spent as she checked the various monitors. This had been a hell of a day for all of them and a day none of them would ever forget. Both for its honor and its horror.

Dr. Caliskan walked over and shook her hand. "Dr. Ricci, you have earned more than just money on this project. You have earned my utmost respect. I hope to do great things together in our future."

"Thank you for believing in me Dr. Caliskan. It has been a challenging program, and I will gladly work on any project with you and this team."

As he walked away to shake hands with others, Dr. Zhou approached her and uncharacteristically said, "I am very proud of you, Sara. You were grace under pressure and the glue that held this together when we needed it the most." A man of few words, he turned and walked away before she could say thanks.

Sara took Dr. Hendricks off speaker so they could talk for a moment. "Julian, it's me. I just wanted to say how honored it has been to work with you. Your attitude towards me gave me the confidence to go back to being myself, and I feel blessed."

"Sara, you added so much to this project and imagine, without the Ricci Gamma Ray Conversion Dish, we would not have had the power to return the array to position."

"And without your critical thinking, the bad guys would have won, and we never would have had the chance. We have a great team and I think you have a lot more projects in your future. Perhaps someday we can get together for a nice dinner. You, me, and your partner. I insist."

"You knew?"

"Julian, everyone knows. Stop living in the dark ages. We love you for you." Julian burst into tears yet again, and they said their goodbyes.

She had just hung up as Omer Celebi came over and they did an awkward fist pump. She was thrilled to see him happy. He had done so much to make this work. "Sara, I now understand why Dr. Caliskan chose you. This has been an amazing project."

"Thanks to you. You are an excellent project manager."

"Thank you for saying so. I certainly hope we can stay in touch. You are perhaps the only one who always treated me with respect and not out of fear of my relationship with Dr. Caliskan."

"Omer, you are too gifted to be living in the past. You don't owe anyone a damn thing. I would encourage you to consider your debt paid in full." Celebi knew what she was saying, but was clearly not ready to discuss it.

"Thank you, but I will await my next role with the Solak Group."

In Rome, Chiara and Giovanna were up late, hoping to catch the news. After several minutes of local events, the camera focused on Carina Ferrari, co-anchor for RAI News 24, in Rome, and the backdrop was a picture of the array in space. "After months of speculation and controversy, the Solak Group, an organization for the betterment of humankind, is breathing a sigh of relief after the successful collection and beaming of energy from the heavens to earth just hours ago. Although there were reports of a near disaster, this effort was successful according to co-chairmen, Dr. Demir Caliskan and Dr. Shen Zhou. According to a written statement by the group, the technology will be donated to the UN in the hope they will use this energy source to help countries wean themselves off fossil fuels. Scientists around the world are applauding the effort while critics continue to say this was all just a pretense to create a weapon in space." While she was talking, they could see Sara on screen, still wearing her Sapienza University jacket, the team behind her in celebration. Chiara patted his knee and Giovanni said, smiling from ear to ear, "I am so proud of my special girl."

Chiara looked at him and said, "You and Annini made a very special daughter. She is an amazing woman, and I am happy to know her. And her dad, too."

The entire physics department at Sapienza University had watched the live feed coming from the SolakGroup.org website for almost twelve hours. It was difficult to understand what exactly happened because the feed was lost for several hours, but something had happened that was not according to plan although it had apparently been corrected. Every time Sara came on screen, the room cheered and a proud Dr. Ferrera was momentarily not concerned about the narrative.

To these students and even the faculty, the room was alive with excitement and the fact that one of their own was there in the room, making it happen was something money alone couldn't buy. When the beam was sent and the energy received, it cemented the deal. The university had already planned an entire year-long marketing champaign around Sara and this accomplishment.

Dr. Ferrera only hoped he could keep her at the university. Every university imaginable would come after her now.

In a private suite at the hotel Port d'Hiver, on Melbourne Beach, Zhou listened patiently on the phone to a Chinese Government official of high regard. Truly honored to be Chinese, Zhou had, his entire life, done whatever the government asked of him. Even when he did not agree. Perhaps for this loyalty, members of the government allowed him relatively free rein, and after the sale of Realtime, they often used his foundation to do things the government wanted done without direct knowledge from its citizens, or the world, they were even involved.

While it was true Zhou had approached the Minister of Trade about eliminating foreign investment, not readily known was that the Minister of Finance had approached Zhou first. The government wanted this, but it had to come from industry. Zhou brought it forward at their insistence, and industry followed. This was important because it gave him status within the government. As he listened, he asked, "The American CIA revealed that a TNA-70 radioscope in Crimea located RF commands coming from Russian to our array. Have you verified this information?"

"Yes, this is a fact. The location was traced to Volokolamsk, and a recent satellite image shows that location is now in ruin. A very large gas leak caused an explosion that leveled an entire block, and many are known dead. It is suspected the explosion was not caused by natural sources."

"Sir, this man Omelchenko, will never stop in his attempt to exact his revenge on me or my foundation. You have seen what he is capable of, and I ask for assistance."

"What kind of assistance?"

"I am grateful for any help in deterring him away from the innocence of my employees. He will gladly kill them all just so I have to live with that regret."

"Out of respect, I will take such a request forward, but you should not expect a reply."

"Thank you for any effort on my behalf." He ended the call and looked out over the water from his nicely accommodated room, knowing he would forever look over his shoulder.

St. Petersburg, Russia

Vertigo, the dark blue superyacht owned by Sergei Omelchenko, left its berth in St. Petersburg and cruised through the Gulf of Finland into the Baltic Sea. On board was a complement of security, Omelchenko, friends, several business owners whom he thought owed him a favor, and a staff of twenty. The head of security, Dima Ivanov was not present but his second in command was running Omelchenko's security detail on board. There were also a few scantily dressed playthings who busied themselves, waiting to be summoned— ready for any request.

Sitting at the fantail under a covered patio to shield him from the cold wind, Omelchenko sat alone with a coffee, reading a proposal. He set the papers down and thought about Zhou knowing he must think himself fortunate having saved his foundation and pulled off the Project Solaris. Omelchenko chuckled. He would allow Zhou to revel in the aura of success, and then scare him, really scare him. After all, Zhou had foreseen the man Omelchenko really was. He laughed again, although nobody around him had any idea why.

The next day, they passed by Sweden, and toward the southern edge of Norway into the North Sea. To avoid interruption, Omelchenko had ordered the captain to turn off its Automatic Identification Systems, the Long Range Identification and Tracking system, and Ship Security Alerting system. He assumed there were those trying to follow him and wished to make them work for it. Although the captain had argued against it, the ship was no longer visible to anyone other than visual witnesses, so when they entered the North Sea a day later, nobody would understand which direction they had taken. Had they gone toward the UK or north to Finland?

The following evening, Omelchenko hosted a party. With the young tarts near his side, they enjoyed the finest food and vodka imaginable until almost two in the morning. When the host finally went to bed, the staff cleaned and prepared for the next day when they also retired, leaving a skeleton crew to run the ship.

At nearly three in the morning, the captain transferred the helm to his first mate and headed to his room. He was almost there when an alarm sounded, causing him to turn and hastily make his way back to the bridge. There was almost no moonlight, so they couldn't see what was ahead of them, but the alarm was coming from their radar, although it was not conclusive what the faint object in front of them actually was. It was large and stationary. The captain noted there were no ships in the immediate area according to maritime records and whoever this was; they were running blind, like them. Why?

Out of an abundance of caution, the captain, without approval, switched back on the distress alerting system and was about to give a course correction when he thought better of it and brought the vessel to a full stop. His intention was to wait to see what this other vessel did. On the bridge, it became tense, as the security team was now awake and active. The captain noted they had entered the deepest waters around Norway and extinguished the bridge lights. The red hue of the emergency lights acted as an omen. Something wasn't right; everyone could feel it.

He thought to awake Omelchenko, but decided he should assess the situation before risking a confrontation with the ship's master given he was likely still drunk. The blip remained stationary in the same position about seven kilometers off their bow, and the security team considered this a threat. Their recommendation was to retreat and put a greater distance between them.

Vertigo was a fast vessel for its size, capable of 33 knots, but nothing this large moved quickly from a dead stop as they used their powerful thrusters to turn the ship. Once complete, the four MTU 20V 1163 TB93 diesel engines would ramp to full power so they could get the hell out of there. They were halfway into the turn when a bright light appeared from the direction of the alien vessel, and seconds later, an unknown force removed the entire superstructure of the ship. The impact was so great, the sixty-eight meter length of the ship immediately folded on itself in the frigid water and was already going down. Anyone not already dead would be in seconds.

In years to come, it might be revealed what happened, but the remnant of the once glamorous ship was now a V-shaped object traveling downward on its two kilometer journey to the bottom of the North Sea. It would likely break in two, long before the end of its journey.

Because of the captain's last-minute action, the International Search and Rescue (GEOSAR) satellite caught the emergency pulse from the vessel. While it could not explain what had happened, it would give investigators a location where the ship went down. An important fact was that the emergency distress signal had not been activated by a human hand. It had been set off by a catastrophic event aboard the ship.

Had any radar been active, it would have shown the blip that had been in front of them was now moving. The Chinese JIN-class 094 submarine, silent beneath the surface, was retreating north toward the Norwegian Sea, apparently taking the long way home.

Apparently, Dr. Shen Zhou had friends in high places, indeed.

Sara sat on the terrace with her dad and Chiara, having a glass of wine and some hard cheese with an herb and garlic artisan style bread that Chiara had made from scratch. With pure extra virgin olive oil and balsamic vinegar from Modena, it was as good if not better than any ristorante in town. Minutes later, Sara plugged her MP3 player into their outdoor system, and the melodic sound of Adele played in the speakers above them.

Sara had flown directly from Florida to stay with her dad and Chiara. She would also take a day to appear at Politecnico di Milano, where she had earned her undergraduate degree, and then on to the University of Milan where she earned her master's. Given the notoriety of the Solaris project, both schools had asked her if she could give a talk about the project and encourage female students to consider sciences, which she gladly accepted.

Giovanni was ecstatic. "And you my special girl are now in demand. This must feel wonderful for you."

"It was a difficult project, but a very rewarding one. It is nice to be recognized, but it's a bit much, actually."

"Are you changing your mind about academia?" Chiara asked.

"Not really. I enjoy the students more than I used to and clearly enjoy a learning atmosphere that a university percolates, but there is something about being out in the real world that appeals to me. Given the notoriety of the project, it behooves me to see what comes my way before I make any permanent decisions."

Giovanna and Chiara both watched her expression change. Thinking she might reflect on Jason, Chiara chose not to sidestep it and said, "Jason must be very proud of you, Sara. Have you spoken to him?"

"No, it has been so hectic. Thanks for asking. He is back in Seattle now, and I know he watched a lot of the video feed with the team there at Versilant." Both Giovanni and Chiara were surprised to hear he was back in Seattle, but said nothing. Sara switched gears quickly. "Chiara, if you can say, how is your investigation going?"

"Oh my. I'll need more wine for that conversation." Chiara rose laughing and filled her glass before bringing the bottle to the table and filling their glasses as well. When she sat down, she replied, "Unfortunately, things have been very slow. We have had no new information regarding our prime suspects, the Brazilian woman Izabel Vargas or her boss, although some say boyfriend Marcon."

"I must assume that is normal, right? Moments to act in between periods of nothing."

"True. Marcon was last seen in Moscow where we think he visited with the Russian Sergei Omelchenko, but there is a new wrinkle." She took a sip of wine and continued, "This is highly confidential, so please do not repeat this to anyone until it becomes public. I mean this. Both of you." As she looked at each of them. "Interpol has confirmed Omelchenko, boarded his yacht in St. Petersburg the day after Marcon left. The vessel had been tracked to the Baltic Sea when the ship suddenly vanished from detection. At first, it was thought she was lost, but other ships reported seeing her as far as Norway heading north, so somebody on the ship purposely turned off its navigation and alert systems. Despite that, a distress signal was received a few days ago and has been confirmed to his ship, *Vertigo*, built by La Ciotat Shipyards in France. Satellite images show no surface contamination in the area, but intelligence chatter suggests the vessel has been lost in water several kilometers deep. Omelchenko's company, Geoentergetics is not talking but they are clearly scrambling, meaning they are aware something has happened involving him."

"I know that the founders of the Solak Group believe that Marcon and the Russian were behind what happened on our project." Sara told them about the incident.

Chiara listened, trying to tie what she had just heard to her own case. "Interesting. Maybe they were eliminated?" She surmised.

"Who would do such a thing? The Russians?" Giovanni asked.

"Perhaps. The CIA recently confirmed a Crimean radio telescope located radio waves transmitting from Russia to a location in space that was at or very close to the location of your array. That had to be embarrassing, and heaven knows, Omelchenko was a hated man in almost every country in the world. The consensus is people liked his money, but not his methods. It is odd, however, that the news and intelligence services still think your project was merely hacked into. Nobody is talking about what you said actually really happened."

"The Solak Group is hoping to allow the hacking story to stay in front and center. Any tie to a weapon will fuel the rumors that almost stopped the project. I'm sorry about your investigation. It must be like starting over."

"It is, but that is how this game is played. Remember, all sightings involved Vargas, not Marcon or the Russian. We suspect they were cleaning and offloading money for Omelchenko, but have no confirmation. We continue to observe Marcon's business and residence, hoping to get a fix on either of them."

"I know this Marcon is a bad guy, but Vargas, is she capable?" Sara asked.

"In Marcon's case, he only talks to an enforcer of sorts, a Greek named Kristatos, and Vargas herself. Given they are his right and left hand, they must be extremely loyal, and extremely capable."

Sara's mind flashed back to Bridget Drummond and could only shake her head at the thought.

"Ladies, I have enjoyed this, but it is time for my sleep," Giovanni said as he rose, kissing both Chiara and Sara. As he walked to the door, he turned and added, "Please you are both welcome to stay up and talk girl talk."

There was an awkward silence when Chiara said, "So, I take it you are not ready for Jason?"

Sara didn't really want to talk about it, but knew Chiara was just trying to help. She rolled her eyes but answered honestly. "Not at all. We talk often and we're good friends. We'll just have to see if we are more than that, given we're so far apart and literally starting over."

"So why try."

"Exactly...Wait, do you agree or just understand?"

"I know you, Sara, but I've never had the pleasure to meet Jason. I'll offer you this. My job is the reason I have largely been alone. But I will not quit my career for any man, even your father. Art Squad is my passion, and it defines me in a way no other single person can, as I imagine science does for you."

"But you're still with someone."

"Yes, and someday, so will you, maybe just not now. That seems natural given all you have both gone through and career wise, you are just getting started. Weirdly, so is he."

"That makes sense." Sara paused and then said, "Dr. Facciolo thinks I can't commit to Jason because I am too confident to 'need' a man."

"I lack her credentials, but disagree. You're just a late bloomer. I was thirty-eight when I met my ex-husband."

"Ah, so here I am, waiting for Mr. Right to come along and sweep me off my feet." Sara said with a laugh.

"Sara, I shouldn't say this, but I just think Jason isn't the one you, but you feel guilty about it because he got hurt."

Sara nodded and replied, "You're not wrong. How will I know when it's right?"

"Trust me, Sara. You will simply know." They both smiled and clicked their glasses. Down the hall, Giovanni smiled as he pulled up the duvet.

52

Sapienza University, Rome

The following morning, Sara got a call from Dr. Caliskan. He had returned to Turkey with an overwhelming positive response to the project. Turkey's UN representative even spoke to Caliskan about making a resolution to the UN to consider the project. But just twenty-four hours later, there was a major setback.

"Sara, I'm sorry to disturb you, but if you have not already seen it, a news story has gone viral about the hacking of our project. That obnoxious reporter at the launch site, the one in the bullet-proof vest, somehow found the connection of a bomb threat at the Sunset Foundation to Zhou. He has said the hack was actually an attempt to divert the array and use the power to ignite a bomb killing thousands."

"Oh crap, here we go!"

"Yes. And it has been of no consequence that the Chinese condemned the story as inaccurate as was a statement released by me on behalf of the Solak Group last night. Despite our success, everyone is now convinced it could be used as a weapon.

I just wanted you to hear it from me and warn you. You might get some pushback from the university."

"Thanks. I actually received a text from Dr. Ferrera to meet him right away. I thought it might be good news, but maybe not."

"Don't let him bully you, Sara. This was an immensely positive project. I have more than enough resources to protect you."

"Thank you, but all should be fine. He has been pretty good with everything so far. Thanks for the heads up."

Two hours later, Sara was in a meeting with Dr. Ferrera. They were both seated in his office, which no longer felt friendly and warm, but downright cold as he sat facing her, saying nothing. His face was serious, his demeanor threatening. Sara was a minute away from just leaving when he lifted the morning paper, swirled it around. "Dr. Ricci, this story is alarming, and it troubles me how I found out about it. Not from you, but from a news story."

"Dr. Ferrera, there is no merit to the story, and even if there were, my NDA with the Solak Group does not allow me to discuss the project outside of my role as a scientist. You, of all people, know this."

"Don't sugarcoat this Dr. Ricci. You blind-sided me." He barked.

"I'm very sorry you feel that way, but do not yell at me. I do not deserve that and did nothing of the sort. Are you not the least excited about the number of scientific advances made on this project? Does it not matter that we foresaw such security risks and put in appropriate controls that worked as designed?"

"Dr. Ricci, the university has developed a year-long marketing campaign with you front and center. How can we do that now when a group of hackers almost used the project to kill thousands? The science is wonderful, but nobody cares about that right now. Frankly, I feel let down after all I have done for you."

"As a man of science, I am alarmed at your perception of this. I am grateful for your help in allowing me to work on this project, but I am not on a tenure track and the money I earn as an adjunct professor pales compared to the publicity generated by my work that the university receives. Are you really going to throw that away at the first blush of a conspiracy?"

"Ah, and now the student is my master. Is that how you would talk to your mentor, Dr. Zimbrean?"

"As a mentor, he would be worried about the science and me personally, not his own assentation to stardom on my coattails."

"What? Is that how you see me?" Red faced, he turned his chair away from her momentarily and now spun it back around. "I have erred Dr. Ricci. Sapienza University no longer requires your services."

"What?"

"You are fired!" He barked.

Sara was shocked, and it took a moment to regain her composure. "I understand." Sara rose on weak legs and started for the door before she turned, fire in her eyes. "When you explain my absence, Dr. Ferrera, be very careful. The solicitors for the Solak Group will be watching to assure you do not slander me or the project." With that, she stormed out of the office. Ferrera knew he had overreacted, but didn't move to correct himself.

Sara fast walked in anger straight to her office, getting hotter with every step. Without further thought, she quickly collected her files, books, and memorabilia. It took six trips, using the only boxes she could find to haul it across the street to her flat. It was on the last trip; she ran into her friend, Amy Keningburg.

"Sara, what are you doing?"

"Hi Amy, I had to get my things."

"Oh my god, you're leaving Sapienza?"

"Yes... I was fired."

"Fired. What the hell? Why?"

"Dr. Ferrera is concerned that the news of the thwarted attack on Project Solaris reflects poorly on the university. He says my services are no longer needed."

"Sara that's bullshit. Come on, bring your stuff back, and we'll sort this out. You are loved here, and that idiot obviously made a huge mistake."

"Amy, I know that, but I'm no longer the forgiving type. Sorry, we'll stay in touch." Amy was crying now, which made Sara cry, but it did not deter her. She turned and headed defiantly towards her flat, carrying her last box of books and papers.

When she arrived, she dropped everything in a pile and poured a glass of wine, heading straight for the terrace as she turned on her small MP3 player to *Beautiful War* by the Dutch band, The Gathering. She was in a very dark mood indeed, so why not choose very dark music?

Later that evening, Sara's phone rang. Annoyed, she saw it was Jason calling and thought to ignore it, but knew she shouldn't. She picked up reluctantly. "Hey, I hope your day was better than mine."

"What happened?"

"I was fired?"

"What? Why?"

"A story broke this morning describing the events of the launch and suggesting the solar array was going to be used as a weapon. Dr. Ferrera thinks that is bad for the image of the university. We exchanged words, and he fired me."

"He's an ass. I read some accomplishments from the project; they're huge. The engineers here can't believe they even know you. Screw him. I'll bet you could go anywhere now."

"Thank you, that is sweet. But this reflects poorly on my record. Fact is, I'm more upset at how it happened than the fact that it happened. By the way, sorry I didn't pick up the other day. It was during the launch, and I couldn't talk."

"No worries. I called to tell you I stopped by your tiny old house. I don't remember you there, but I remembered the house."

"That is nice to hear. I loved that place."

"So, who carved Sara + Jason?"

Sara laughed, "Mostly you. I wasn't strong enough to dig the blade into the hardwood."

"Dann and Susan have been telling me all the stuff that happened. I can't believe it, but I guess in between all the bad stuff, we were an item."

"Yea, kind of."

"You must be mad that I can't remember it."

"Not at all. I'm just glad you're healthy and alive."

"Dann says our relationship was one-sided. Me wanting you, more than you, wanting me."

"Jason, I'm weird and never having been in a relationship, so I really didn't know what to do and still don't. We had some great times, but the one thing we always fell back on was regardless of how we might have felt about each other, I live in Italy, and you live in Seattle. Neither of us could reconcile that."

"I recall the issue, but not much more than that, so it's probably best."

"Yes, perhaps."

"Hey, relax. You'll get no pressure from me. I'm just happy to not be in a hospital."

"How is Versilant?"

"So far, pretty good. I'm starting slow, taking in small doses at a time. While I might not recall a specific project, I can get there pretty quick skimming notes and specs."

"Good news. Anything fun?"

"We're adding a few new nanobots to the platform, but we're just starting. If you get bored, fly over. The guys tell me you were a big help."

"Thanks, and I'll let you know since I'm in between careers."

"Okay, robot girl, I have to go, but let's stay in touch and seriously, I really value you as a friend. You know that, right?"

"I do, and I feel the same. Besides, you're my official bodyguard remember?"

"Always." Sara hung up and felt calm. Chiara was right. Just let it go and see what happens. The future was the future, and with any luck, the past is the past.

53

Rio de Janeiro, Brazil

In his study within their private sanctuary, Marcon and Vargas sat discussing aspects of his legitimate business, Povos Engeria. He had not yet told her of the failure and his life being spared by the Omelchenko. Sensing something was troubling him, she asked, "Cristiano, are you ever going to tell me what happened? It is written all over your face."

He paused but replied, "It is best you know. We failed to punish Zhou. The British scientist deceived us, and everything went wrong from there."

"So, the scientist is dead?"

"No. Antonov and Albescu and the entire Volokolamsk team are dead. The scientist was rescued by SRI and Royal Marines, costing seven additional lives and loss of the Romanian plant for at least six months."

"Where is Diabo in this charming story?" Diabo is a slang Russian term for the devil.

"Mind your tongue, Izabel. He is likely many people's version of the devil, but he'll also kill you for saying that."

"What is his hold on you Cristiano?" Izabel asked bewildered.

"No hold. He has been very good to me over the years. Yes, I take many risks for him, but it pays very well and being associated with him often allows me success even before negotiations start. Look beyond the man himself."

"I have and someday, my love, your relationship with him will get you killed."

"Not today, Izabel. He spared me you know."

"Is that why you called after leaving Volokolamsk?"

"Yes, I went to tell him of the failure in person. He was rather gracious and said we would create a new plan."

"And this gives you cause for concern? I would think you'd be elated."

"He left on his yacht the next morning after inviting me to go with him, but I chose to be with you. He has not been seen or heard of since. Norwegian authorities say they received a distress beacon from his yacht; the type triggered by an event, not by human hand."

Izabel did not mouth her desire for Omelchenko to be dead, but it was difficult to observe Marcon so concerned. What the hell? She looked at him and said cautiously, "Cristiano, this man is not your father."

"I know this, but I was the last person to see him the day before his disappearance. Dima Ivanov will come for me to answer his questions."

"What the fuck for? You didn't kill him?"

"I know, but I need to go to him and settle this."

"Let him think what he wants, Cristiano. If what you say is true, you'll be walking into the lion's den."

"Perhaps, but it is the way things must be done." He leaned down and kissed her. She was scared for him and even for herself, but allowed his affection and then some.

The plane touched down on a private runway in Domodedovo Airport, south of Moscow. Marcon and his own security team left in three Mercedes S550 sedans to just outside Moscow's second ring to the corporate headquarters for Geoentergetics. Marcon had not called ahead. Two cars arrived under the glass awning to protect the vast company entrance from rain and sleet. Security was high, and no sooner had the cars stopped than the six of Marcon's party were met by a dozen of Omelchenko's. The third car was secretly parked around the corner. Marcon was met outside the car and was told only he could enter. They knew exactly who he was.

He argued, but this was not a debate and he imagined Ivanov watching this on a monitor, laughing, as he relented.

Marcon was taken to the fourth floor and placed in a conference room, alone. He poured himself a coffee and had taken his first sip when the door opened and Dima Ivanov, head of security entered with a folder and sat down, facing Marcon.

"You saved me the trouble of hunting you down."

"There is no reason to hunt someone in plain sight. You have known exactly where I have been since I left."

"You are correct."

"Say what you must Dima. My relationship with Sergei is complicated, but highly lucrative. I fear he has been killed."

"I was disappointed he spared you."

"Yes, you must be heartbroken. Please, let's get this over with so we can move on."

"Marcon, you are just a criminal Sergei used to get things done and insulate himself. Do not think for a moment you were anything other than a tool. How did you kill him?"

"I did not, and you know this. The only way to eliminate a vessel of that size was by a military asset. I have access to neither, nor do I have a motive. What you say may be true regarding Sergei's thoughts of me, but I saw him as a mentor. I would give my life to defend him."

"He spares your life when he shouldn't and 24 hours later, he is gone."

"Twenty-four hours later, he was in St. Petersburg on a trip he asked me to take with him. It was two days later when contact was lost. Sparing my life was a gift. Why would I then kill him?"

"You're well informed Marcon. How do you know this? Because you arranged it?"

"No, but it makes me wonder. Why were you not on *Vertigo*? Head of security begs off and suddenly the ship is gone. Perhaps you arranged his fate."

"Be careful Marcon, I am the one in power here, not you."

"You have no power Dima." Marcon yelled. "You inherit none of this. You're just acting out because he gave me the work that you felt you and your team should be tasked with. Let's dispense with these fucking games. I had no means to pull this off, nor would I. My life is altered negatively by his disappearance."

"Says the man who recently took over a satellite array in space and almost leveled a city block in China. No, I think I am not done with you. You are capable of this I am certain."

"I am not alone, and my men have instructions should I not conclude our business soon. This will get messy, Ivanov."

"Yes, we know Marcon. But did you know your men can no longer take your commands?" Marcon rose and glanced out the window and down to the entrance. No men, no cars, as Ivanov sat in the corner sure of himself.

"And you and I are alone. I can kill you ten different ways before anyone can enter that door you weak piece of shit."

Ivanov pulled a PSS-2 Silent Pistol out of his coat and said, "You were saying?"

Sara began her second week of life no longer attached to a university—the first in years. Still not ready to explain to her dad what happened, although she should, she filled her days saying hello to all those that had reached out to her. She also worked feverishly on the three technical papers she was writing or co-authoring with the Solak Team regarding Project Solaris. All the while, she was still angered by the whole sequence of events and had refused two calls and a text from Dr. Ferrera.

It was a few days later when Dr. Zimbrean called from MIT, and Sara answered immediately. "Dr. Zimbrean, it is so nice of you to call."

"I am pleased to hear your voice and should I forget, tremendous job on Project Solaris. It warmed my heart to see you in the control room, although I would have preferred to see you cloaked in an MIT jacket. Many of us here watched the entire video feed."

"Thank you," she said with a laugh, "It was an amazing project despite the moments of drama."

"Sara, that is partially the reason for my call. I have spoken to Dr. Ferrera, and these are his words, not mine. He has made a mistake which he would like to alter. He knows he overreacted."

"Dr. Zimbrean, I know he is your friend, but I have been through too much to look the other way. Whatever happens will happen, but I am done with him, although perhaps not the university."

He paused but had expected this response. "I understand. What are your plans?" knowing she was not without cause.

"I'm working on papers related to the project. The Solak Group is pushing to publish them before the next UN Climate Change Committee meeting, which is just three months away. Meanwhile, I'll wait for the next project. Money wise, I'm good. I earned enough to cover me for a while."

"Okay. If you need any help, let me know. I don't have to say that you are always welcome at MIT. Please take care and call or text me if you want to talk."

"Thank you. Talk to you soon." Sara disconnected the call. She was upset with Dr. Ferrera, but at the same time, she understood why he was angered. After all, he had vouched for her, but there was no question he had been out of line.

Feeling the need to connect, Sara called home days later. The phone rang twice when Chiara picked up. "Sara, it is late. Are you okay?" Sara had paid no attention to the time and at first only wanted to talk to her dad, but it was clear Chiara would not wake him except for an emergency. Sara explained what had happened and Chiara replied, "Sara, for now, this is our secret. It will only upset Giovanni, so we will not discuss this tonight. I think you have handled this correctly, but if they contact you again, you should at least hear them out."

"Thank you. I'm not sure what to do, but have a fairly good idea."

"Your instincts are good. Listen to them."

"Thank you Chiara."

"All my love, Sara." And the line disconnected.

Sara had just returned from a run the following morning when her cell rang and, looking down, she noted it was Dr. Ferrera. She hesitated, but answered. "Hello Dr. Ferrera."

"Sara, are you still in Rome?"

"Yes, Dr. Ferrera. I live here."

"Ah... yes. I know. It's just that I saw you cleared out your office."

"That is what one does when they have been fired."

"Yes, about that. I think we should talk."

"Dr. Ferrera, you said what you felt. I guess we both did so, given that, what is there for us to discuss?"

"Sara, I have been told to assure you that the university wishes to resolve this. They very much want you to remain part of their program. Our program."

"I would consider the fact that you had to be told the basis of our problem. If that is all, I wish you well Dr. Ferrera."

Sara was ready to hang up when she heard him say, "Sara, I am truly sorry for my actions. I overreacted and I'm asking for your forgiveness. At least give this some thought. I understand you're not happy with me and you are welcome to work for someone else, but please, think of the students. The university!"

Pulling the phone back to her ear, she said, "I will," and hung up the phone. Dr. Ferrera knew she was feisty and in that moment, almost missed the more vulnerable and insecure woman she had portrayed just six months earlier. Clearly, that was gone.

He had really messed this up, and she hadn't been wrong. He had been using her to advance his own status within the university, *but really, who wouldn't?* Here he had worried about her screwing this up for him, and now the university would no doubt make him pay for his actions.

Izabel Vargas was becoming nervous as she paced back and forth like a caged animal. The house staff were giving her wide berth and avoided eye contact if they had happened across her. Izabel had been trying to get hold of Cristiano for five days, with no success. His trips to Russia were always for one day. One fucking day because Omelchenko made him travel twenty-two hours for a fifteen minute meeting. Holding a glass of Tohu Sauvignon Blanc from Argentina, Izabel waited for Kristatos to arrive.

When the elevator sounded, Izabel went to greet him. The doors opened and Kristatos lumbered out with a look of concern.

"Any news?" Izabel said in haste.

"No. the primary security team does not answer. I was able to contact the backup team, and they say he was taken to Omelchenko's residence three days ago."

"Why?"

"We can only assume Ivanov is interrogating him."

"But this is so stupid. Cristiano had no hand in this. He looked up to that bastard for whatever warped reason."

"Izabel, Dima Ivanov dislikes Cristiano very much. Omelchenko always gave Cristiano the big projects and looked at him with respect. He did not do that with Ivanov and worst, left him to play bodyguard. I can only imagine he was quite unhappy when Omelchenko spared Cristiano's life."

"What do we do now?"

"We go there and make a case to get him released. There might still be some honor among thieves."

As was the case just days earlier, the NetJets Gulfstream VII landed at Domodedovo Airport. Ground transportation arranged by Ivanov was there to greet them and they were brought to the residence. Kristatos had, of course, planned, knowing there was no way into the compound without help. He had also given a stern warning to Izabel. "Say nothing and do not react to your emotions. This man, Ivanov, is a bit of a loose wire. We must take care and not give him an excuse to kill us both." She nodded, but with her anger was visible. "Izabel, I mean no disrespect, but my words are fact. Once we are inside, I cannot do or say anything to protect you."

"I understand."

They waited for fifteen minutes when Dima Ivanov came out to see them in the main hallway. Apparently, they would not be invited in.

"Kristatos. It has been a long time."

"It has. I am asking you to part with my boss. I would like to take him home."

"He is not here. He came to Geoentergetics a few days ago, but I have not seen or heard from him since. Perhaps he got lost?"

"He had multiple security details. One is missing like him, the other says he was brought here. I just wish to collect him."

"I'm not sure how to help you Kristatos. He came to me rather than I find him, and we talked out our differences. That is that."

"Okay, Ivanov, we'll play by your rules. Might you be open to a financial arrangement?"

Ivanov laughed and spread his hands around him. "No, Kristatos, I am well in that department, but thank you for offering. Good luck, and I hope you find your lost dog."

Izabel was staring at Ivanov with blood in her eyes, but he was only amused as Kristatos grabbed her and lead her outside and back to the waiting car. He motioned her in and gave her a sign to be silent. The car was most certainly bugged. They arrived unharmed at the airport and boarded the same plane when he finally spoke.

"I am sorry Izabel, but you got that look and Ivanov was just wanting to see how far you might take it."

"I was ready to kill him. So, do you think Cristiano is there?"

"He is there, unless..."

"... He is already dead?"

"We have to accept this is a possibility, but I think he is there. Ivanov was hiding something."

"Why the game?"

"It is his show. All these years being the heavy but never making the rules."

"I would like him to die, and he will if Cristiano is harmed."

"Difficult, but not impossible." Kristatos said as he smiled.

Marcon rose when asked and was brought into the study where he used to meet Omelchenko. Ivanov was letting the circumstance get to his head. Marcon sat and Ivanov said causally, "Your lieutenants were here asking me to hand you over. Ballsy, I think. They even offered to pay."

"And did you strike a deal given you apparently think this is all yours?" waving his hand at the opulence of the room.

"That was rude, Marcon. Please recall I'm trying my best not to just kill you."

"You will anyway. How about we make it a fair fight? You and me to the death. No weapons. Mano-a-mano?"

"Perhaps, but I think for your crimes, a trial is necessary. I'm putting together a tribunal to hear your case before you are sentenced."

"And the charge?"

"The murder of Sergei Omelchenko."

"Ivanov, you know I would never harm him. Why this silliness?"

"Because I am in charge, not you. I decide now and I want you to know your fate is in my fucking hands." He practically screamed. Two guards entered, and Ivanov told them to take Marcon back to his cell. Marcon acted as if he were a broken man, and the guards chuckled as they led his weak and lifeless form back to his room.

They had just rounded the corner when Marcon struck. They were both close to him, too close to use their weapons when Marcon belted the guard to his left in the throat, crushing his windpipe. It wouldn't kill him, but would incapacitate him and remove his ability to yell. Just as quickly, he grabbed the second guard by the head and twisted violently, breaking his neck before turning to the first and doing the same. Death in seconds, but no blood, and very little sound.

He pulled both of them into a room and locked the door from the inside. From the bodies, he removed a pistol, two assault rifles, four throwing knives, and a cell phone. His Russian was lacking, but he needed to contact his security detail at some point. He then changed into the larger guard's clothing to blend in. The knives went into his new tactical pants and the pistol in his waistband. He placed the assault rifles over his shoulder and went to the window. Off to one side, he glanced out and saw nothing. He quickly reset the security sensor on the window and as it was searching for the network, he pried the upper and lower contacts off and placed them together before he opened the window and climbed out.

At least five-meters off the ground, he climbed out onto the ledge, closing the window behind him before climbing up the stone blocks to the roof sill. He was up and over in a minute. He needed to make his way toward the back of the residence and then down near the trees. The good news was he was momentarily free. The bad news was he was still in the compound and would have to make his move before they let the dogs out, which they usually did at seven o'clock every evening. He had heard them each night and took note.

56

Paris, France

Dr. Shen Zhou was having a glass of champagne as he worked the room of wealthy patrons in the famed Galerie d'Apollon (Apollo Gallery) at the Louvre Museum. He was attempting initial support for the Nile Basin Project. The premise was to fund a series of wetland projects to improve the habitat for the very creatures the Nile Basin has used for food for centuries. In the current state, the wetlands were being damaged or eliminated, altering the entire ecosystem of the region. Some of these patrons were members, but most were not. But influencing them often indirectly influenced a member.

He loved the Louvre Museum, and having it to himself for this private event was expensive but worth every cent. Although

Zhou looked confident—the gracious host—he was far from settled. Two days ago, he learned of the likely demise of Sergei Omelchenko, which caused him no concern, but the taking of his entire vessel meant that at least fifty or more other soles had perished. Of course, some of these were soldiers and others were likely criminals in their own right, but at least half were guilty only by association. This troubled the more humane side of him. He continued to mingle, mindful that if those around him only knew what he was really thinking, they would run out of the building with justification.

Kristatos and Vargas had struggled since their return from Moscow as they thought of how to assist Marcon, if in fact he was still alive. The unseen security team was still there, and Kristatos had positioned them near the house to assist. Meanwhile, they had been discussing Omelchenko.

"Assuming what we have heard is true, to take out a vessel the of that size, this must have been sanctioned by a government. They are on the only ones with such firepower. Russians?" Izabel asked.

"Most likely, although the whole plot against Zhou makes me wonder if it could be him?"

"He has no reputation for such things. But it offers an explanation. Could the Chinese government do this knowing he was after Zhou?"

"Perhaps, but why? Like Russia, I am not aware that the Chinese government is very supportive of their super rich although Zhou is more than meets the eye." Kristatos added.

"What do you mean?"

"Cristiano told me Zhou was asked by his Government to come to them and request the end of foreign investment in the telecom sector. By him coming forward, others would follow, and they did. Cristianos analysts had said, the government even uses his company and his foundation to pursue projects they cannot. Perhaps on the threat of the Russian involvement in redirecting the solar array to kill thousands of their citizens, Zhou appealed to them, and they accepted the challenge."

"If we could prove this Cristiano can be free."

"Perhaps, but I think Ivanov has a personnel war with Cristiano. All this nonsense about Omelchenko is just an excuse."

"What about the bitch that caused all this to happen, Dr. Hendricks? You realize if she had just played fair, nothing else would have happened."

"True, but killing her does not help Cristiano. Let's focus on him first."

"Agreed. I am worried about him." She looked down, saddened. "I've never really worried before."

"He is a very accomplished solider Izabel. I have no idea where he is, but if he is there, he is waiting for his time." They had no idea; Marcon was now heading off the roof and had already sealed his fate.

Marcon had gone to the darker side of the roof and climbed down, using the stone blocks as a ladder. No easy feat, but there was no other way. As it was, he knew the residence had vast security systems and could not believe he had not yet been discovered. He imagined a room full of techs looking at hundreds of outside monitors, which was true, but they were likely concentrating on where there were holes in personnel or sightline. Marcon was using this to his advantage.

He reached the ground and walked casually in plain sight toward the trees to the back of the property. His goal was to aim for the stone fence that surrounded the entire estate, knowing in advance the trees and all vegetation had long been removed at least four meters from the wall. This was a security measure to allow sightlines from two guard towers. Glancing at his watch, it was almost five, meaning he had just two hours. Marcon tucked into the shadows, planning his next move, when all hell broke loose.

They must have discovered him missing because every security apparatus on the compound seemed to come alive at once. Marcon stayed close to the house while the troops were spreading out toward the walls. After fifteen long minutes, he himself headed in that direction, acting as if he were one of them. As he approached, voices were coming to his left. Hiding in the shadows, he dropped the rear guard with a throwing knife. The moment the first guard realized his friend was down, Marcon threw the second knife into his throat. Before he could react, Marcon ran to him, pulled him down and held him as he bled out before he went back behind a large tree and waited. Two more guards appeared and were about to come upon the bodies in the tall grass when Marcon came out from behind the tree, slit the throat of one and broke the neck of the other. The last thing he did was pull out the Russian phone, contemplating the strange keypad and placing a call to his security team. He had no idea where they were or even if Kristatos had deployed them, but took the chance. His instincts were rewarded when the phone quickly answered. They were very near the residence.

He was succinct. "I'm out of the residence and going toward the north wall and then into the Moskva river. The current will take me towards Moscow. Try to intercept me five to ten kilometers downriver from the house. The area will be hot." The call was ended, and the team immediately headed in that direction and the team leader texted Kristatos to explain the rendezvous. Kristatos read it and smiled. Marcon was alive and on the move.

Pulling the assault rifle forward, Marcon got the hang of the unfamiliar weapon and placed it into single shot mode. He moved forward near the edge of the tree line, where because of the vegetation removal, it was impossible to use the trees to breach the four meter high walls. He laid down flat in the grass, a miss on their part as this should have been maintained to a much lower height, allowing him some cover. With the rifle aimed at the tower high above him, he waited for the guard to come into view. Through his scope, he saw the tip of a gun several times, but never the guard holding it. They were well trained. He was about to create a reason to force the guard to come closer to the edge of the tower when the guard's face came into view, and Marcon expertly pulled the trigger once, without hesitation. The guard's head burst on the impact from the high-power rifle, but the shot gave away his position, and the opposite tower began shooting in his direction. He pivoted in the grass, took aim, and killed the guard before abandoning the two rifles. With only two throwing knives and the pistol, he ran to the wall and climbed for his life, blind to what was behind him. He was going to make it or die trying.

Sara arrived at the Milan apartment to spend a few additional days with her dad and Chiara having taken the train from Rome. When the time was right, Chiara had told Giovanni about the episode at the university and he was concerned for Sara, but knew she had done nothing wrong. They were all out on the terrace having a glass of decent Chianti when he asked, "So, have you spoken to him?"

"You mean Dr. Ferrera?" Her dad nodded. "Just once." Sara responded. "He apologized, knowing he did not have the authority to fire me, which was his only real concern—that this might reflect badly on him. It did, and he was placed on probation, or so I'm told by a friend at school. You remember Amy?" Giovanni nodded affirmatively.

"Has anyone else called from administration?" Chiara asked.

"Yes, the Rector actually called me, and I was honored to hear from him. I was professional and honest, telling him I would happily promote the school, and that they were welcome to use my image in their fall campaign. It is good for me, women of science and the university, but I stopped short of any additional commitment to them."

"What was his response?"

"I think he understood and only said good luck and others would reach out to me."

"You handled that well my special girl. What is next for you?"

Sara laughed and said, "I honestly have no idea."

Days later, Sara was in the kitchen with Chiara when she asked about her case involving the missing art. Chiara glanced around to make sure Giovanni was not within earshot and answered softly, "The loss of Omelchenko is public news. Most all news outlets are saying the Russians themselves did this. At first I was skeptical, but a Putin loyalist was just named the new head of Geoentergetics, which to me confirms it. Putin has gone on TV to deny this, but it is well known how he feels about oligarchs such as Omelchenko. It is said that when the radio waves were traced to Russian soil, that was the kicker."

"But with Omelchenko gone, you have lost your art, yes?"

"No, I don't think so. Please recall it is unlikely the Russian ever had the art in his possession. All of our leads and sighting have been Vargas. These works, despite their history and admiration, were just tools to launder or convert currency. And then there is the latest?" She said with a smile.

"What?"

"Izabel Vargas has been confirmed by several sources as the host to a recent showing to sell the Raphael and the Rembrandt. We have Interpol tracking her even though we are a bit surprised."

"Surprised that she is selling?"

"No. The hastily and public way she did this. Until now, she has been very careful, but this, this was an amateur hour for the likes of her. It is almost like desperation. But that's okay, we'll take it. This is as close as we have been."

"Is she acting alone?"

"Maybe? Marcon gives her a lot of free rein, considering who and what he does. It seems though that the news of Omelchenko's demise is what prompted the opportunity to sell. They can make well over one-hundred million euros, if not more, by selling art that isn't even theirs." As close as Bulgari was to the truth, the fact was that Vargas had to sell to raise immediate funds to help Marcon. She and Kristatos had access to some credit but cash? For that, they needed Marcon, and he wasn't there. Mercenaries at their disposal didn't take American Express.

"So, I noticed you didn't want dad to hear. He remains overprotective?"

"No. he is much better. I just try not to make a habit of discussing my work with him, and seriously, I get it. After losing your mom, he is terrified of losing either of us. And it's not like we help matters, always finding our way into the thick of things. He is a former pension administrator, and I can only imagine risk to him is only having five back-up pencils should the lead on his first one break." Sara laughed just as he walked into the room, asking about dinner.

Chiara glanced at Sara and smiled as Sara noted her dad was a few pounds heavier than the last time she was there.

Kristatos was happy to know Marcon was on the move, but very concerned for his friend; of all the places to be hunted, Russia was the worst. The recovery team was six men. All experts in the country and able to move freely, they were a blend of Russian, Ukrainian, and Polish soldiers and had worked in this theater for years. On the opposite side of the river, they would wait and work their way downriver. They had access to weapons, money, and a plane ride out and Kristatos hoped to hell they needed all of it.

Izabel had a different idea. "I think we must go back to Russia. We have to be there for him."

"Izabel, no one is happier than I to know he is trying to get out, but any attempt for us to get into Russia will cause our death or worse, make him risk himself to find us. We must stay here."

"Then you stay. I'm going to Russia."

Kristatos looked at her now in a way he had not before. "You will do as I say. This is not a debate."

"Really. So, you would keep me from leaving?"

"Yes, it is for your own good."

"When Cristiano is back, we will revisit this conversation." She yelled, fire in her eyes.

"I sincerely hope we have the opportunity." He said with cold, dead eyes, causing her to back off and look away.

Nearing the top of the wall, Marcon was singularly focused on getting up and over. Using every small handhold and foothold he could find; he was trying to get over the wall quickly. He had been nicked on the shoulder, but adrenaline was so high; he had not noticed it until now. He switched his weight to his other shoulder and brought his leg up over the wall. Without pause, he went over the half meter thickness and started down the other side.

Reaching for a handhold, a rock cemented in place, and he pulled on it before attempting to get a foothold. He reached his other leg down to a second foothold, which felt solid. As soon as he let go of the original foothold, his handhold broke free of the wall. Marcon was holding the rock, but nothing was holding it as he fell backward, slamming into the ground, knocking the air out of him in the three meter fall. It took a second before he summoned all his strength to roll over, trying to jump up as he did so. He managed, but fell over in excruciating pain. Looking down, his right femur appeared detached from his pelvis, meaning he either broke his hip or dislocated it. The pain was intense, so he imagined it was dislocated. Despite that, he put the pistol grip into his mouth, bit down and attempted to reconnect the hip to no avail. There was no more time to dwell on it. If he tried any harder, he would pass out, which meant his death. He reluctantly dragged himself toward the water. It would be freezing, but that would also keep him from going into shock.

At the water's edge, he painfully pulled off his shoes and withered out of his pants, taking a few minutes to avoid passing out. He tied the shoes together and placed them around his neck. He next tied both pant legs closed and pulled himself into the water. Fuck, it was cold.

Moving forward, he dragged the pants behind him to fill them with water. Once done, he floated onto his back and rolled the waistband to trap the water inside, making a life vest of sorts. He placed it over his head and used his good arm to pull him toward the stronger current.

Shots were going off at the residence behind him, although he had no idea what they were shooting at. He hung on now, letting the current pull him downriver.

The extraction team arrived three kilometers from the house on the river's edge and, although they did not expect to find him this close, they looked first before they followed the river east. The team leader noted the sporadic gun fire upriver. It was dusk, and they had maybe thirty minutes to find him, or they would have to use their flashlights, which would give away their position. They broke up to cover more area and at each inlet turned in to see if he was there. They had traveled two kilometers east when darkness set in, but they elected to use the moonlight and avoid flashlights for now.

Twenty more minutes passed when one of the team made an animal sound. That was a signal. Someone had found him, and they converged on a sand bank four meters offshore. Marcon was lying on it, his upper body on the sand and this lower body in the water. He was unconscious, and they quickly pulled him to shore unaware of his injury. They dragged him out of the frigid water to assess his condition and it was then the team leader turned on a small micro light and jumped back, startled. Cristiano Marcon was a pale bluish gray. His right femur was broken or detached from his pelvis; his breathing was very shallow. Marcon was in dire shape.

They quickly wrapped him in a blanket and immobilized his lower body before giving him an injection of morphine. Quickly, four men carried him on a nylon stretcher with a man in front and back, acting as sentries. They made their way north towards the forests, heading for St. Petersburg. That was their way out. Three hours later, the team leader called Kristatos.

"We have him. Heading to the safe house. His condition is critical." He ended the call. There was nothing else they could do.

Kristatos hung up, the look of concern painted on his face as he went upstairs to tell Izabel about the status. He didn't want to, but she needed to know. She let him up and knew immediately something was wrong.

"They have him, but he is badly injured."

"What? What is wrong?"

"I don't know; it is possible to capture cell phone data, so we spoke for just seconds. They have him stabilized and are on the way to the safe house outside St. Petersburg."

"Did you speak with him?"

"No, only the team leader. Cristiano was unconscious."

"We have to wait, yes?"

"For now, yes." Izabel just nodded, and he took his leave. Neither said it, but the hatred for Dima Ivanov was very high. Kristatos understood him and knew that he might lose his life, but should Marcon die, Izabel was right, so would Ivanov.

It was morning the following day as Ivanov causally drank a cup of coffee. Marcon had somehow escaped, and eight of his men were dead. Ivanov himself had killed another this morning for allowing it to happen. It was assumed now that Marcon had somehow breached the wall and exited by the river. The bodies of the men he had killed were in that direction. How in the hell he killed the two tower sentries was unknown? Assault rifles are great, but as a sniper rifle, he had to give the bastard credit. The man knew how to shoot. Kristatos had mentioned a second team, and perhaps they had been mobilized to help him. He had men heading towards St. Petersburg and all private airways between the residence and there, including Moscow proper. Ivanov had a very long reach.

His thoughts began to focus on revenge. Kristatos was first, as they had some history, and he wanted Marcon to know he was coming for him. Next in line was the other lieutenant, the one everyone said might be a love interest as well. Since she thought she was so tough, he would kill her with his bare hands. Again, more breadcrumbs leading to Marcon. Last in line was

Zhou. Marcon had failed to avenge Omelchenko, but Ivanov was far less complicated. He would just kill him. It was the least he could do for Sergei.

Although Kristatos had not told Vargas, he was heading to St. Petersburg right then. The team needed all the help they could get, as Ivanov would certainly assume that area as a destination even though it was vast. Loaded into two Mercedes G550 wagons, they left the HQ of Provos Engeria, heading to the airport. Kristatos was in the lead vehicle with three others, and the second SUV had four men as well. They were coming around a sweeping turn when the driver pointed to a flash up on the mountain. Despite going fast, before they got a sense of what was happening, there was a second flash and the SUV behind them was blown into the air, killing all instantly. Kristatos yelled at the driver, realizing what the second flash was, but there was nothing they could do before the lead SUV shared the fate of the first.

Ivanov had just won the first round. Kristatos was dead along with the team coming to rescue Marcon. One down and two to go.

Polícia Federal arrived on the scene first and the Fire Department moments later. The officer in charge knew the vehicles and recognized the markings of an assassination. He radioed for the Special Operations Command, COPESP. They had met Kristatos a week before who explained Marcon's disappearance and that he might need help. Marcon was a former captain within the COPESP and his first thought was *they should have stayed closer to him.*

It took four hours before a field coroner could assess the scene and prepare the dead. Kristatos was identified by the large ring he always wore, and they concluded he was the likely target.

Elite forces helped the Polícia comb the hillside for evidence, but short of scuffed boot prints and burn marks, there was nothing else. The assassin was long gone. It was close to eight in the evening when they finally made their way to the Marcon residence. The COPESP commander knew Izabel and thought it was best for such information to come from him. He explained the hit, and she told them about Marcon and the likelihood that the assassins worked for Dima Ivanov, head of security to Sergei Omelchenko. The commander wrote this all down and wished her a safe evening. The implication was, *you're next.*

She was rightfully scared and pragmatically knew she needed to make plans to escape this surrounding. Her mind went to the two paintings from Omelchenko. She smiled and would start there, knowing they were worth perhaps one-hundred million euros.

61

Copthorne, West Sussex, England

Sara walked off the plane in London refreshed, heading to the home of Julian Hendricks. They were going to spend the weekend putting the finishing touches on the three technical papers they would send to their editor on Monday.

Sara took a taxi to her house and as they left the Gatwick airport; she noted the two MDE buildings from her past, wondering if the Managing Director, Sophia Antonion, was watching her. What a silly thought as they turned in the opposite direction toward Copthorne. The taxi arrived in less than fifteen minutes and as Sara paid; she got her first glimpse of the money pit. Although Sara preferred to stay in hotels, Julian had insisted she stay with her. Sara relented, knowing Julian was still affected by her ordeal in Romania and didn't have many friends. They intended to make this a-work-hard, play-hard weekend.

Sara knocked, and Julian answered happily. They hugged, and Sara came in for a cup of tea. The weather was fair but damp, and Sara immediately noticed the house offered little protection from the outside. Poor Julian.

Both wearing sweaters, they started on the first paper about the solar panel design and went through it, which took them into the early evening. Julian took her into town for a nice dinner at a local pub, and it was some four hours later when they returned. Both were tipsy as Julian unlocked the door and flicked on the light, which, of course, didn't work. Both laughed at the curse of the money pit as they walked in and Sara closed the door. Looking at her watch, it was after ten. Tomorrow was going to be a bear of a day.

Suddenly, a light came on and Julian screamed, but a hand quickly covered her mouth. A gun was aimed at Sara and a finger to the assailant's mouth said, stay quiet. She understood the consequences.

There were two men, one who was blocking the stairs, and another who quickly moved behind them, blocking the door. Another light came on, and an attractive woman sat looking at them. Her voice was stark. "Bring them here."

The armed men ushered them forward into the living room and once right of her, she motioned for them to sit, which they did. Guns were still trained on them in the muted light. "Do you know who I am?"

Julian said nervously, "No. Why are you in my house? What the hell is this all about?"

"My name is Izabel Vargas."

"I have no idea who you are and don't really care. Get out of my fucking house." Sara meanwhile was shocked. This was Izabel Vargas? The woman the Art Squad was after, but she glanced away to hide her expression. It all but said, *I know who you are.*

"I'm here because my boyfriend is missing and might be dead. All because you thought yourself clever. The Russian project failed and because of that, they killed everyone involved. Their blood is on your hands." Hendricks gasped thinking of that reality as Vargas continued. "Worse, the dead may include my beloved Cristiano. After a few details are taken care of, you will die for this." Sara tried, but could not contain herself and gasped.

Izabel looked up and stared directly at her. "Who might you be?"

"I'm nobody." Sara mumbled.

"You flinched when you heard my name and jumped when you heard of Cristiano. Who the fuck are you?" She was up out of her chair and in Sara's face now.

Hendricks all but screamed, "Listen, if it's me you want fine. Do what you must, but she has nothing to do with this. She just works with me."

"You shut up." Vargas said sharply and looked back at Sara. "I asked you a question. Answer it or die wishing you had."

"I'm Sara Ricci. I do not know you, but the name of Mr. Marcon came up on a search a private security firm did for me."

"And why would you research him?"

"I didn't. At our launch site, a student was acting strange, and he ran when we tried to confront him. I had a friend look into who he was, and he has been an activist student for anti-renewable projects. Rumor is Mr. Marcon was a financial backer to these causes. That is all I know."

"This is not over cute one. Let's go." The gunmen immediately motioned for them to head outside toward a van. They thought to scream but didn't. When questioned, neighbors would not recall any sounds, so perhaps they should have. They were pushed into the van, and all went black moments later.

Sara awoke not understanding how long she had been out. It was dark, and she was in a chair in a cold room, devoid of furniture or anything else. It looked like a warehouse. Julian was next to her. Sara could smell her perfume and called out to her softly, not wanting to alert anyone that she was awake. In the background, the sound of a commercial jet plane was landing, and soon, another was taking off, so she suspected they were back by the airport or very close to it. For a second she panicked, thinking this might have something to do with MDE Enterprises, but dismissed the idea. Sara could hear voices, but not clearly. They were muffled and coming from another room.

From a perch on top of a small building to the left of the warehouse, agents from Interpol, the Metropolitan Police, and two investigators from the Italian Carabinieri Art Squad were looking down on it. Interpol had verified that Vargas was inside having arrived in Gatwick the day before on private wings. They had also traced the warehouse to a holding company owned by Povos Engeria.

Interpol had alerted the Metropolitan Police, formerly known as New Scotland Yard, the day before, and they had been surveilling Vargas. They lost her briefly, but she showed up again here. Both Interpol and the Art Squad suspected the stolen art was inside, and this was where the illegitimate sale would take place. The only unknown was when would the buyers arrive and second, who had they taken into the warehouse.

Thirty minutes before, a van had pulled up, and two people, perhaps women were dragged inside; dead or unconscious. Nigel Hughes, Detective Chief Inspector (DCI) of the Metropolitan Police, wanted to act on seeing the bodies, but more was at stake here and they collectively waited for the art buyers to show. They hoped this would not drag out into the morning when the area around the industrial complex would become much more crowded, the situation harder to manage.

Inside the building, Vargas had gone into the room where Sara and Julian were tied up. Sara was wide awake, and Julian was just coming to as she walked in. "I won't keep you too long. After some business, I will be back here to help you into your next life."

"Please, she really has nothing to do with this. Just let her go." Julian pleaded, meaning Sara.

"I'm not so sure, but anyway, it's not your call. You are both secondary to the reason I am here, and I'll decide what to do with you later."

"You heartless bitch." Julian yelled, and Izabel intently hit her in the face with her fist. Julian had never been hit in the face and never by someone who obviously knew how to fight. She was shocked as her lip split, and she was bleeding a significant amount. Sara lurched forward but didn't get far, as her restraints held firm. Vargas walked over and smirked before saying softly, "Go ahead cute one. Get angry. There is something about you I just don't like," as she belted Sara for her troubles. Vargas looked over her shoulder at the guard. "This one I do not care about. If you can handle her, she's yours. The other one is mine. Only mine!" The guard smiled and leered over at Sara as Vargas left for the other room.

62

It was just before midnight when a BMW M760i sedan drove up slowly and two people, a man carrying a large aluminum case and a woman, climbed out and were escorted into the warehouse. Within ten minutes, a second car, a Mercedes S550 arrived, and two additional men got out, both with large cases, and entered the warehouse. The art buyers and their money had arrived.

The intel from the Art Squad was spot on and teams prepared to rush the warehouse from the front. All windows and a rear door were being monitored by the remaining troops and all were aware there may be hostages.

On a count of three, the Police DCI, the Carabinieri and an Interpol agent flew through the door. One guard nearest Vargas spun and fired wide and DCI Hughes shot on instinct, putting the guard down before he could get off another shot, and immediately shot above the head of the second guard who surrendered. Everyone in the room flew to the ground, yelling and screaming to avoid being hit. From a separate room, there was a muted scream.

To the left, Vargas took advantage of the sudden confusion to save herself, running across the room and crashing headfirst, arms ahead of her as if she were diving into water, as she smashed through a painted over window, hoping to tuck and roll on the exit to the outside. She made it out with minor cuts, but as she put her hands down to facilitate the roll, a piece of glass sliced into her right hand. She screamed but executed the flip and was almost on her feet to run when she ran headfirst into a waiting Interpol agent. Despite her forward momentum, he was completely rigid, his Walther PPK fixed on her forehead. She stopped when the barrel of his gun touched her forehead and he used it to push her down into a seated position. Vargas looked up and pleaded, "You don't understand. If I don't complete this transaction, he is dead."

The policeman unphased shouted, "Who is dead?" Realizing her mistake, she went silent. The policeman gave her a handkerchief to wrap her blooded hand, cuffed her, and brought her back into the warehouse.

Lead Art Squad investigator Chiara Bulgari, gun out, noticed Vargas being monitored by Moreau, the Interpol agent, and rushed to the walled area, looking for a way in. The wounded guard had tried to get his gun only to be hit again by DCI Hughes. Shots then rang out from the next room, some coming at them through the walls. They all dropped and

Bulgari, looking up, saw the outline of a false door and slammed her body against it twice.

The door imploded inward, and a confused guard shot wildly, but Chiara dropped to her knee and fired. He was wearing a bullet-proof vest, and fell back only to get back up when she shot again. This time she got a leg, and screaming, he stayed down. That scream became a chorus to the screams of the hostages inside.

Chiara kicked his gun out of reach and held aim on the guard. Nigel ran in, assessed the situation, and took over, cuffing the injured guard as Chiara ran over towards the hostages, stopping short in horror.

"Sara?" she yelled, rushing over to pull off her makeshift hand cuffs. "What the hell are you doing here?" As soon as her hands were free, Sara hugged her and screamed, "Please help Julian! I think she has been shot."

Chiara had noticed her slumped over and went to her on the opposite wall. There was no hiding Chiara's face as it became serious. She turned and yelled, "Get an EMT in here now!" She gently undid her constraints and eased her down onto her side. Within a few minutes, both rooms were secure as EMT's in either room worked on the wounded. Sara was not medically inclined, but the movements were obvious. Julian was dead or dying. She wept as Chiara came by and asked her if she was okay. She was, other than a welt on her cheek, a shiner on her forehead, and her clothes half off thanks to the guard who thought he was going to have some fun before the shooting started.

Sara looked at him on the floor in pain and without warning, jumped up and kicked him like a soccer ball right in the face. DCI Hughes immediately jumped between them and shouted at Sara, but thinking to himself, *wow, nice shot.*

Chiara grabbed Sara and pulled her back, saying calmly, "Sara, he can't harm you."

"I know. I just needed to hurt him. Disgusting piece of crap." Chiara wanted to laugh, but knew that would be highly unprofessional. Looking at Sara, it was clear he had tried to make an advance on her.

Back in the other room, preliminary statements were being taken by various agents. The buyer agents were trying to claim ignorance, although that was difficult given Rembrandt's *The Storm on the Sea of Galilee,* (1633) and Raphael's *Portrait of a Young Man* (1514) lie in front of them, flat and undamaged on professional stretchers. Not to mention the three aluminum cases with as much as $150 million in cash they had brought in with them from their cars. Police would confiscate that for now.

A dejected Izabel Vargas sat there, knowing it was over and that she had failed. She mumbled several times, "He is lost now."

Interpol Agent Moreau walked over to Bulgari and asked, "She said something similar outside. What is she referring to?" Chiara explained her tie to Cristiano Marcon and his possible death at the hands of Omelchenko's agents. She had no idea, nor did she care. Marcon was not in her fight.

Just as she concluded it was time to get the site ready for forensics, Vargas, who was standing handcuffed, slammed her body into DCI Hughes who fell over, as she kneeled down in a deep squat attempting to grab a weapon on the floor from the guard who dropped it. Difficult with her hands still cuffed, she was limber enough to pull it off and was now holding the gun in her right hand behind her back. She could not aim normally, but she turned her back to Bulgari intent on trying. Agent Moreau, standing near the door didn't hesitate and shot Vargas center mass. She went down with a thud. The gun harmlessly fell to one side, and Moreau walked over and kicked it away.

A few minutes passed before the room had resettled and was back in control. Chiara had radioed the room was clear again, and they were coming out. The EMT from the other room had checked on Vargas. He looked up at Chiara and shook his head. She was dead.

When the door to the outside opened, Chiara was a bit surprised at the number of media outside and a helicopter overhead hovering with a light shining down on the warehouse as she and the able-bodied walked out, some escorting the buyers and guards. The EMT's would follow with the dead or wounded.

In Milan, it was late. Giovanni often struggled to sleep when Chiara was not there these days and walked to the kitchen to get some hot milk when he stopped midstream and stared back at the television, which he had accidentally left on.

"This is Norman Stokes for BBC late edition. Our top story this evening comes from outside London where agents from Interpol, Metropolitan Police and the famed Italian Carabinieri Art Squad successfully raided a warehouse next to Gatwick airport. Several suspects are injured, and at least two are known dead. All roads into and out of this industrial area remain closed at this hour. The two paintings, a Rembrandt and a Rafael were stolen from museums over thirty years ago and have been recovered along with one-hundred-fifty million euros in cash. This footage is live as the scene is unfolding."

On the television, Chiara, his Chiara, had just walked out of a warehouse followed by police guiding handcuffed people out and into police cars. That was followed moments later by three sets of EMT's wheeling out three gurneys. Each had a police escort and on one, the EMT was sitting atop the wounded doing chest compressions. Giovanni was about to turn away when his heart almost stopped. Last out of the warehouse was Sara, who looked half naked but for a blanket wrapped around her being supported by a policeman. Her face was bandaged. *My God, what the hell happened? Why is my Sara there?* He ran and grabbed his phone frantic to talk to Chiara, but there was no answer.

Epilogue One

Spring had officially begun as an older man stood with a cane and walked stiffly towards the door of the dacha, 110 kilometers west of St. Petersburg. The only way here was by foot or by helicopter, as any road was well over thirty kilometers away.

The door from the dacha opened onto a small deck. The unobstructed view was of a large meadow surrounded by a dense forest of mature trees. He got the door open and walked out on to the deck, each step harder than the one before. Ten to twelve steps was the limit before he had to sit as he found the chair and eased himself down into it, admiring the view, thinking of last week's news.

In this location for almost three weeks, he had recently used a special satellite feed to get some information from the outside world. Much had changed in a short time, none of it good.

First was confirmation that his friend, Sergei Omelchenko had, in fact been murdered. His yacht had sunk in deep water with over sixty people aboard, all presumed dead. Some debris had been located and a weak metallic signal had registered at a depth of over nine-hundred meters, which was believed to be the remains of the *Vertigo.* Solicitors for Omelchenko would determine to what extent it was observed further.

Also distressful was news explaining why he could not get hold of his key lieutenant, Kristatos. He too had been murdered along with seven of his men. No doubt Ivanov's doing.

Most unsettling was a fine art sale gone bad, taking the life of Izabel. Her actions and failure only brought sorrow and loss, although he was puzzled. *What was she doing selling Omelchenko's art? Was she doing this to raise cash to get him out of Russia, or was this a hundred-fifty million exit strategy?* He would never know.

His thoughts were interrupted when a soldier came out onto the deck. "Mr. Marcon, we have a window to depart in less than an hour. Are you ready?"

"Yes," said Marcon, as he pivoted on his good leg and headed back inside. They had used actors' makeup to present him as an old man, trying to get him past Ivanov's security team, which had been monitoring private aircraft out of St. Petersburg. As he hobbled inside, he smiled, knowing that someday soon Ivanov would pay for this limp with his life.

Marcon's days as a soldier might be over, but in some respects, his days as a criminal were just getting started.

Dima Ivanov was at that moment several thousand miles away from Russia. With Marcon still temporarily in the wind, he had looked forward to killing his bitch, Vargas, but the police beat him to it. Losing the art was unfortunate, but Ivanov had no instructions from Omelchenko's business associates to locate such assets, so he concerned himself with other things. He was satisfied the thief, Vargas, was rightfully dead.

Exiting the elevator, he used his passcode to enter his suite at the Grand Hyatt, on the top floors of the Jin Mao Tower in Shanghai. He had rented the room for three nights but had only been inside the room for a few hours. Here on the 66th floor, this room looked directly at the Shanghai World Financial Center building, formally the world's second tallest building.

It was dark and nearing eight o'clock when Ivanov, dressed in a tyvek suit, booties and a hairnet to contain any DNA transfer, pushed away the credenza and opened the curtains wide. He then took a special tool out of an accessory bag and placed the suction cups on the window of his darkened room on the lower portion of the window.

Once secure, he activated the motorized device and in a few minutes; it had etched a two-inch hole in the five millimeter thick glass, approximately thirteen inches off the floor. He tapped it with a special tool and removed the glass plug. The glass had two panes, and he repeated the process on the second piece. When he pulled the second plug, cold outside air hissed in, which he sealed with a rubber disk.

Ivanov lay prone on the plush carpeted floor and pushed the barrel of the silenced VSS Vintorez sniper rifle through a matching hole in the rubber disk out into the cool evening air. The front of the rifle was on a stand with sharp tips that penetrated the carpet to stay firm. The butt of the rifle was anchored to a motorized lift, which he could manually move in four directions to center the front of the rifle. He moved it down and then slightly to his right until his sight was in line with a small conference room on the 64th floor of the Shanghai World Financial Center building, one-hundred-seventy meters away. As seen through the high-powered scope, a dozen men and women sat around an oval table in the brightly lit room. Papers were everywhere on the table, and most had a laptop at their fingertips. A dinner was being prepared in the adjoining room. He could see everyone clearly except the man whose back was facing him now. He was talking, and the table was listening intently. Ivanov had been watching him for over an hour.

Doing some breathing exercises, Ivanov then accessed remote instruments he had set up the day before, and took final air temperature and wind readings before making tiny adjustments in the barrel location to compensate for these factors. Trusting his setup, he softly clicked off the electronic safety and finally placed his finger on the remote trigger. He paused for a second, holding his breath, and then pushed the button activating the trigger.

The head of Dr. Shen Zhou blew apart as the 9x39mm subsonic round torn across the expanse, through two layers of glass, killing him instantly, and showering those around him in glass, blood and human tissue.

Two down, two to go. Satisfied, Ivanov placed the rifle in a golf bag and went out into the foyer, removed the outerwear carefully, folding it inside out before placing it in his small suitcase. Moments later, he was on his way to the airport.

Epilogue Two

Lieutenant Chiara Bulgari and Captain Marcello Abruzzo of the Comando Carabinieri Tutela Patrimonio Culturale (TPC) or informally, the Carabinieri Art Squad were standing on a makeshift platform outside their headquarters to the clapping of a small audience. Behind Bulgari and Abruzzo was the entire TPC team, and directly in front of them were reporters.

Both dressed in Carabinieri uniform, large pictures of the Rembrandt and the Raphael sat on easels behind them. The originals were in a temperature controlled room under massive security in an unknown location, even they didn't know. Giovanni and Sara Ricci stood silent in the crowd, excited about this celebration.

Bulgari had the mic and explained the raid and some minor details that led them to the warehouse that night. The moment she stopped; reporters vied for a question.

"Is it true several died in this raid?" one asked.

"Sadly yes. Those responsible for this illegal sale did not yield to police and started a gun battle. As a result, two people were wounded and two were killed."

"Were the paintings damaged by gunfire?" said another.

"No. Other than a few scuff marks, they are in very good condition, although both had been cut from their original frames many years ago."

"Where are the originals being held?" asked the reporter from RAI News 24.

"No comment."

"Have you identified the woman who arranged the sale?" asked the same reporter.

"Yes. Her name will be released soon. She tried to kill a policeman and was subsequently killed herself."

"The warehouse is tied to an entrepreneur, Cristiano Marcon. Was the woman killed related to him?" said a woman from Sky TG24 news.

"We believe that is possible, but not our concern. It was she that attempted to sell the stolen art believed to have been purchased illicitly by a Russian oligarch. I am not aware of any police action related to Mr. Marcon."

"Who is the Russian?" said the same woman.

"No comment."

"A woman was seen clinging to life as EMTs were trying to save her. Did the Police shoot her?" Chiara looked toward the voice, and it was a man who had a journalist badge but no cameraman nor visual branding. Perhaps he was freelance.

Unhappy with the question, she said smartly, "I'm sure you meant to say, is she okay? The short answer is no, she remains in critical condition. The next twenty hours will be critical for her."

"Did the Police shoot her?"

She ignored him as another question came. "Who owns these works now that they have been recovered?" asked another.

"As is our custom, the pieces in time will go back to the museums from which they were taken if that is the wish of the owner or their trust. It is our sincere honor to return them after so many years of loss."

The questions came so fast, there was not an opportunity to answer them all, but one question by a woman also with RAI caught her by surprise. Chiara knew this reporter fairly well, and they had worked together in the past. "Is it true the young PhD student involved in last year's ruckus with Maximillian and Bridget Drummond was there and wounded at this scene?"

Chiara paused. "Yes. Dr. Sara Ricci and a colleague were being held captive at this location by the same woman. The reason for their captivity is unrelated to the art thief and sale."

"Was she injured?" the same woman asked?

"She was treated for minor facial wounds, but based on what we saw..." Chiara paused and smiled at Giovanni and Sara before adding, "This brave little lady gave more than she got."

The reporters gasped and Chiara was still at the podium twenty minutes later, hoping for an opportunity to sit down.

The normally placid house on Lake Lowell in Caldwell Idaho, was suddenly alive. Purchased as a retirement home by former Sergeant Major Harley Sykes and his wife, Annabel, a decade before, they now lived here full time. Overlooking Lake Lowell, it was one of only a few lots with such a view, and Harley had built a small dock for his rowboat. Gas motors were not allowed on the man-made reservoir.

Although there were a few pictures of their family inside the modest house, its walls had never hosted a family dinner or a retirement party. Not even a birthday party. Harley didn't believe in them.

Today, however, was a new day. Harley had surprised Annabel a few months before by asking her if she could get the kids up for a barbeque. The kids meaning thirty-six old Jason and thirty-three-year-old Rachael. Shocked by the request, Annabel had made the arrangements before Harley could change his mind.

Rachael had taken a rare three-day pass from Fort Benning where she, a second lieutenant, was stationed, having just started her fourth tour. She would be a lifer like her dad. Jason had driven over from Seattle for a long weekend in his late model

Toyoda 4-runner. Shocked at the request, they both came largely to see why they had been invited. There had to be a special reason.

Annabel and Rachael were cooking side dishes as they watched Harley and Jason outside through the kitchen window, which faced the water. They had been smoking a brisket for ten hours and Harley was describing something about the lake, or so it seemed, before they headed inside.

Food was eventually placed on the table, and the Sykes family was about to have its first meal together in fourteen years. In fact, the only other time they had even been together was in the hospital in Seattle, when Jason had been infected by nanobots over a year before.

Harley raised his glass, and the others followed. "This meal has been a long time coming. I know now that is because of me... and I apologize for that."

He paused and took a breath. All eyes at the table were on him as whatever they expected him to say, this was not it.

"Listen, I know I'm a better soldier than a husband and god knows, a better soldier than a father. While the army will never be far from me, seeing Jason and Rachael injured because I failed to trust my shot was my first epiphany. The second was coming so close to losing Jason for the second time earlier this year. This is my way of saying; this family is all I really have to show for myself in this world and I'm going to try to not be such an ass. Cheers!"

They all sat in shock before they slowly raised and clicked their glasses. Annabel had never heard such words from Harley's stern mouth and looked first to Rachael who smiled and shrugged before she looked to Jason, whose mouth hung open similarly amazed as he still held his beer glass in the air. It was a new day in the Skye's family.

Sara had moved things around several times, but she rearranged the flowers and swapped pillows on the small sofa once again. The entrance and the main room and kitchen were bright, the colors especially warming. With the windows open and the glass wall to the terrace open, the sounds of the city hung in the background as birds chirped nearby. Suddenly, she heard the familiar exhaust of her dad's vintage 1958 Alfa Romeo Giulietta Spider Veloce coming down her street as it slowed and pulled into the narrow drive. Sara poured some wine into four glasses, so it could breathe, and hit her MP3 player. Not too loud, *Paradise* by British rock band Coldplay came to life, as she walked to edge of the terrace and looked down.

One floor below, her dad, Giovanni, dressed in his best spring fashion had walked around and opened the door for Chiara as she looked up and smiled. The kind of smile every man wants to receive, and every woman wants to give. Such looks said they were in love.

A few minutes passed before they arrived at the door. As her dad entered, he handed Sara a nice bottle of 2017 Castello Vicchiomaggio La Prima and kissed her on both cheeks. Chiara handed her flowers, doing the same as Sara opened her arms wide holding the gifts in each hand and said proudly, "Well here it is."

Giovanni looked the room over. "My special girl, it is lovely, please show us around."

When Sara finally decided it was time to leave Rome, she initially considered buying some land in the mountains towards Vincenza, with a view of Lake Como, but Giovanni was insistent it was too far away from universities and transportation suitable for her freelance physicist lifestyle. Sara had just recently started her small one-person company, Ricci Analytics.

She wanted a tiny house like the one in Seattle, but small plots of land in Milan did not exist in residential areas within the old city, and tiny houses could not be permitted. Giovanni had been willing to sell the flat in Rome and use the proceeds to buy her a nice flat here, but she was adamant. She had to do this on her own.

Chiara contacted some friends in real estate, and they found a small one bedroom terrace flat on Via Santa Rita Da Cascia and Via Giacomo Watt, near the Naviglio Grande canal within a few kilometers of her childhood home. Although it was in dire condition, the price was right, and it had good bones. After five weeks of renovation, she had just moved in, hence the housewarming party.

She led them out onto the small but well-appointed terrace after handing them each a wine glass. They had just sat down when Jason walked in and placed a stack of firewood next to the fire pit in front of them before sitting down on a log bench next to Sara and said hello.

"Jason, it looks wonderful. I had no idea you had such talent." Giovanni said with affection as he looked at the aftereffect of his work.

"Thanks." As he looked around before adding, "It was a great way to get back in shape and I'm glad it turned out so well." He was referring to the disaster this had been a month before. With Sara's help, the inside received new paint, new floors, and curtains along with new fixtures, cabinets, and appliances. The old terrace, the remnant of an unkept herb garden, had been in ruins. Jason gutted the entire space and together, they redid the floors in handmade Italian terracotta tiles, built a BBQ area, an oak pergola with outside seating for six, and a smaller covered area with conversation seating directly off the small house so Sara could sit outside even in the rain.

"Very impressive. When do you return to the States?" Chiara asked.

"Next week. We have a few more days here, then a quick trip to Montreux for the publication of Sara's papers regarding Project Solaris. I'll head home from there."

Chiara added, "Well the place looks incredible. Sara, you must frame before and after photos, I just can't believe the difference."

Sara smiled as she silently moved her finger in the carved letters on the end of the log bench that said, 'Sara + Jason.' Betty in Seattle had offered it to Sara, and Jason's company, Versilant had it shipped here.

Whatever happened would happen, but for now, she and Jason were happy to be friends, and occasionally on this trip, friends with benefits. Sara handed each of them a glass of wine and all smiles, they did a quick toast to her new home in the middle of crowded Milan.

The festive mood was broken by Sara's phone. Not recognizing the number, she picked up as she stood, leaving the terrace. "Ricci Analytics, Sara Ricci speaking."

"Is this Dr. Sara Ricci?"

"Yes, it is, how can I help you?"

"I have little time," said a man in a mild Scottish accent, who seemed to pant. "But I have come across something that makes little sense to me. It involves..." Silence filled the phone, then perhaps a minute later, the sound of air blowing before she heard a loud thud. Sara waited for a response, but nothing came.

"Hello, are you there? Hello?" she asked. Nothing. She pulled back the phone and checked. They were still connected. She placed the phone back to her ear. She heard muffled sounds, but couldn't make them out.

Faintly, she heard a voice say in Spanish. *"Tus secretos deben morir contigo espía."* Followed by a loud gunshot. Sara jumped, causing her to drop the phone on the floor. She reached down, excitedly picked it up, and immediately hung up. She ran to her computer and wrote the incoming phone number on a pad. She quickly typed into her browser to translate, *"Tus secretos deben morir contigo espía."* The translation came up immediately, "Your secrets must die with you spy."

By now, Jason, her dad, and Chiara were in the house, noting her odd behavior and her pale and shocked face.

Jason asked, "Sara, what just happened? Who was that?"

Sara turned to him white as a sheet. "I don't know, but whoever it was, they were just murdered."

Sara takes on a unique project for a friend and one she thinks will take little of her time. It isn't long before she finds herself in trouble and has no idea why, but someone clearly thinks she knows more than she does. Join Sara on her next action-packed adventure.

Like Deadly Discovery?

Other titles in the Sara Ricci Scientific Thriller Series:

Book 1 - Deadly Dissertation

Book 2 - Deadly by Design

Book 3 - Deadly Discovery

Book 4 - Deadly Dilemma - *coming in late 2022. See an excerpt on the next page*

Excerpt

From Deadly Dilemma

The late afternoon air had become positively stifling as hot afternoon heat blended uncomfortably with the high humidity coming off the Caribbean Sea. The ensuing heat index was so uncomfortable, it easily disrupted the human body's natural ability to regulate one's internal temperature. With his core temperature rising and his body sweating at unhealthy levels, thirty-four-year-old Cameron Fernsby, a lanky assistant professor from the University of Glasgow in Scotland, slowly sipped a homemade concoction of mineral infused water, hoping to replenish enough liquid and salts to keep him moving. A not so easy task as he slowly hiked through the dense, unforgiving Columbian jungle—and its many ways to die.

Fernsby had not wanted a field assignment here or anywhere else, but his physics department chair, Dr. MacAididh in Scotland, had threatened to sack him if he didn't pick up the pace and get himself published. Shortly after that rude pep talk, the University of Glasgow partnered with the Universidad del Magdalena in Santa Marta on an experiment to make water from air. The experiment was being sponsored by the Vand Corporation in Denmark and at the urging of MacAididh, Fernsby had reluctantly applied for and was accepted for the project. He was ten months into his one-year sabbatical and unsure if he would survive the next few months, although bitching about the miserable weather was a positive sign. It meant he was still alive.

The first few months had been rewarding as he worked with grad students planning the experiment. Senior to these young researchers by ten years, if not more, he felt empowered and enjoyed the respect they offered him. That was a far cry from Scotland where students considered him a complete dufus and reciprocally, he considered them pampered little brats.

Soon they were preparing the experiment site close to the main campus, and eventually began to install hardware received from Denmark. Just before the start of experiment, security had been increased with soldiers from the Columbia Army, the local regiment, Grupo Gaula Magdalena and Fernsby assumed this was done by the Vand Corporation although in his many talks with them they had said nothing about this.

A decent scientist, Fernsby fully understood the physics of the experiment, and initially, it seemed to work fine, but output soon began to degrade. He felt changes were being made to the prototype unit inconsistent with the process, as he understood it, although he said nothing at first. He did this in part because he was technically only responsible for tuning the microprocessor. When he did finally start to raise concern, he received no conclusive answers and considered appealing to the lead engineer at Vand.

No sooner had he mouthed this concern when odd things began to happen. First, his lab equipment, notes, and even personal effects appeared to have been gone through. Colleagues at the job site began to distance themselves from him and eventually stopped sitting with him at mealtimes. As he sat alone, at least one guard was always watching him. No one else, just him. That was bad enough, but not long after, they removed his access to restricted areas, citing security reasons, which took away his access to a phone that could call out of the country. They even blocked his Wi-Fi access, leaving him alone and cut off from the rest of the world. He had a personal cell phone, but it didn't work in Columbia.

Clearly he had stumbled on to something, but given the way the soldiers were focused on him, he also knew it was unlikely they would just let him leave. It was then he decided his only way out was to escape, but he reasoned that if he was going to risk his life, he should understand why. To him, someone was trying to sabotage the experiment. He just didn't know precisely how or even why, but needed to find out. But who could help him?

He knew he should have just called Rada De Clecq, the head engineer in Denmark, but he lost his phone access before he could. His co-workers at the job site refused to even talk to him, so they were out. Colleagues in Scotland could likely help, but similarly, he couldn't get hold of them and even if he could, might he be placing them in danger?

The only other person Fernsby considered was an Italian physicist whom he had never met. He had received her contact information from a friend and thought that if he could escape, he could alter his cell phone plan to call her and explain the odd changes to the experiment. The questions he intended to ask her were written in his journal, and depending on her answers, he could then consider calling De Clecq from the safety of Scotland instead of this hellhole.

After a few days of planning, Fernsby reluctantly escaped under the veiled protection of night. Since his escape three days before, he had left the desert region of Santa Marta; and made his way into the forest, intent on hiking to Maracaibo, Venezuela, one-hundred-sixty kilometers away. Estimating a fifteen day journey, he could finally return to Scotland and the University of Glasgow, leaving all this madness behind him.

Major Sebastián Da Silva of the Columbian Army's 1st Division, Grupo Gaula Magdalena had risen quickly within the ranks of the Unified Armed Forces of the Republic of Columbia. At just thirty-eight years of age, he had a fierce reputation for getting things done and he strictly followed the motto of his regiment, Patria, Honor, Lealtad... *Homeland, Honor and Loyalty.*

Standing now in front of his intelligence officer, he sought an update on the disappearance of a suspected espía, or spy, Cameron Fernsby. Of course, Fernsby was not a spy, but he had become a big problem for Da Silva who was being paid to sabotage the experiment. Labeling him an espía, gave him unlimited power to act as he pleased.

"Status?" he barked to no one in particular.

A young man said loudly, "Major, we believe Fernsby left in the late evening three nights ago."

"Who saw him last?"

"A cook at the job site cafeteria."

"When?"

"Just past nine o'clock, the same evening he disappeared."

"Any idea where he went?"

"Based on questions he had been asking and evidence in his room, we think he went into the jungle likely heading for the Venezuelan border, the fastest route out of Columbia."

"On the surface, a poor choice given the ruggedness of our jungles not to mention the drug cartels who rule the mountains. But Fernsby is an avid runner and seems resourceful. Do we have a team going after him?"

"Yes sir. Command Sergeant Acosta and two men left yesterday."

"He has a two-day head start. Keep me informed." With that, Major Da Silva walked out of the room, satisfied. They would soon have him. Even people born in the jungle often died there, so this pale white man didn't stand a chance.

Six days later, Fernsby was still trekking through the dense jungle and the Da Silva was still empty-handed. That said, Fernsby was fading. The heat, exhaustion and limited food intake were getting to him as he left the region of Magdalena and entered La Guajira, almost halfway to his destination.

The entire time, every imaginable combination of bugs, snakes, and noises filled his mind with horror throughout the day and especially at night. He could not readily fall asleep despite his exhaustion and when he finally did, something would inevitably crawl on him and wake him up, usually in a panic.

It was bad enough to have limited sleep, but hiking here was unlike anything one might expect. There were no trails meandering through the forest. Under the dense canopy of the forest were decades of growth that you simply zig-zagged and fought your way through. The game was to locate the smallest trees and shrubs you could walk climb over, or the tallest you could walk under, so every kilometer traveled forward was at least two in total. At that moment, he would have paid a king's ransom for a machete.

Although his pace had slowed considerably over the last few days, Fernsby hoped to reach the town of San Juan del Cesar with the water and food he had remaining. That town was large enough to escape detection, and he could replenish his supplies there. As he hiked on, perhaps a few kilometers from the town, he was completely unaware that human eyes were upon him.

Command Sergeant Raul Acosta was near Fernsby when his satellite phone rang. He stopped, held up his fist for all behind him to stop, and answered. He hung up moments later and turned to his men. "A cartel scout saw Fernsby an hour ago. I have the coordinates, and it looks like he'll bypass Cherúa and head for San Juan del Cesar. We need to stop him before he gets there, or we might lose him. As a precaution, men from the local Policia are on their way from San Juan del Cesar and will hike towards us. Major Da Silva is with them. Let's move, double time."

Fernsby continued, unaware that teams were now coming at him from both directions. His thoughts were of the Italian scientist. He needed to call her to understand what he had uncovered, but his phone would have to be modified to make such a call. Knowing he was near a major town, if he could get a cell signal, perhaps Vodafone, his cell carrier could set him up to call internationally. Tired and perhaps less irrational than normal, he stopped and pulled out his phone, knowing the moment he turned it on, they could track him. But he considered it a risk worth taking. He put the SIM card back in, turned it on, and hit the shortcut to Vodaphone.

It actually took less than ten minutes, but soon, armed with his list of questions, he pulled up her number and hit send. A woman answered as his eyes darted all around him, "Ricci Analytics, Sara Ricci speaking."

"Is this... Dr. Sara Ricci?"

"Yes, it is. How can I help you?"

"I have little time," Fernsby replied, "but I have come across something. It involves..." He suddenly froze. Were those voices?

He pulled the phone from his ear and stayed completely still until, sure enough, the sounds of men speaking Spanish were nearing. Shit. Was it scouts from the cartels? Local hunters? Were Da Silva's men right behind him?

Suddenly, something hit him in the shoulder so hard he spun completely around and fell to the ground, the cell phone gone from his hand. In shock, he didn't feel the pain, but as he glanced over; he noted his shoulder was a mass of blood. *Shit! What the hell just hit me? A bullet? An animal?*

Unable to move, he tried to understand what had just happened and immediately regretted his decision to contact her. As the sounds of the voices grew closer, in pain and resignation, he momentarily closed his eyes.

When he opened them, a young soldier was standing above him. Command Sergeant Acosta causally pulled his IWI Jericho 941 pistol from his holster and pointed it at Fernsby. "Tus secretos deben morir contigo espía," and shot him in the forehead. Fernsby was dead instantly.

Acosta removed his knapsack while another soldier searched Fernsby's body. Nothing was in his pockets, but in the knapsack were his remaining food and water plus a computer and a small black notebook. A cell phone was in the dirt close to his body. Acosta ignored the computer as it wasn't powered on, but opened the notebook and read a series of questions at the last few entries. He smiled and then looked at the cell phone as his facial expression went from a smile to a frown. The phone said a call had just ended a few minutes before. He placed both items back into the pack and turned, facing his men, "Let's meet up with Da Silva."

It took just an hour before the two squads met. Acosta explained the shooting to a nodding Da Silva who said, "You and your men did well. I'm surprised he made it this far?"

"Major, there may be an issue." Acosta reached for the knapsack and pulled out the small black book, which he held open to reveal the questions, and held it out for Da Silva to read.

When finished, Da Silva turned to Acosta and said quietly, "We were right to watch him. Fernsby clearly understood the changes being made to the experiment."

"I'm afraid there is more." Acosta handed him the phone, and Da Silva immediately understood.

"So he made a quick call to this person just now. Not enough time to ask these questions, but perhaps enough time to explain his deadly dilemma."

"I thought the same. What do you wish?"

Major Da Silva looked around then said quietly back to Acosta so others could not hear, "We can't take a chance. Find this Dr. Sara Ricci and kill her."

Made in the USA
Coppell, TX
01 April 2023

15068002R00223